For Matt & Dawn,
I hope you like
a sad love story.

Bill

Moonglow

A love story

by

Bill Tucker

Goose River Press
Waldoboro, Maine

i

Library of Congress Control Number: 2008926793

ISBN: 978-1-59713-066-0

First printing, 2008

Goose River Press
Waldoboro, Maine

Once upon a time,

a girl with moonlight in her eyes

sang for me.

Her name was

Betty Lee.

Acknowledgements

I believe that most writers have friends, or if not close friends, associates, that read their manuscripts and offer valuable critiques about the books they write. Some of the more careful ones help get rid of the typos that the writers miss no matter how many times they read their own work.

Two such couples who read *Moonglow* in manuscript were John and Elsie Martinez and Jim and Joy Godbold. These people have read the manuscripts of all my books and have offered me some friendly and very insightful suggestions. John Martinez is an educator who has a chair named for him at Tulane University in New Orleans and Elsie is a published author who also critiques the work of others. Jim Godbold is a retired full colonel in the Marine Corps and an author of a marvelous memoir about an astonishing career. Joy is a well-read lady with a wonderful feel for the romance in a good love story.

Two ladies from the publishing industry have been of enormous help in getting this book in print. Yessenia Santos and Lydia Zelaya, of the Permissions Department of the Simon and Schuster publishing house, have guided me through all the complexities of acknowledging the copyrighted work of other authors quoted in this book.

And, of course, my wife, Betty Lee. She labors over manuscript preparation and doesn't hesitate to tell me when she thinks I'm going down the wrong road. She loves lyric fiction and, like me, is not a fan of books whose authors think that a corpse in the first paragraph is necessary to get the reader's attention.

Thanks to all of you.

Chapter One

"Let's all turn to number one-oh-one, Brethren, and sing together this great hymn of praise to God's bounty," evangelist Andrew Herbert Osgood directed and struck a pose of readiness as the six or seven hundred people rustled through the books to hymn one-oh-one, found it, and waited for his gesture to begin.

"Let's stand as we sing."

Reverend Osgood always got a better effort when they stood. Acoustics being what they were in a big tent, you just couldn't get the best out of them sitting with their bellies all wrinkled up, women especially. The men didn't sing much anyway.

With a perfected motion of his expressive hands, Reverend Osgood drew them out of the collapsible funeral-parlor chairs that were neatly arranged, row after row, on the sawdust covered ground. The canvas tabernacle seemed to heave with palpitating anticipation. The deep influx of air into expanding female bosoms and the resigned sighs of tired-footed men added sibilance to the night.

Evan Sherman stood by his mother's side and his eyes wandered over the familiar forms in the rows in front of him, pausing only to make certain of the ownership of each young female backside before passing on to another. He paused for some time when he came to Irma Freeman. Her soft-hipped voluptuousness was curvingly evident through her light summer dress and Evan remembered the day in the woods. The first vision of a sweet breast's nakedness, lovely soft cones emerging from a slowly peeled bathing suit, floated before him, and he lost himself in it for several time-less seconds.

"Bringing in the sheaves—" The jarring words burst upon the May night. Nasal, toneless men's voices, indifferently mouthing the words; women's voices, searching for the notes in wavering tremolo, abandoning each in vain search for the next—flat alto, screaming soprano, straining tenor, rumbling-monotonic bass—set up disturbances in the air, formed wave after wave of discordant sound. The cacophony could be heard on Main Street six blocks away between the steam-engine exhausts at the railroad station.

Evan was startled from his dreamy contemplation of Irma Freeman. His unopened hymnal was dangling from his right hand, and he stole a furtive glance at his mother, Martha. She was obliv-ious to him, perspiringly out-singing a painfully strong-voiced woman directly in back of her. The contest went on and he returned to Irma, who was now partly obscured by the ever-shifting, restless movement of the singers. He shifted slightly himself. The view was not improved so he gave her up and went on with his scrutiny of female buttocks until he stopped at Sarah Casey. Involuntarily he examined her hunched behind, identified it with her chicken-breasted, flat-faced frontside and wondered frowningly why he was doing so. Then he remembered.

I wonder if Henry ever fooled around with her. Being right next door would make it easy. .

"We shall come rejoicing—"
What if he got caught?
"Bringing in the sheaves—"
He never had anything to do with her that I can remember. He said it was an analogy, her living next door like that other girl did.
"Bringing in the sheaves—"
What if he did and Mr. Casey caught them doing it?
"Sewing seeds of gladness—"
Evan grunted as Martha's elbow sharply prodded his ribs. He

looked up at her questioningly, and she dipped her head toward her opened hymnal. Immediately he began singing the familiar words without opening his own book and sang on until the hymn reached it's ringing climax

The next selection was "Love Lifted Me" which the Reverend Osgood allowed them to sing while seated, but when he called for "Onward Christian Soldiers" he made them stand again. Both of these Evan sang from start to finish. His voice was fairly good and sounded better in his own ears than it actually was. He was caught up in the strong tempo of the music. To him the sounds were consonant and pleasing. When the last verse was completed, he reluctantly sat down hoping for a few brief moments that another selection would be announced. When it wasn't, he reverted to his earlier thought, dwelling at length on the hypothetical relationship his mind had synthesized between his cavalier brother, Henry, and the banjo-butted Sarah Casey. With the help of a thousand other originators, Henry had coined the *banjo-butt* in a moment of inspired invention.

Reverend Osgood stood tall and cadaverous behind the rough wooden lectern that rocked on the uneven boards of the rostrum whenever he touched it. For thirty seconds he did not speak and the heavy breathing died down and the chairs scraped and creaked no longer and nobody coughed or blew his nose. Ten seconds of complete silence caused faces to burn and throats to tighten in strange self-consciousness.

"We're going to give something to God tonight," he said. Everyone heard him because he said it loudly. It was not a shout. He said it easily and confidently, leaning across the lectern with his elbows and crossed forearms supporting his weight. But his voice was vibrant and compelling and the night breeze that was cool now and flapped the tent occasionally in quick unpredictable gusts carried it over the crowd so that all heard.

"Most important of all, Friends, are the souls we're going to give Him. We're going to deliver up to Him some puny, degraded souls," said the Reverend Osgood and then he paused to look searchingly out over the crowd as if trying to select or divine which souls would be delivered.

"We're also going to give Him something else, Friends. We're going to give Him what we've grown to think more of than our immortal souls—what we spend on new automobiles, and new dresses, and bootleg whisky, and cheap women. We're going to give some of our precious money."

So began the prologue to the offertory. The Reverend Osgood went on to explain how difficult it was for a rich man to enter the kingdom of Heaven. The harangue lasted for two minutes. He called for volunteers to take up the collection.

I should have asked Henry about Sarah when he was home on leave.

"Who'll give ten dollars? Come on, Friends. Let me see your hands."

The volunteers plucked a dozen ten-dollar bills from twelve upraised and somewhat reluctant hands. The donors struggled with the expressions on their faces, trying to make them register unobtrusive generosity instead of contemptuous triumph.

They sent him overseas so fast I'll bet he didn't get around to telling all those girls in New Jersey goodbye.

"Who'll give five dollars?"

Irma Freeman looks good without her clothes on. Only one I've seen. Her father's a preacher, though.

"Who'll give two?"

"One dollar, Friends. Don't be ashamed to give a dollar."

All those girls at Milcrest that Henry said did; nice girls, too.

Several hundred dollars were waved in the air by those who were unashamed. Those who didn't, were so depression ravaged they didn't have a spare dollar.

4

He said it was after he decided not to be a preacher that he did it. He must of decided mighty quick or went up there knowing it.

The plates, from which the varnish had long since vanished and with the felt in their bottoms worn down to the bald fabric, and the insides white and grained from the nickels and dimes and quarters from countless passes through a myriad reviving contributors in countless small towns, were passed by the volunteers.

Two consecutive hymns were sung and everyone was tired and accepted the uncomfortable chairs with considerable relief when they were finished. The Reverend Osgood had insisted on every verse and toward the end many of the men abstained from the singing altogether and devoted their attention to the pain in their tortured feet. A few, those who had waved the ten and five-dollar bills in the air especially, sourly questioned themselves concerning the motives that had prompted such spontaneous acts of sacrifice.

Evan, who knew the selections by heart, shifted until the provocative backside of Irma Freeman was again within his full view and, while rivaling Martha herself with his vibrant notes, drew upon his memory to outline in his mind what was under Irma's dress. The picture was thrillingly complete when he sat down.

I'll bet being a preacher's daughter doesn't have anything to do with it as far as Irma's concerned. Look at Henry. But I don't think Henry really had the call. He never acted like he really had it. I think that maybe I had it more than he did.

"The twentieth chapter of Exodus, Friends," the Reverend Osgood said and looked musingly out into the faces that swam mistily before him in the yellow light of incandescent bulbs that straggled in a thin string the length of the tent. Here and there a face reflected the pride of its owner in recognizing the contents of that particular part of the Bible. "The twentieth chapter of Exodus," he repeated. "The Ten Commandments." Here the Reverend Osgood paused again as if in thought.

"For the benefit of those of you who don't remember," he continued, "I'm going to refresh your memory by reading them aloud."

The commandments were Reverent Osgood's subject for the evening.

She'll probably go up to Milcrest next year, if she doesn't get sent off to some girl's school. If Henry'd still been up there, he'd go after her, like when I saw him and Irma standing outside when we had the dance at the Legion Hal. But that's not anything. I've done that myself; kissed a few girls—Irma once.

The Reverent Osgood read from the twentieth chapter of Exodus. He read beautifully and swayed gently forward and then backward as he let the words, resonant and meaningful, escape from his lips. It was as if he were reading poetry he had written himself, each word carefully selected so that only those of perfection remained. Everything was stillness and there was no rustling in the crowd to distract from his voice. He was about half way through.

Being off away from home sure made a difference in him. Maybe a lot of the guys act like that. Don't have their folks around to watch them so close.

"Thou shalt not commit adultery," the beautiful voice of the Reverend Osgood read.

Adultery means after you're married. That's supposed to be worse than if you do it before.

Evan looked over the crowd of steady middle-aged married people sitting under the tent, people who had been married so long that they had begun to look alike. Pillow breasted, age-shattered women and stolid railroad-ruined men, coupled so long together that nothing could divorce them one from the other although they may have hated each other for twenty years, sat and watched and listened as the Reverend Osgood told them not to commit adultery.

The young people sprinkled among them smiled inwardly and felt uncomfortable at the sides of their parents.

Henry must have gotten over the girls a little bit to want to join the Army so bad. I bet he's over in England or France somewhere right now wishing he had stayed home. There's plenty not going in for some reason or another. The impassioned reading was over now and the Reverend Osgood put aside his Bible deliberately and paused artfully before he went on. This was a powerful part of his technique. The pauses made the congregation uncomfortable and caused them to feel a certain hotness about the face similar to that felt by the young people when he had spoken about adultery. Everyone wished he would continue. His pale face hung phantomlike and bodiless above the lectern and his presence so permeated the physical confines of the tent that everyone waited in the acute awareness and maddening anticipation of a mass séance.

"You're all sinners," he said loudly at last and pointed an accusing finger at them. His long arm shot over the lectern and the finger prodded the air before him. The words seemed to split the silence and they rang painfully in their ears. "And so am I." The Reverend Osgood magnanimously included himself. "We're all miserable, shallow-souled sinners. And you know what's the worst thing, Friends? We're not worried about it." He paused again. "If we were worried about it, we would be doing something about it. We've forgotten the Old Testament God who wouldn't take any sniveling excuses and said 'Thou shalt not.' He didn't say under certain circumstances maybe it's all right. No rationalizing, no maybe, no excuses. No, Friends. He said unequivocally, 'Thou shalt not,' and He laid down the laws."

The Reverend Osgood started at the beginning of The Commandments and, with considerable embellishment proceeded to go through them again, one by one. His treatment of the first several of them was creditable but his natural predilection for the virtue of abstinence caused him to save his best efforts for the later commandments whose negative aspects appealed to him strongly. By then his voice was filled with sincere passion.

"Thou shalt not—"

Henry said some of the football players didn't want to go, some of the big guys. That shows it's not being afraid that's got anything to do with it.

"Thou shalt not—" the Reverend Osgood exhorted. His voice was not so beautiful now. From the low rumbling mellowness and resonance of the scripture reading, it had with each succeeding sentence climbed to a slightly higher pitch until now it was thin and nasal and accusing. His attitude held promise of its going still higher, growing still more accusing. There was an uneasy movement in the crowd.

Mamma wants me to stay home till I get called. She doesn't want me to go. Says since Henry went she doesn't see why I should have to go.

"Thou shalt not—"

It's a good thing Henry found out as soon as he did. What if he'd gone on through and maybe into seminary before he really found out?

"Thou shalt not—"

Mamma always said God intended one of her boys to be a preacher, and she never gave him a chance to find out if it was him. She said it was decided before I was born and I don't guess she could figure on it being anybody but Henry. But I always felt like I had the call more than he did. When Brother Freeman was talking to all of us summer before last down at the church about needing some of us to make the decision, I felt like I had it.

"Thou shalt not covet—"

The Reverend Osgood stood aside from the lectern now and flung the impassioned words first at one side of the aisle divided congregation and then at the other, stalking back and forth, pointing his accusing finger. There was a seething unrest in the crowd, a strained coagulation of emotion evident in their burning faces. The tall gyrating evangelist seemed to have transfused them with the fervor that twitched in his own mobile face. Martha was transfixed.

8

"...nor thy neighbor's wife." Again he bent, pointed, and glowered.

"...nor his manservant." This he said after he had crossed again. And here he left off with the enumeration of the things not to be coveted. Sometimes he did not mention the manservant in order to take advantage immediately of the strong admonition of coveting another man's wife. But somehow it spoiled the rhythm and lately he had been leaving it in.

How odious it was to covet another man's wife, he said. With what repugnance must God look upon a man who covets another man's house. What a terrible and basic sin was this thing of covetousness. And why count one sin more than another? Is it worse to steal a man's ox than to covet it? Is it worse to lie with another man's wife than to covet her? Who will escape eternal hell fire that waits for those who live with avarice and deceitfulness and profane the name of God? What's to be done with the rich man with the poverty stricken soul? How are we to escape the whirling vortex of iniquity when we reject the regeneration of God's love?

"I'll tell you, Friends—" the Reverend Osgood began to issue the invitation.

Evan had worked himself into the proper frame of mind for a personal regeneration. He had been listening to this last litany of human iniquity. As he became aware of the closing words of the Reverend Osgood he looked at Martha to see her leaning forward stiffly in her chair, captivated, the catalepsy of religious emotion in every straining limb. Her fervor, like that of those about her, crackled in the air and he was suffused with it. Like Martha, he leaned forward in the chair, straining for the words. Before his complete submission he brought back in fleeting recollection the prurient thoughts of moments before and, with the goadings of a Christian conscience, despised himself.

"...you can stand down here and say, 'Andy, I've decided to be on God's side.' That's all you need to do, Friends."

The last hymn was "Rock of Ages," the invitational. The evangelist's voice was beautiful again and could be heard over the wavery voices, full of urgency and importunity. There was the radiance of conquest on his face as the people with burning faces dribbled into the aisle to answer the call. Sarah Casey reached the aisle first, even before Martha. There were tears shining in her eyes. After Sarah and Martha came the others, seventeen in all. Among them were three men, a nine-year-old boy, and Evan.

Chapter Two

Evan Sherman looked anxiously at the young woman as she flipped through the registration cards on her desk, her fingernails clicking rhythmically against the cardboard. When she stopped and examined a card closely, he leaned as far as he could across the counter that separated the registration clerk's desk from the rest of the office. Of the three desks on the business side of the counter, two were empty. It was after five o'clock and they were alone in the office, except for a student at the other end of the counter.

"Daniel Sherman, Ridgefield, Mississippi?" she asked.

He had told her twice his name was Evan Sherman, but she looked steadily at him. Her unsmiling eyes demanded an answer. She was working overtime, and it was obvious she resented it.

"Well, that's right, Daniel Evan Sherman, but I go by middle name, Evan." He didn't dislike the name Daniel, but he knew its origin was his mother's insistence on something biblical. He was just grateful it wasn't Zechariah she had selected to satisfy her religious impulse.

"You can call yourself Joe Palooka, Mr. Sherman, but your college record has to show the name on your birth certificate."

"Yes Ma'm."

"Freshman theology?"

"Yes, Ma'm."

The young woman studied the card for a time and then wrote something on it. There was no front panel on her desk and she sat carelessly with her dress pulled up past her knees, her bare legs spread, so that the white flesh disappeared into dark inviting invisibility where the chair creased the bottom of her thighs.

Evan was on tip-toe, pressing further across the counter, his attention riveted to the card in the hands of the spread-legged girl. She was ten feet on the other side of the counter, but he strained to see what she was writing.

"Got your bursar's receipt?" she asked.

"Yes, Ma'm."

Evan produced the receipt from the folds of his new wallet and held it across the counter. She did not get up, but looked at him and the extended paper slip for a few moments.

"All right," she said. She wrote something else on the card. Pushing her chair back she pulled open a bottom desk drawer and withdrew a large sheet of paper. Her legs flared widely, exposing her pink covered crotch. Evan did not notice.

"Want me to fill a form out?"

"No. You just sign it." She got up and came to the counter and penciled an x by a line with "signature" printed under it. "Right here," she said.

Evan signed his name with his new fountain pen.

"I could fill it out," he ventured.

"We fill out all deferment requests."

"When you think they'll get it?" he asked apprehensively. "I mean, you fill them out right away, don't you. I wouldn't want—"

"Don't worry, Deacon. These folks ain't going to let the Army get you. Anybody can see you're a lover, like me, not a fighter."

The young man at the end of the counter had spoken. He lounged easily with his elbows on the counter and looked at them coolly with eyes so blue there did not appear to be any pupils in them. A deep cultivated wave corrugated his blond hair and his extravagantly broad shoulders refused to be narrowed by the bulk of his body that sagged between them. He was big and good looking and it seemed to agitate the girl that he had spoken.

The day had been long and tiring for Evan. He had walked dazedly about for hours enduring the endless agony of registration. He was lost and friendless in the midst of the confidence and good humor of the upper classmen. He was uncertain and fearful, awed by everything and everyone. He longed to find his room in the dormitory and lie down and shut it all out of his mind for a while. So when he heard the soft but somehow derisive voice, he turned in a quick reflex of confrontation. Belligerence showed in his burning face and the clenched fists pressed tightly to his sides.

"You talking to me?" he asked offensively.

"Now don't get all exercised, Preach. You're liable to get mad and hurt somebody." The blond young man walked a few steps until he stood next to Evan. He limped badly. "You are a preach, aren't you? Theology student, gospel monger, preacher, you know."

He didn't give Evan a chance to answer but turned to the girl and said:

"Better cross your legs, Mona. I can see your squirrel. What you trying to do, get the preach all excited?" He turned back to Evan. "Well are you?"

"Yes, I'm a theology freshman. Why?" His voice was still defensive.

"Oh. No reason. Just asking." He shrugged his giant shoulders. "Had a preach for a room mate last year until he moved over to Seminary. Hell, excuse me, Preach, of a nice fellow. Took me all year to corrupt him." He chuckled as if savoring the memory. "Where you staying?"

"I don't know. They haven't assigned me a dormitory room yet."

Evan had begun to relax. There was no danger here. This was an upper classman and these were the ways of upper classmen. Candid, easy, assured. Let the fluid go back into the gland, save the adrenaline for another battle.

"That's good. You can come in with me. This other guy was older but I never had a room mate like that preach." He shook his head to show how much he appreciated his former roommate.

"Freshmen have to stay together, don't they?" Evan asked. His ignorance of college procedure was stamped on his face.

"Supposed to, but they don't. Half of them know somebody up here and move in with them. Anyway you wouldn't like the freshman dorm. I didn't know anybody so I stayed in it for a month until I did know somebody, then I moved. You wouldn't like it."

Evan thought a minute. A warning went up in his mind. *Don't get started off wrong,* he admonished himself. *He said something about corrupting that other guy. I better not.*

"I better stay in the freshman dorm, but thanks anyway."

"Okay. Suit yourself, but you won't like it." He turned as if dismissing Evan.

"Hey, Mona. Give me a deferment form," he said to the girl who had crossed her legs and pulled her short skirt down to where it just split her lovely knee caps. Her face had stopped burning. The thin ankled shapeliness of her legs was appealing in this position. Her feet were nicely packaged in a pair of high-heeled pumps.

She glowered at the broad-shouldered blond for an instant then reached down and jerked open the bottom drawer and extracted one of the long sheets of paper. She was careful not to spread her legs. The blond watched her with bold admiration in his eyes as she came to the counter and slapped down the sheet of paper.

"You look good today, Mona," he observed.

"I look good to you any day. So does any other woman," she said bitingly.

"No." His face sobered with mock seriousness. "There's some that don't look so good to me. There's an old lady, for instance, who works in the cafeteria that doesn't appeal to me at all." He grinned up at her from his bending position over the deferment form. Their faces almost touched. Evan, who was about to leave

14

and had begun piling his books into his arms from the counter, thought he was going to kiss her. But he didn't; he just looked up into her face and grinned.

"Oh, you're disgusting," she said and flounced into the back of the room. As she walked he watched her, still smiling.

"That woman has evermore got one lovely ass," he said, as if confiding in Evan but loud enough for her to hear.

"Hey, Preach. Where you going?" He had observed that Evan was leaving.

"You wait a minute, and I'll buy you a cup of coffee. I got something to show you anyway."

Evan hipped his books back on to the counter and waited. He hadn't been in the cafeteria, didn't even know where it was. Since his early breakfast at home, all he had eaten was a bag of salted peanuts and a bottle of pop just before he got off the train. That had been nine-thirty in the morning. Now he was suddenly aware of a stomach-griping hunger.

"Here you go, Mona," the blond said and picked up the form he had signed and held it across the counter. Mona came from the back of the room and his eyes caught every movement of her fluid flat-bellied walk.

"Don't you think this is getting silly, Melvin?" she asked and jerked the paper from his hand.

"No, Mona, I don't. It amuses me." There was none of the earlier playfulness in his voice. His eyes held hers coldly, until she wavered and looked away.

"Come on, Preach." He walked past Evan, toward the big double glass doors that opened out on to the campus quadrangle. Evan hurriedly scooped his books from the counter and followed.

"Mel," Mona called hesitantly as he swung the silent glass pane open and turned to let Evan pass before him.

"Yes?" There was condescending patience in his voice.

"I didn't mean—" she began and stopped helplessly. Her eyes

pleaded with him.

"Forget it, Mona." Now his voice was tolerant.

"But I didn't mean—"

"It's all right, Mona, for God's sake. I'm not that sensitive. I like being Melvin Stuart, 4F, unfit for duty. I'm lucky. Now forget it like I tell you." He dismissed her.

"Mel," she called again after he turned and started through the door. There was a rising note in her voice, fear that the closing door would keep him from hearing. She ran to the end of the counter, ready to call out again, his name already formed on her lips. But he stopped. With the door propped open with his hip, he waited, not answering, with indulgent patience.

"You're not mad at me?" Her voice was lowered. She was standing next to him in the doorway, fidgeting, as if she wanted to put her hands on him but was afraid someone would see. Evan heard her troubled voice and saw her troubled face and felt like an intruder, but he did not turn away or stop listening.

"No, Sugar. I'm not mad at you." Melvin smiled reassuringly. He stood looking at her for a moment and then quickly stepped inside and pulled her to him. He kissed her on the mouth. One of his broad hands straddled her buttocks, the other held the door ajar. The blinding brightness of afternoon was gone when they stepped outside. Half the quadrangle was in shadow, and the buildings that walled the green island of the inner campus were no longer austere and foreboding, as they had first appeared to Evan. Suddenly he was very tired. He wanted to sit down and drink that cup of coffee Melvin had offered him.

He shifted the heavy load of books to the other arm, and as he did so, looked back at the administration building to see Mona framed in the glass doorway a hundred feet away. She stood motionless, looking after them. Melvin was smiling when Evan turned thoughtful and quizzical eyes to him.

"Mona's worried about me; this little limp keeps me out of the army. Me being 4F bothers her. Thinks I brood over it. Mothers me. She'd make some man a fine mother."

Evan's face was noncommittal. There was nothing Melvin had said he could comment upon.

Melvin slapped his left leg. Evan became aware of the limping gait again.

"Born with it. One inch shorter than the other one now. Wasn't much when I was little. One wouldn't think an inch would make such a difference."

There still wasn't anything for Evan to say. He smiled compassionately.

"I fill out deferment forms two or three times a semester. Get Mona to send them in. Makes the guy at my draft board mad as hell. He's written twice to tell me that it's not necessary to apply for deferment. I went by the last time I was home and asked him to do what he could to keep me out so I could finish my education. He spent thirty minutes trying to explain why I didn't have to worry about it without hurting my feelings. Dumbest bastard I ever saw." Through all this Evan could see the outrage in Melvin's eyes and he could not understand it.

"What did you think of the tail on Mona. I thought you were going to crawl over that counter to get a better look at her crotch, Preach."

"I guess I missed it. I was looking at the cards she had. My name's Evan, Evan Sherman, if you're looking for something to call me." Evan couldn't keep all the irritation out of his voice.

"Okay, Evan. But the next time you're over there, take a look— it's worth it. They can't take away the vestments for looking, but it may take you until you're a sophomore to find that out."

The cafeteria was already full of students and it was only five-thirty. The boiling anthill of strangers brought the lump of fear into Evan's throat again and he looked helplessly at Melvin who had stopped just outside the main dining room and was peering intently inside. He seemed to be searching for someone and his eyes went from one cluster of students to another, examining the group at each table silently and thoroughly. Shrill female laughter penetrated the din, and he looked across the dining area in search of its source, found it, reviewed the faces which made no apparent impression, and then turned back to Evan. He stood looking at him a moment quietly, smiling at the uncertainty that was in Evan's face.

"Put your books down over there, Evan." He pointed to a row of shelves littered with books. Neat stacks of stiff ones, carefully isolated from the darkened, secondhand, much used ones thrown against the wall, showed the presence of so many freshmen, stiff, new, isolated from their fellows with the same distrust of the conglomerate that their books seemed to have of the dog-eared confidence of the pile.

Evan made another neat stack. He pushed aside other books to make an island of his own. He turned back to Melvin, relieved to be free of the burden.

"You looking for somebody?" he asked Melvin.

"They're not here yet. Come on, we might as well eat while we're here."

Melvin spoke to several older students as they made their way into the serving line. After they selected their food they found an empty table and sat down. Melvin began to eat hungrily. The food was bad but Evan was too hungry to really notice. He ate with increasing relish as the food soothed the burning in his stomach. All about him the hostility seemed to drain from the faces. He could hear individual voices now. Everything was quieter; the day-long scream of urgency that had been inside him, against his eardrums and in back of his eyes, echoed briefly and died. He noticed that half the students at other tables near his were girls, pretty girls, bare legged and pretty. And they were confident, they had a place here. They smiled easily. He thought about Irma Freeman from back home. She was imaged before his eyes and he looked about thinking that perhaps—but no, she wasn't going to Milcrest, some school in North Carolina she had said. The thoughts of home began to flood in and he thrust them aside guiltily, refusing to be homesick the first day. Then it occurred to him that the first day was over, all except finding his dormitory room. And it hadn't really been so bad, now that he had time to think about it, not really bad at all, just tiring. There had been so much to do and it was all done now and tomorrow was Saturday and the next day Sunday. Two days with nothing to do but get used to it before he started classes. All the worry had been for nothing

"What are you studying, Melvin?" He asked between mouthfuls. Now he was proud of the fact that he was sitting with this upperclassman. The girls at adjacent tables gave Melvin lingering glances of open admiration. Just by association he had become superior to the other freshmen who sought consolation and safety in each other.

"Law. Second-year law. You're associating with a five year man, Evan." He grinned up from his plate. "I thought you could tell by looking at me. Can't you see it in my face, defender of the people." He struck a pose, turning his profile to Evan. "If I had a pair of suspenders, I'd look like William Jennings Bryan." His voice was glib and derisive.

There was surprise on Evan's face.

"What's the matter?" Melvin asked.

"Five years," Evan said, incredulously. Here was a man who was starting his fifth year of college. Melvin must be twenty-three, maybe twenty-four, years old. And he was studying law. Law school at Milcrest; he had never thought of it. Preachers and the liberal arts, church secretaries and history teachers, all those; but law, nobody from Ridgefield that he knew had ever had a degree in law from Milcrest. "I guess it never occurred to me they even had a law school at Milcrest. I thought it was—"

"Just a preacher factory? Well, it's a lot more than that. But the lawyers from Milcrest are known as the good Christian lawyers as opposed to the dirty, conniving shysters the other schools produce. Nobody thinks we're very smart," Melvin grinned. It was obvious that he was not deprecating. "Old man that originally endowed this school was a lawyer, big Christian, too. Richest man in the state seventy-five years ago. Regular Robin Hood—took from the rich man and kept it so he could die and leave it all as a monument to clean living and brotherly love. Probably been a communist if he hadn't been so rich. And when he put the part about teaching law in the will he didn't turn it over to the church men—made it a separate endowment. Just to be on the safe side, you know. Religion tempered with reason—very clever old beaver."

All this meant little to Evan, except that now he knew there was more scope to Milcrest than he had thought. There was a law school and this added something, elevated it somewhat, picked it out of the ranks of small church colleges, gave it the worldliness of the university. And what was that about the Seminary? He had mentioned his roommate going over to Seminary.

"What was that you said about your roommate going over to Seminary? I mean, you said it like it was just across the street."

"It's right here on the campus. Over on the west side of the golf course. I guess you haven't had a chance to see it yet. Dormitories and classes all in the same building. It's the biggest one on the campus."

"I thought Seminary was in Pineville."

"Oh, you can go to Pineville if you want to. Pineville's the only other one in the state—gets students from all the other schools in the south. Lots bigger than the one we have here. You probably won't want to though. All the guys like it over by the golf course. Kind of point of vantage you might say." There was a gleam in his eyes. The golf course was meaningful.

Evan flushed, remembering what his brother, Henry, had said about the ministerial students taking girls into the bushes along the golf course. *But surely not after they were in Seminary. Practically ordained, some of them already ordained. Of course not. That's not what he meant.*

"We don't lose many to Pineville," Melvin said musingly except that the innuendo was still in his voice, directed to Evan.

And it was absurd, Evan thought, *even if that was what he did mean, because there was no way to know that I could even interpret it like that.* Evan changed the subject.

"How long does it take to be a lawyer, Melvin? How much longer you got, I mean?"

"Three years pre-law, three years law. This year and one more, Preach, then I can go forth and spread the gospel of the law. We're a lot alike, you know, in our professions, I mean. Both saviors of a sort. You'll save them from hell; I'll save them from jail. But if I'm lucky, I'll get paid more eventually." Melvin flashed a quick smile. "Our educations are alike, too. You get three years of pre-God and two years of God. The doctors have it over all of us though. They have a lifetime of being God." He said this with a sigh, a feigned resignation.

Evan winced. *There were rules about it. Melvin is breaking them talking like that. You can't even think things like that. Where was his fear?*

"I better go see about my room," Evan pushed his chair back, starting to get up.

Melvin placed a broad hand on his arm. The movement was restraining, not really forceful, but his hand was heavy, purposeful.

"Wait a minute, Preach. There's something I want to show you. A couple of things, in fact." His voice had in it the same quiet restraint as his hand.

Evan remained seated.

"I got to do it before six." Not much determination, just a little, high and dry in his throat.

"You just wait a while. We'll get that all straightened out."

Melvin looked at him reassuringly. The blue eyes did not offer him a choice.

"There they are," he said, as if speaking only for himself, and rising, beckoned to someone in the front of the dining hall. Evan was conscious of a small eddy of movement, response to Melvin's signal, as he followed the direction of his gaze.

He stood up as they approached the table, uselessly, for he was examined briefly by the two girls, and by the two boys not at all, and then ignored as they turned to Melvin.

"Who's this?" Melvin nodded toward the taller of the two girls. His eyes had not left her face since she had come up to him. Evan looked from one to the other, sensed the intense attraction, spontaneous and physical, Melvin had to this strange girl. But he could see none of it in her pale face. Hair black as night framed the paleness, draining the color and expression, leaving only the gray eyes, the pencil line eyebrows, the lips red with lipstick. She stood only four or five inches shorter than Melvin's six feet two. There was no physical extravagance to any part of her seemingly perfect body. The bulk of Melvin seemed to subdue everyone in the group, except this tall girl.

The other girl was watching them closely. She shifted uneasily and small red splotches of color showed on her sallow cheeks. She started to speak, mouthed something, soundlessly stopped, and then stood uncomfortably examining Melvin's profile.

"Molly, this is Melvin." The introduction was made by the taller of the boys who had all the appearances of being from the country. Only a few seconds had elapsed, but he seemed to be allowing them, waiting to see the impact of her register in Melvin's face. As the country boy paused, Evan broke his attention from the two of them long enough to look at him, to examine his country face and lanky frame. The mark of the summer sun burned from under his collar. Where it creased his neck there was a white line that grew wide and then thinned as he shifted his head. A smile exposed his large teeth to the gum line. The other boy was quite short, not over five foot six. He didn't have a country look about him.

"She came down with me yesterday, from home. She lives in town." He was no longer speaking to Melvin. It was for everybody else's benefit, as if being from town gave her some special distinction. She hadn't walked behind a plow, he seemed to say. She was a town girl. There was admiration in his voice; he was proud of her. "She's going to do religious studies, ain't you, Molly? Give the preacher something to think about while he's making up his sermon."

"She and Evan here ought to get along fine then. Evan is a preach," Melvin said and jerked his thumb toward Evan who nodded his head in confusion. He had hoped he would be spared their attention. The four of them examined him silently for five seconds.

"What about Fred?" Melvin asked. He no longer looked at Molly but at the tall red-necked boy. "Have you seen him yet?"

"Yeah, I saw him. He said about eight o'clock it ought to be dark enough."

"What does your almanac say about the moon? Did you think about that? Are we going to be able to see?"

"Sure, I thought about it," the country boy said with contempt. "Moon's full. All you had to do was look—it's up now. You'll be able to read the paper by it at eight o'clock."

"Where is my bird?"

"Over in my room. Don't worry; nobody's going to bother him."

"Everything's ready then, I guess. You got him fixed up today?"

"He's ready. Couldn't be better. Sharp as a razor." He paused and looked down uncertainly, obviously wanting to say something else.

"Maybe you better pay me now, Mel," he said still studying the floor about his feet.

Melvin looked up sharply and the pupils disappeared from his eyes as he stared hard at the side of the country boy's red face. The others shifted uneasily before Melvin reached for his wallet.

"Okay," he said. He took out two tens and a five and handed them over. They were quickly pocketed.

"You got a good bird there, Mel. I don't have to tell you though. You've seen him. You saw what he could do up at the place. You wait and see."

"We better go," Melvin said shortly. "It's after six."

"We didn't eat yet." the country boy said.

"You can eat later."

"We'll just have a cup a coffee."

They filed up to the cafeteria counter and returned with their coffee to drag chairs around the table until all six were squeezed together in a tight huddle. They sucked on the steaming liquid without talking. Melvin sat impatiently between Evan and Molly, drumming his fingers on the table. The sallow-faced girl was on Evan's other side and she looked accusingly at Melvin from time to time, oblivious of the others at the table.

And to Evan all that had been said was meaningless, something they all were aware of except him, something that had taken from Melvin the attitude of bland indifference and caused his eyes to become animated with excitement. Evan gave up trying to piece it together and sat thinking about Melvin and the two girls. The sallow-faced one was jealous of the other. Evan speculated that she was his girl or maybe had been his girl and still wanted to be. But she was jealous of the tall girl who was really beautiful. Funny the way she hadn't opened her mouth the whole time, only sat there looking around serenely like she knew something nobody else knew. And that other fellow, the short one, hadn't said anything either but nobody seemed to know he's even alive, or care. Evan realized that he hadn't really been introduced to any of them. The only name he knew was Molly.

It's been over an hour, Evan thought, *and I haven't seen about my room. I ought to get away somehow before they close. It's after six. Maybe it's too late already. Of course it's too late. Why didn't I go on? I don't even know where to go.*

With the thought, a wave of panic came over him.

He turned to tell Melvin he had to go and saw that he was getting up.

"Goddamn it, come on," Melvin commanded. "It's almost six-thirty."

The jealous girl got up immediately and stood by his side. There was a belligerent possessiveness in her attitude as she stood there, a sort of defiance. The others also got up and started to move toward the front of the dining room. Evan hung back uncertainly.

"Come on, Preach," Melvin turned back to him.

"I have to see about my room." He did not want to speak. He wanted them to go on and leave him free to do what was to be done. He had hoped they had forgotten about him and thought if he just stood there they would go on without even noticing.

Melvin walked back the few steps that separated them until he stood only a foot away. Evan found it difficult to keep his eyes from wavering as Melvin looked at him.

"Come on, Evan. I said I'd take care of that," Melvin said levelly and waited until Evan made the first movement. He let him pass, and then walked back himself to where the jealous girl waited anxiously for him. She breathed a shallow sigh of relief and victory as he came back to her. Her large firm breasts jounced elastically as she walked and Melvin turned to her and flashed a quick smile. She smiled back happily.

Chapter Three

The books were heavy in Evan's arms, so he sat down on the steps and slid them onto his knees. The others sat down too, and they waited silently for Melvin and the country boy to come back out of the dormitory. Molly had walked beside Evan across the campus and now sat beside him, very closely, so that her thigh grazed his in the movement of crossing her legs. This physical touch caused a shiver of thrill to run up his spine. Nothing showed in her face that was indistinct and phantom-like in the moonlight. She returned his gaze and he quickly looked away. He was afraid to look again and wanted to say something but could think of nothing.

Melvin emerged from the dark doorway carrying something in a sack. Close on his heels was the country boy who looked apprehensively about, his movements nervous and furtive.

"Let's get the hell over to the woods," he said as they came down the steps. "This is against the law, you know. They'd throw our asses out of school if they followed us and saw it."

What is it? Evan groped for some escape, some answer. *What are they going to do? How did I get into this? Against the law? God, what are they going to do?"*

But he walked with them between the two dormitory buildings, crept along with them through the shadows of the other buildings until they reached the fringe of trees that lined the golf course. Evan gave up his thoughts of escape as they entered the woods.

The moon was the only light now, and it was bright. There was as much light as there would be until the moon went down, and even in the woods the figures around him were distinct; it was just their faces that he couldn't see. Evan followed blindly, not allowing himself to think about anything. Melvin was ten yards ahead of him, hurrying, intent on whatever it was that he was to do, so that if he had had the courage to ask him, it would have been too difficult. And he did not want to know. Whatever it was, it was better not knowing, because there was nothing he could do now; he had come too far.

Then they all stopped abruptly, and he saw the other group standing in the clear space, maybe thirty feet square, between the trees. There were four of them, two boys and two girls, and Melvin went up to one of the boys and spoke to him. Evan heard his name. This was the Fred that had been mentioned before. They were all quite close now. Most of them seemed to know each other and he found himself standing where he was obscured by the others in his group. Molly stood beside him.

"You got the wire?" Melvin asked the one he had called Fred.

"Over here," Fred turned and showed him a roll of chicken wire lying on the ground.

"Well, let's stretch it."

They made a ring of the wire as the others watched. Evan scraped up a pile of pine needles and put his books on them and then came back to watch them stretch the wire and prop it up with pine branches where it sagged. When the ring was complete they paused a moment, studying it.

"You ready?" Melvin asked.

"Who's going to hold the money?"

"Do you have it with you?"

"Yes."

"I trust you. We'll keep it until it's over, Okay?"

Fred looked intently at him. He was as tall as Melvin and his big frame was lithe and powerful. They would make a good match,

Evan thought as he looked at them.

"Okay, let's go."

As they moved apart to pick up the potato sacks that were lying on the ground, everyone but Molly and Evan came up to the side of the chicken wire ring. Then they followed and stood together looking first at Melvin and then at Fred.

Over the edge of the ring each was bent with the potato sacks extended almost to the ground. Each clasped the bottom of the sack with one hand and held the top with the other. In this position they remained for what seemed a great span of time, the sacks held quiveringly vertical, indistinct shapes in the uncertain light of the September moon.

The spectators crowded closer, straining to see, careful not to collapse the fragile wire ring. Molly stood by Evan's side transfixed, her eyes wide and staring, absorbing the filtered light, grown darker in her pale face.

And Evan, rigid and expectant, thinking of nothing, free of his old fears in the face of this new one, recoiled convulsively as her hand, colder than the September night had made it, closed about his. But he held it, too tightly until the warmth growing in her caused him to ease his fingers and allow her hand to lie quietly in his.

"Now!" Fred's voice stabbed into the night.

Both he and Melvin released their grips on the bottom of the sacks and snapped them upward with the same motion, identical and simultaneous, as the rest strained even closer, widening their eyes to see.

The relief flooded over Evan

A cock fight. My God, a cock fight. And I didn't know. The sacks, the ring, against the law, not even a murder, just a cock fight and I didn't know. They even mentioned birds and he paid the redneck. Kiss my ass!

But he was caught up in it. The cocks hit the ground on their feet and walked indifferently and jerkily around the ring until they sensed each other and, when they were close enough to see, the hoods came up and after that no one knew which one was which because they were just a violent, prolonged explosion of shadow and strange noise.

Molly began to squeeze his hand then, pulsating and spasmodic, and, when he could drag his eyes away from it to look at her, he saw that her eyes were wide and reflected some of the moonlight. Her lips were parted slightly and the lipstick was black on the phantom of her face, so he caught the tempo and squeezed her hand back.

The shadows burst apart and one of the cocks went for the side of the ring where Melvin stood, trailing a dark line of blood, crashed into the wire wildly and then was back in it again without any choice.

None of them knew when it was over, not Fred or Melvin even. The country boy couldn't be sure. The bird flopped in its dying convulsion and they stood, all ten of them, as they had been, straining and silent spectators in the night shadows.

Then the victor began to crow and Melvin moved and Fred was beside him as he tore open the twisted ends of chicken wire. They both squatted beside the dead bird. Molly withdrew her hand, making no other movement, just taking it away so that Evan's was suddenly cold with the moisture of it before he realized it was gone. He looked at her and she was as she had been in the cafeteria, serene and apart from him.

"Goddamn it, Coley!" Melvin cursed.

"Yours?" the country boy asked although he knew it was and had known since the first spur had drawn blood.

"Goddamn you, Coley!"

"It was a good bird. I never guaranteed anything. That was a good fight."

Melvin and Fred stood up. The moon lit Fred's face. He was smiling but there was no humor in it, just a dull grinning mask. He held out his hand.

"Let's have it," he demanded.

Melvin glared up at him, and Evan felt they were teetering on the edge of another pit of violence. Thus they stood for a few moments while the others shifted uneasily about. The smile never left Fred's face, and when Melvin finally twisted his own mouth into the sardonic smile of the vanquished, they all sighed in relief.

"You wait a minute," Melvin said and then turned to face Evan. "Come here, Preach."

At first it didn't register; he had become anonymous in the darkness of the woods.

Preach. Preach. That's me. He wants me to come over there.

"Wh-what?" croaked from Evan's throat.

"Come in here, Preach."

Evan's feet were leaden. As he passed, he looked at Molly, and she was far from him, watching his movements with a mild interest. And the others were just spectators, waiting for the next thing to happen. He stood at last by Melvin.

"Say a few words over the deceased," his twisted mouth demanded.

Evan tried a feeble smile that died on his lips.

The girls that had come with Fred giggled.

"But, Melvin, I don't—"

"Preach," Melvin said again quietly. He put his hand lightly on Evan's shoulder. "Just a few words."

Evan opened his mouth to protest again, but couldn't. Instead he shouted:

"Lord have mercy on his soul." His voice shattered the night quiet and rang in his ears.

Melvin squeezed his shoulder and then patted it gently.

"Thanks, Preach," he said and reached down and picked up the dead bird. He sent it arching into the trees.

"Okay, Fred," Melvin said and drew his wallet from his pocket.

He counted ten ten-dollar bills into Fred's hand. Fred watched it closely.

"Okay?" Melvin asked easily

"Right."

"You take the wire."

"Right."

"Come on, Preach. You did great. Get your books. You'll stay with me tonight."

As they left, Molly took Evan's hand. They walked together until Molly turned to go to her dormitory. Neither of them had said a word.

Chapter Four

Apprehensive and defeated, Evan stayed with Melvin. He stayed even after that first night, not because he was intimidated into it, but because in the light of day there were no ghosts and because he wanted to and because it was the easiest thing to do.

Nothing was said about the cockfight. Only once in all the time afterward was it mentioned, so Evan never had any certain knowledge of what had prompted it. He only sensed that Fred embodied all antagonism for Melvin. He was the supreme adversary, and he represented whatever struggle was at this point necessary in Melvin's life.

About a week later, Evan asked Melvin if he had seen Molly again.

"Yeah. I saw her a couple of days ago walking across the quadrangle. Must have been between classes."

"Was her hair as black as it seemed when we were in the woods?"

"Black as a raven's wing and almost to her waist," Melvin said and gave Evan a curious look. "I noticed the hand holding the two of you were doing. I do believe you're smitten with the stunning Miss Sullivan."

"Her last name's Sullivan?"

"One hundred percent Irish. Just one generation from the Emerald Isle. Parents came over just after they married."

"How do you know all that?"

"That redneck she came down with told me."

"You plan to date her?"

"Not yet." Melvin smiled and Evan knew the Molly Sullivan subject was closed.

For the most part Evan and Melvin got on well together. Under the hard shell of Melvin's cynicism could be detected a strange sentimentality. Of all the things that came to frustrate him, his physical inadequacy was the most tormenting. In this, there was nothing that could be said to comfort him. He hated being 4F, unfit for service. He despised Evan for not wanting to join the Army. He detested him for having two legs the same length. But the hate was sporatic and short lived. Once it was spent he stopped railing at Evan, forgave him his cowardice, his hypocrisy, his two legs the same length. He helped Evan with his studying. He was a brilliant student and what was obscure to Evan was clear to him. Bitterly he philosophized; cogently he explained everything, even the Bible, which he interpreted with his mind alone and without skepticism. At this, Evan was amazed. Melvin was not religious; he sneered at the "preachers." He seemed to have no compunction about his rational blasphemy.

But he was a good teacher. Evan thrived on it and his grades were of the best in his class.

The days went by and Christmas was near and everybody went home for the holidays.

Seated on the train and looking out at the bleak country-side that was unfamiliar and held no promise in its sameness, Evan thought of Henry. He remembered Henry's homecoming of a year ago from this same train that was overheated and strong with woman odor, woman fragrance. He turned and let his eyes run over some of the girls that were sprinkled about the length of the car. Molly's pale face loomed before him, suspended in his imagination. He had not seen her often after that night. He had never spoken to her. He sighed, remembering.

Henry was in England now, not far from London the letter had said. He hadn't been able to tell them exactly where, just England. And a year ago he had come home to tell his father that he was joining, and had told Evan about the girls and the golf course, and about not being a preacher. That had only been a year, almost to the day, and now it was he that was going home. How different it was! What kind of ride home had it been for Henry? What had he been thinking about? The girls probably.

There had been moments of doubt during this first semester, long agonizing spells of wondering, during which he could see no direction, no purpose in his life. The eventuality of becoming a preacher could not establish itself and he fought it, creating now an imperfect picture of himself walking in the everyday paths of righteousness. But that had come and gone. Now he was comfortable with his decision. He was going home.

The monotonous country slid by speckled with window grit. With his chin cupped in his hand and his elbow supported on the narrow windowsill, Evan looked unseeing through the glass. All that was necessary now was for Martha to reinforce it all, give him the comfort and the approval. All that had spilled from the flood she poured over Henry, Evan had gathered and used, and used again. There was infinitely more. There would be long evenings when they could talk. Martha's face lingered in the window, obliterating the coldness that hung over the fields.

The buildings along Railroad Boulevard were obscene. They were dirty and offended the eye. The dirt was railroad dirt and they had been corrupted by it. The one-floor buildings were mostly shabby grocery stores that offended the eyes of those passing through on the train. It was the only part of Ridgefield they would ever see, and looked like the crummy railroad outposts of hundreds of other identical towns covered with the identical spew of identical steam engines.

Evan stepped down from the train directly in front of the depot.

He stood on the asphalt pavement and looked expectantly about, seeking the change brought about by over three months of Ridgefield without Evan Sherman.

But everything was the same. The Beanery still squatted to his left and the iron benches were still pushed up against the front outside wall. The plumes of black smoke rose in the same pattern from the same smoke stacks in the shops. The same figures inhaled the same dead station house air, while the same overalled men occupied the same positions in the same attitudes of three months before. The three months had been a brief closing of the eyes.

So nothing was changed at all. There was still the room without Henry, forsaken and lonely, perhaps a little colder now that Christmas was near. Martha was the same. They talked into the night when his father, Amos, a conductor on the railroad, was gone, and doubts only came to disturb him before Martha subdued them.

His father moved at the same distance, drifting beyond the focal point of Evan's consciousness as before, but now there was something undefinably different. It seemed to probe unceasingly for recognition. There was something in Amos Sherman's eyes. He looked at Evan oddly at times. Sometimes he would sit and study his son's profile in silence, and there was a feeling in it that made Evan turn in his chair, the hair rising on the back of his neck. And Amos would turn quickly away.

On Christmas Eve, Martha was melancholy and depressed. She spoke often of Henry and shook her head forlornly at the prospect of the first Christmas without him. They were all affected. The coldness was in Evan's bones, as it had been when he lay in the bed without Henry's warmth and listened to the receding anguish from a despairing train whistle rise in the night.

At midnight they got up and prepared for bed. Evan lay in the dark, waiting for her to come.

They knelt beside the bed.

She called upon God.

She demanded protection for Henry from the treachery of night.

It was already light where Henry was.

Evan went back to school two days early. They all knew it was early, so the lies about having to study seemed necessary. Martha's protests were mild and quickly abandoned. Amos accepted it in silence, realizing his inability to penetrate Martha's religious armor was partly responsible for driving him away from her. He had a strong feeling of kinship with this son. It came up to tighten and burn his throat when he saw the panic in the boy's face. He longed to say something to him, formed the phrases in his mind, mouthed them to himself, always retreated in the face of what Martha had armed Evan with, afraid the pity would be misunderstood

So Evan escaped back to Milcrest. The campus, and everything there, was something he wanted to put his arms around and hug to him. In the early evening he walked across the quadrangle. Half way across he stopped and put his suitcase down on the grass that was already damp with quick December dew. He looked about for several minutes searching for some sign of life. Nothing stirred. The campus was deserted and quiet. He strained to listen for some sound. There was no sound to be heard.

A thin sigh escaped him. He smiled wryly for his own benefit and picked up the suitcase. There would be someone in the cafeteria.

Suddenly he was hungry. As he walked, the hunger mounted and the poorly cooked, tasteless fare that came from the cafeteria kitchens appealed strongly, and he quickened his pace.

The dining room seemed vast in its emptiness. A few students were scattered around and a half dozen faculty members clustered at several tables close to the serving line. They watched him inquisitively as he walked toward them, lost interest and resumed their eating and conversations.

There wasn't much to offer in the way of food. A lone colored girl stood behind the counters taking short orders, doling out the bready sandwiches, dishing up the ever present frankfurters and beans. The steam-table trays were empty for the most part. The cashier sat at a table drinking a cup of the bitter coffee that had been made for breakfast.

Evan asked for a plate of beans and frankfurters. He sat down and ate hungrily.

When the hunger was gone and the plate empty he leaned back and stirred his coffee, absently watching the faculty members as they talked. A tall, gaunt associate professor of history inhaled deliciously on a cigarette, sipped his coffee. Evan wished that he smoked.

His thoughts drifted. They settled on the days he had just spent at home and he determinedly closed his mind to them. The seemingly endless evening devotionals with Martha exhausted him.

In his mind's eye, he saw the dimly lit corridor of the almost empty dormitory where he must go. For two days, he would be essentially alone, and the prospect of this disheartened him.

He could go to a movie. Yes, that was it, a movie. The day would be all right. He could study a little, read a novel, loaf around, and walk down through the woods in back of the Seminary building. Abruptly he got up and rushed from the dining hall.

He slid his new suitcase under the bed onto the same dustless rectangle where the old one had lain for over three months. He walked from the room, closing the door loudly in the stillness. His footsteps echoed hollowly as he walked from the building. He caught the bus into town and went to a movie.

It was nine-thirty when he walked back out on the sidewalk in front of the theater. The movie had been a comedy, and the two hours of it had refreshed him. He felt good again. He walked buoyantly down the street and halted in front of the drugstore. A malted milk would be good before going to bed. He hesitated, thinking about the expense added to that of the movie. Nobody would be there to talk to. He went on. Maybe he should walk back out to the college. It would do him good. Two miles in the biting air would make him sleep well. He passed the bus stop.

Many of the houses still had the Christmas decorations in evidence. Through a window in most of them could be seen the colored lights of the Christmas tree; holly wreaths and cardboard Santa Clauses clung to the front doors in familiar shadow. Now and then colored lights were strung thinly from the roof edges of those more determined to enter the mood of festivity.

Most of the houses were ablaze with lights. Every window he could see was a rectangle of yellow. Occasionally mirthful voices drifted out and rang penetratingly in the cold night. This all seemed strange to Evan. Ridgefield was not quite as large but practically everyone there would be in bed by now. College town, that must make the difference, he guessed. It was some bigger, too. Then he passed a large house where a number of figures could be seen gaily active through the broad windows. Couples were dancing determinedly in the midst of all the others who ignored them, intent on their own conversations, their own pursuits of happiness. The sound was jubilant and appealing as it came to him. He paused on the sidewalk to watch. While he was watching he remembered. It was New Year's Eve.

New Year's Eve. The indefinable, reasonless joy of it was transfused into him from the swaying window-framed shapes and he smiled to himself. He felt the ecstatic swell of happiness that gave a springy jauntiness to his steps. He skipped half a block.

Anyone would think I'm a fool, he grinned to himself.

It lasted all the way, for the full two miles.

His heart pumped as he climbed the steps in the dormitory building. His last display of goaty joy, leaping and running across the quadrangle, had taken his breath. Walking down the dark corridor he shucked off his top-coat. Tiny beads of perspiration stood out on his forehead; the blood was hot in his face now that he was in the closeness of the building, and his underwear was cloyingly damp. He hurried to take off his clothes.

The unexpected light blinded him as he swung open the door. His darkness dilated eyes recovered blinkingly. He saw them before they could move, before the ecstatic faces could register outrage, still coupled under the brightness of incandescent light, in Evan's bed.

They were discovered. Mona looked at him---stricken, unbelieving. She was sitting up now with one white perfect leg stretched in front of Melvin, the other bent under her. She hugged her small breasts in her arms.

"Get out, Sherman!" Melvin hissed between his teeth. He sat unmoving in the bed. His face was ashen and savage.

Evan fled from the room. He groped blindly down the corridor, found the stairs and stumbled down them, out into the night again.

He sat on the bench and leaned against the tree gulping the cold air. His mouth was dry; every gasping breath was painful. The raw air stung through his clothes to his damp skin. He began to shake violently and went back inside the dormitory and searched for an empty room on the first floor. When he had found one, he lay down on the sheetless mattress until the shaking subsided. He got up and pressed his forehead against the cold window pane and thought of nothing. Eventually he removed his head from the cool relief of the glass and stared into its transparent blackness. For ten minutes he stood without moving.

He went over to the cold radiator and turned the valve. If he was to sleep here, the room must be warm; there was no cover. He could use his topcoat. Better get out of the damp underwear.

When he stood naked, except for his shoes, it began to crush in on him. His own body precipitated it. He held it at bay for a while as he put all his clothes back on except the underwear and topcoat.

He lay down and pulled the coat over him and surrendered to the thoughts that came rushing in.

Mona. Registrar's office Mona. Melvin told me she was married; her husband away in the war.

She walked swayingly before him. She sat down with her legs carelessly spread so that his eyes were dragged to peer between them. She shifted so that he could see.

But he had seen it all, the act, her nakedness, her complete nakedness.

Irma Freeman's body was outlined through the filmy summer dress.

She stood in the woods with the wet bathing suit about her ankles. She stretched and preened, had pride in her body. The white shanks of her legs, long, smoothly curved, were profiled against the dark woods. She turned to face his hidden eyes.

And before the cockfight, the girl with the large breasts pressed against Melvin. She clung to him fluidly as he kissed her. Melvin's large hand covered her breast briefly before she dragged it away. Molly stood beside him watching them. Her lips were parted slightly. She had pressed his hand and looked at him strangely. But just once and never again.

She was naked, completely naked. He had seen the act, the coupling, the savage marriage.

And Irma Freeman naked in the woods.

And the girl with the big breasts naked with all her clothes on.

And Molly with the nakedness in her eyes.

And the compelling voice of Andrew Herbert Osgood: "Thou shalt not commit adultery."

The room was warm and Evan's eyes were still opened against the blackness when the twelve identical notes were chimed from the Presbyterian belfry in town. He did not hear them, but the new year had begun. With sudden hunger, men kissed other men's wives at parties all over the land. And the wives responded with searching, open-mouthed abandon. A drunk was run down and killed by another drunk in Memphis and Seattle. Babies were stillborn and breathed not one breath of the year of our Lord nineteen hundred and forty-three. Guns boomed, men died, couples fornicated, women conceived. At hourly intervals the year of 1942 reached a climax and lay back spent after the giant historical orgasm.

And in the land where time begins Henry stood in a dark doorway and drew a young Englishwoman to him.

"I don't have much time," said Henry. "They're shipping me out. If I could just have that to remember when I'm over there." And after an adequate pause, "Couldn't we go to your place."

And, when it was New Year's at Milcrest, he was getting out of bed, leaving her, assuring her he would write, while he knew that in a week's time he wouldn't remember her name.

Chapter Five

Evan avoided Melvin for two days. He waited until he could see him walk out of the dormitory and start across the campus quadrangle before he went back to his dormitory room to shower and change his clothes. He spent most of the time holed up in his borrowed room thinking about his own reaction—the moral and physical shock of Melvin's and Mona's sexual union. He would examine himself standing before a large mirror one of the room's regular occupants had installed next to his chest of drawers. He postured in an attempt to avoid the appearance of holy disapproval he knew Melvin would expect. He also took inventory of his physical attributes and shortcomings.

Evan was a very good-looking eighteen-year-old freshman. He stood a fraction over six feet, a slender 170 pounds; well muscled enough to look good in a pair of tennis shorts and a tight polo shirt. His auburn hair and hazel eyes went well with the summer tan that would stay with him through the winter months. Except for Melvin, Evan Sherman was as physically attractive as any male on the campus. Unfortunately, he had so little social confidence that his naiveté brought looks of dismay to the faces of the girls in his high school, who found him delectably attractive. The few he kissed didn't completely discourage his fumbling attempts to feel them in sensitive places, but even a mild resistance would so discourage him that he would never try again. He seemed to be oblivious to the second looks he got from the coeds on the Milcrest campus. The only girl he had noticed enough to think about was Molly, and he thought about her constantly. Now he thought about Mona; he couldn't keep the picture of her—naked and shocked—from appearing again and again on his mental screen. And he had to go back and face Melvin.

He went back to his dormitory room and waited for him.

"Am I going to get a lecture about the evils of lechery, maybe a few verses of scripture that condemn poor Mona as a poor-man's Mary Magdalene?" Melvin stood in the doorway, relaxed, leaning against the door jamb with his arms crossed. When Evan started to answer, Melvin held up his hand.

"Before we get started on the sanctimony, I'll tell you bout Mona. I told you she was married, but I didn't tell you the guy she married two years ago was a miserable, brutal, abusive, stupid son-of-a-bitch. She was twenty-one and should have had more sense, but now there seems to be some strange sense of urgency with young women. Maybe it's because of the war, some fear that they will be left out. She tried to leave him but he came after her, abused her until he had to go back to his army unit."

Evan was sitting on the side of his bed and began to stand up, started to speak, but again Melvin held up his hand.

"Not yet," he said, and Evan sat back down. "Mona and I sleep together, rarely, only when she needs me. It's always when she needs me. She says I'm the only one, and I believe her. I stayed here for the Christmas holiday, because she doesn't have any place to go." Melvin came in and sat on the side of his bed facing Evan. "Now, I'm ready for the sermon."

"I don't have any sermon, Mel," Evan said. "I really don't care what you do, but I think you're just trying to justify what you're doing. That's the kind of thing my brother did when he was here last year, before he joined the Army. I never could understand that. He was supposed to be studying theology. He said it wasn't adultery if neither of you were married.

"Don't agonize over your fallen brother, Evan. He had a lot of company out in the Seminary woods." Melvin was leaning forward with his forearms on his knees. "It's amazing how many women on campus think it's sinful to sleep with anybody but a Seminary boy. Those guys are very convincing, but it takes some of the ladies until they're juniors to go out in the woods for their holy couplings."

Evan flushed in sudden anger. "That's a lot of crap, Mel." He said it as evenly as he could, but his voice had begun to rise. "Why can't you leave the theology students alone? I don't care what you think about the preachers—just keep it to yourself."

Melvin leaned forward, looking intently at Evan's white face, his bloodless lips.

"You're a dumb young punk, Evan." There was a deadly calm in Melvin's voice but it was controlled and level. He sat on the edge of the bed with his forearms resting on his thighs and his hands hanging between his knees. There was no evidence of the physical movement that Evan braced himself for. Melvin's face was soberly expressionless. Nothing could be read in the shallow blue discs of Melvin's eyes. "You'll be a dumb punk when you get the diploma that says you're an honest to God holy man, only you won't be so honest to God, just holy. You'll be twenty-three years old and you'll go out and start telling the poor devils two or three times your age what they've got to do so they won't be left out." He paused, caught his breath, and rushed on.

"You'll sit at the table of one of your good parishioners and eat the food bought with the money he cheated the widows and orphans out of. You'll shake your head with him over the soul of the poor bastard who got caught sleeping with the church organist that you had just drummed out of the church. The same one you'd been wanting to get into ever since you saw how nice her ass looked spread out on the organ seat. And you won't know the difference."

Melvin shrugged his giant shoulders almost imperceptibly. "Okay. The way you look at it, it is a lie. Maybe not a third of the preachers have ever been out in the seminary woods with a woman. Maybe not one in ten, or in a hundred. I only know a few who have and it doesn't make any difference to me one way or the other. They are probably some of the best of the whole lot. I've seen the rest of them, too, Evan, and I swear to God I don't know where they come from. The misfits, mercenaries, maladjusts, queers, fools, cheats, liars. One hypocrite or another. And there are the cowards, Evan—physical, moral, intellectual—whatever they are."

He nodded to Evan who was standing in a quivering fury of indignation before him. "You're not a physical coward; you just don't have the foggiest idea why you're here. I'd rather see you out in the woods. There seems to be fewer hypocrites out there."

Evan hit him flatly in the face. He hit him as hard as he could, and it popped Melvin's head back. Before he could do it again Melvin's hand had closed on his throat, just tight enough to bring tears into his eyes, tight enough that his clawing hands couldn't remove it. Melvin held him at arms length and wiped a trickle of blood from the corner of his mouth with his other hand. He examined the hand silently and then ran his tongue over his gums tenderly, surveying the damage.

"I wondered when you were going to get around to doing that," Melvin grinned. His teeth were pink with the diluted blood on them. I'm not through yet, Evan."

"Don't do that again" he said softly. There was more menace to the words than if he had shouted them.

The beds were a few feet apart. He sat down on the other one facing Evan. They held each other's eyes briefly.

"Every once in a while I find a good one. So I won't say there aren't any. There just aren't many. And remember this. The sex part is incidental. I'm not trying to justify it or myself. I'm just saying it's not that important. You've got more to worry about than that. I'll tell you something, Evan. My father is a preacher."

Evan's eyes widened. He never was prepared for what Melvin

said. This must be some new lie. The protest was on Evan's face.

"Why, you said—"

"Yes, I know. I told you he was Delta-country landed gentry. He was, but he wasn't my father—he just happened to be married to my mother—just her husband. My father's a preacher. Do you know how many people know that? Just three, Evan. You and me and my mother—of course I'm not counting the preacher. And do you know how I know? I know because I stood outside in the hall when I was four years old and watched my real father and mother, and it took me ten years after that to know enough to remember. I don't look like him at all except for the eyes."

Melvin had lapsed into silence. Evan sat four feet away wanting to drop his eyes from Melvin's face, too ashamed to do it, ashamed for Melvin to see the pity.

Melvin got up.

"Save that pity, Preach. If you think I'm disillusioned, you're right. There isn't time for illusion any more. I think you'll need that pity for yourself anyway."

He walked to the door and swung it open. Evan was still sitting on the side of the bed with his back to the door.

"One more thing, Preach." The way he said "Preach" made the anger flare suddenly in Evan's eyes again. "What you think of Mona is your business. But if you ever say anything to embarrass her about what you saw, I'll slap your face inside out."

Evan got up and went to the window. He watched Melvin limp down the outside dormitory steps and start out across the quadrangle. There was something pathetic about his shambling gait. His hands were shoved into his trousers pockets. Evan turned and crossed the room quickly. He let the door slam loudly as he bolted into the corridor.

Halfway to the administration building he caught up to him. He fell in stride and did not meet the questioning glance. When Melvin shrugged and turned away, Evan asked:

"Where you headed?"

"Administration building," Melvin answered. He turned to look at Evan again, who looked up sharply and Melvin grinned at him. Evan hesitated and then grinned himself. They walked on in silence.

Mona stood behind the counter watching the lone student, who was in the office, write his name on a scheduling card. She looked up as they came in and, recognizing Evan, flushed deeply and turned her burning face back to the cards before her, appearing to scrutinize it closely. She twirled a pencil nervously in her fingers, and, when the boy finished, she asked him several unnecessary questions that caused him to look wonderingly at her, and then at Evan and Melvin. When he had answered them he stood uncertainly, waiting until she dismissed him with her eyes. At last she turned defiantly toward them, because she couldn't delay any longer.

"Yes?" she asked, and because her bottom lip quivered a little she took the inside of it between her teeth.

Melvin and Evan slid down the counter until they were in front of her, and didn't speak until the door had closed behind the boy.

"Take it easy, Mona." Melvin looked at her solemnly until some of the panic drained out of her face. When she thought she had sufficient control she sacrificed the comfort of Melvin's face to let her eyes flicker to Evan. He smiled thoughtfully, reassuringly, pursing his lips, showing no intent to embarrass her

The tension ebbed slowly, and her shoulders slumped forward as she allowed herself to relax. She looked tired. A feeble smile struggled on her lips and her face brightened a little.

"You might as well get used to Evan, Mona. He'll be around for a long time," Melvin advised quietly.

Evan thought he should say something. They were both looking at him. He had to be careful, not smile when he said it.

"I've got a miserable memory," softly, levelly, no smile

But it must have been wrong, the way her eyes flared.

Shouldn't have alluded to it at all; just kept my big mouth shut.
She was all clouded up again, looking at him coldly, not letting his eyes get away like they wanted to. He didn't dare look at Melvin. He felt like a fool.

"Good," she said softly at last.

She warmed.

She smiled widely. Her eyes were almost happy.

She was very pretty.

Evan sighed in relief.

"Give me a form, Mona. They're really after me now. Been over three months since I sent one in," Melvin said.

Mona got the form, and Melvin began to fill it out. She leaned close to him across the counter. He stopped writing and looked up into her face which was inches away. Evan thought that he was going to kiss her.

"What are the poor civies going to do when the sailors get here, lover? You know how the women love a uniform. I don't think we'll have a chance."

"Some girls don't go for the bell bottom trousers," she said meaningfully. "There'll be a few left for you draft dodgers."

"All the same if they offer me a commission, I think I'll take it. Nothing less than a full Commander, though."

"They might offer you Captain of the latrine," Mona offered thoughtfully. She had fallen in with the banter. Evan was amazed at her recovery. He had never heard a woman talk like that before.

"Head, Mona, head. Let's be careful of our terminology. In the Navy it's a head."

"Pardon me."

"That's okay." He leaned across the counter and kissed her on the mouth. "Come on, Evan. We better get out of here," he said and pushed the deferment form across the counter.

"You finish this for me, Mona, before Evan has to start forgetting all over again."

It was a nice day, bright, gusty, and cool on a Mississippi January afternoon.

"Where now?" Evan asked.

"Thought I'd walk down to the woods."

"Mind me coming?"

"Of course not."

"I'm sorry I hit you."

"So am I. You busted my lip on the inside."

Evan didn't comment on it further. They rounded the dormitory building, started toward the woods.

"You're wrong about the preachers, Mel," he said after several minutes of walking across the spongy golf course grass.

"Maybe so." Melvin agreed off-handedly. His voice showed a distaste for the subject now.

"That's a terrible thing for you to believe. Maybe a few of them shouldn't be here, but you can't—"

"Look, Evan, you—"

"No. Let me finish. You may be right about me. I don't think so though. Maybe I'm a coward for not wanting to go into the Army. At times I believe I am, and then I talk myself out of it and start feeling pious as hell about the whole thing. I have shortcomings like anybody else and I'm working on them. If I'm a hypocrite and a coward, okay, then I'm a hypocrite and a coward, but you can't condemn them all. And I can't worry about the others. If there are some bad ones, there's nothing I can do about it—only myself. I'm the only one I have time to find out about. If I let myself worry about the others, I never could see through all the misery I'd be letting myself in for."

Melvin studied Evan's face while he talked and, when he finished, looked at him curiously a few moments longer and then turned to look thoughtfully into the dark line of trees they were approaching. The closeness of the woods made it seem cooler and Melvin shoved his hands deeper into his pockets and hugged his sides with his arms. The day was bright and the thin wreaths of misty clouds were motionless in the sky. As they got closer to the woods, Melvin could detect the smell of the river two miles away.

"Everybody lies to himself a little," Melvin said musingly, more to himself than Evan. "Life is too brutal and human beings are too flawed to bear it without the lies. Has it ever occurred to you, Evan, how many chances a man has to play the hero and how many times he plays the fool instead? How many guys do you suppose there are in the world just waiting for their chance to prove something, and, when it comes, they're hiding behind the kitchen door waiting to pinch the maid on the ass or sitting on the toilet reading a story about a brave young airplane pilot in Collier's magazine."

Melvin's voice trailed into silence, as if he were continuing what he had been saying in his mind, because it was easier than the effort of speaking. His jerky shambling gate infected Evan somehow so that his own movements were erratic. They slouched on toward the gray undefined tree trunks ahead.

Melvin continued aloud now:

"Maybe it's all illusion, all mind." He tapped his temple with his forefinger to indicate the dwelling place of what it all meant.

Melvin chuckled and took a sidelong look into Evan's perplexed face. He broke out into a loud hoot of laughter at Evan's confusion.

"Don't take me so seriously. Anybody with half an eye can see there's nothing to it. Where is the comedy? Couldn't have something like that without a sense of comedy. I would have been born a girl and been named Pearl and all the rest which is too absurd for people so civilized and who take themselves as seriously as we do. There's a certain amount of justice nowadays, too. Mama couldn't have coped with that scarlet letter. It would have been just too much for her."

Evan didn't know what Mel was talking about. He hadn't read Hawthorne's *Scarlet Letter.*

They were in the woods now. The ground was spongy with leaf-mold under their feet. A cool dampness enveloped them, and the light that filtered through the evergreen foliage made varying patterns of lacy shadows fall across their shirts as they moved along. There was no underbrush and the trees were widely spaced as if by design. Occasionally a patch of velvety green moss could be seen between the grotesquely gnarled roots of some enormous oak tree. Evan stopped and ran his hand lightly over one such patch. It was cool and alive and close-knit as a carpet. The smell of the river hung in the air, and Evan pictured the tumultuous swiftness of the water as it raced over a gravel bar. Beneath the surface he could remember the slick splotches of variegated clay.

Something plopped at his feet, startling him from his reverie. He caught a glimpse of a big gray squirrel as it bounded into a beech tree. The limbs shook convulsively for a while and then were still.

"What makes you think you had the call, Evan?" Melvin was propped against a tree waiting for him.

"What?"

"Come, let's walk a little farther." Melvin said and began shambling slowly ahead. When Evan caught up to him he said, "What makes you think you have divine calling? That's what they call it, isn't it? I mean, when did you know? How did it come?"

Evan began hesitantly to tell him about the night in the canvas tabernacle. It sounded ridiculously uneventful and meaningless in his own ears. He tried to think of how he had felt and found that he could not remember feeling anything in particular. There was the gushing pain of embarrassment in him when he realized he was ashamed of what he was saying. He was not doing it justice, what he was saying was not adequate. The thought flickered in his mind that he must tell him about Martha and Henry before there could be any meaning, but he could not bring himself to mention them. Irma Freeman in a gauzy, summer dress floated before him and his voice trailed off in disgust with himself.

They had reached the clearing in the pine trees when Evan finished telling about it. He was surprised when he recognized it. It hadn't taken long to get there, not like the other time, and it was different in the day-light. There was no sign to link it with the breathless violence of that September night. Now the place was cool and bright and detached from the wavering uncertain figures with the craven faces leaning over the chicken wire, bathed in moon glow and shadow so that there were no eyes, only black pools of straining emotion.

Evan wrenched the eerie picture from his mind, and as it vanished and the winey freshness of woods came into his nostrils again, the disgust and depression of moments before vanished also.

"I've meant to come back down here before, but I never did," Evan said.

Melvin had stretched full length on the ground, careful not to disturb the dry pine needles on top of the cushiony mat, and lay in an attitude of complete relaxation, looking up through the branches overhead.

Evan stretched out beside him.

"Why?" Melvin asked.

"I don't know. I just did."

They lay in silence for a while.

"Was that all there was to it? I mean what happened at the revival meeting that night, Evan?"

"I can't explain it, Mel." Evan said sullenly.

"No, I don't suppose so." There was a note of contempt in Melvin's voice that Evan caught. He didn't reply to this and pressed his lips tightly together hoping Melvin would let it drop. After a few moments passed and Melvin didn't speak, Evan asked:

"What was the cock fight about, Mel?"

"Just a bet."

"That was a lot of money."

"It was that kind of bet."

"I got the impression it was more than just a bet. Who was this guy Fred?"

Evan waited for an answer, and, when it didn't come, said, "Okay, forget I asked."

"No, I'll tell you, if you want to know. You remember the tall girl that was with us that night?"

"The one with the—"

"Yeah," Melvin interrupted "the one with the big tits."

Evan flushed deeply.

"Yes, I remember her," he said.

"Well, she's Fred's sister."

Evan remembered the two of them pressed together in front of the dormitory after they had come out of the woods and while Melvin kissed her his hand had cupped over her breast and Fred was standing there close enough to touch them, watching.

Evan shivered again.

"Let's go back. I'm getting cold," he said.

Evan would occasionally see Melvin and Mona having a cup of coffee together in the cafeteria or sitting on one of the benches in the quadrangle. When Mona saw him, she would smile and wave for him to come join them. He did on a few occasions, but only briefly, and then he would move on. If they continued their physical intimacy, he was unaware of it.

Melvin never called him *Preach* again, and waited for Evan to talk about his faltering convictions and the boredom he had come to feel with the theology lectures, the homilies and prayers, that seemed to drone on until he was on the edge of coma. Melvin would never tell Evan what to do. He would say, "Give it some time. You'll know when the time comes. I don't think you're ready for any big decisions yet."

As Melvin seemed to lose his cynicism, at least where Evan was concerned, they developed a friendship that became less and less fragile Evan told Melvin more about how his mother's fundamentalism and religious strictures had affected his and Henry's life, and had driven his father ever closer to agnosticism. In turn, Melvin recounted the nonspiritual history of his family.

"It took six generations of Stuarts and one hundred and thirty years to reduce the twelve thousand acres of Mississippi Delta cotton fields to the ten acres where the old house still stands. Twenty-four rooms and my mother still lives in it with a maid and a cook. She seems to think she's part of a southern aristocracy that doesn't still exist, if it ever did. Fortunately, there's still enough money to last until she's gone." Melvin paused and seemed to be considering what he would say next. "I won't consider the old place mine when she dies. I don't have any Stuart blood in me, so I'll sell it, if I'm still around in thirty or forty years."

Chapter Six

Evan settled into the academic routine of finishing the second semester. The course work was so unchallenging that he asked, and was granted, permission to audit a course in Contemporary American History. The lecturer was spellbinding when he detailed the changes in the last forty or fifty years that affected modern social structure, and college life became much more comfortable.

The change in Evan's attitude, from sour endurance to a much more pleasant enthusiasm, prompted Melvin to ask:

"Did you get Molly to give you another hand squeezing?"

"What?"

"You don't seem as suicidal as usual. I figured something besides that wonderful new course you're taking must have happened."

"Do you think Molly is Catholic?"

"Of course, she's catholic. She's Irish."

"I wonder why she came to a Protestant school like Milcrest."

"Milcrest isn't a protestant school. They just have a protestant Seminary. A Hindu, anybody, can come here. Anyhow, Molly isn't practicing to be a nun."

"Do you think she would go into town and see a movie with me?"

"How would I know? Evan, don't you realize there are a couple of hundred girls on this campus who would jump at the chance to go damn near anywhere with you, unless they think you're a little funny?"

"What do you mean, funny?"

"You've been on this campus for over six months, and, as far as I know, you haven't had a date. I've seen the second looks the girls give you, and you don't even give them a smile. They talk to each other. Maybe they think you don't like girls."

Evan got the point.

"For God's sake, Mel! You don't think I'm that way, do you?"

"No I don't, but you can't keep acting like you're a monk. Go stand outside Molly's classroom building and wait for her class change. When you see her, ask her to have a cup of coffee with you in the cafeteria. You'll find out what she thinks."

The first day Evan didn't see her. The next day he saw her coming out of a classroom building across the college quadrangle.

"Hello, Evan. I've been waiting for you," she said before he had a chance to say anything. He didn't know how to respond, so he waited until she gave him a questioning look.

"Molly, do you have time to have a cup of coffee with me?"

"I have all afternoon."

During the two months left in the semester, Evan and Molly became friends. On their first date, Evan held her hand briefly, toward the end of the movie, but made no attempt to kiss her when they lingered at the front door of her dormitory. He wanted to ask her what she meant when she said she had been waiting for him, but didn't. He was afraid she would fault him for the lack of courage he knew he had.

As the weather warmed, they would find a secluded place where they could sit and talk. By the library, there were private benches in a labyrinth of evergreen hedges. For Evan, their talks became a confessional of sorts. He told her of his boredom with the repetition and sanctimony of his courses in theology and his reservations about the religious restrictions imposed on the life of a minister. She told him her major wasn't Religious Studies, as the red-

56

neck boy had said at the cockfight, but Music with a preferential interest in Religious Music.

"Are you certain the life of a minister is what you are really prepared to accept?" she asked after Evan had repeated his complaints several times. She didn't seem impatient with the indecision that Evan was sure Melvin would consider repetitive whining, but it was evident that she wanted him to do something. "If you aren't, you can always change your major. The courses you've taken can be used as electives in an Arts Degree"

That instant Evan gave up Theology as a major.

He turned to Molly and looked into her wondrous eyes that had turned from grey to violet in the twilight. He cupped her face in his hands and kissed her until her lips slightly parted.

This was the last time they spent any time together before Milcrest became institutionally involved in the war.

In late May, the Navy V-12 program came to the Milcrest campus. The V-12 program was designed to give officer candidates preliminary training and the opportunity to take college courses. At first, there were only a few officers in summer suntan uniforms to be seen walking importantly from building to building and drinking coffee all to themselves in the cafeteria, as if harboring from the prying civilian eyes the momentous secrets of a nation at war.

Then a bus-load of sailors came and they could be seen about the campus, hurrying on one esoteric mission or another, ignoring all others save themselves, except for the covert officer-aware scrutiny they gave all women, young and old alike, dwelling longest on the young ones with undulating walks and lingering smiles.

Then they began to pile in. Almost every bus and train brought them. Some came straight from high school graduation exercises, still in civilian clothes, to be transformed over-night into blue-bold saviors-of-democracy-for-mankind, especially the women in it.

The university's conventional system of two-semesters in an academic year was changed to three semesters. Civilian students had a one-month summer vacation, while the navy students concentrated on the non-physical aspects of naval officer training. This was another source of irritation for those students who considered a three-month summer vacation was something guaranteed by the Bill of Rights.

After giving it some thought, Evan began to like the new arrangement.

"You know, Mel, I think I can get a Batchelor of Arts in just two more years, if I take a few extra courses. I'd need only nine more semester hours than my regular schedule, only six more, if I had taken that course I audited for credit."

"What's your hurry? You that eager to get into Seminary?"

Evan hesitated and then decided he might as well tell Mel he had given up on Theology as a major.

"I'm not going to Seminary, Mel. I've changed my major."

They were walking together to have lunch at the cafeteria. Mel stopped on the sidewalk and turned to look at Evan:

"You want to tell me why?"

"Because I was never intended to be a minister, Mel. As you know it wasn't my idea. I've been fooling myself about *having the call.* I don't have any idea what that means."

"Was it all that crap I laid on you about the misfits and hypocrites who stand in the pulpit?"

"That was part of it. I just needed somebody else besides you, somebody with no reason to have a personal prejudice, to help me sort it out."

"Somebody with gray eyes and jet black hair all the way to her waist? Somebody like the most beautiful girl on the campus?" Mel knew the answer, and he smiled as he waited for Evan to confirm it.

"Well, yeah, Molly. She's catholic, but she's pretty passive about religion. She's not majoring in Religious Studies, as that redneck said. Her major is Music, with a special interest in religious music, because she likes it."

They were sitting in the cafeteria before Mel asked:

"What are you going to tell Mamma when you go home?"

"Nothing about any changes. I think I can dance around the subject for a month."

"You'll eventually have to tell her."

"Maybe not. She doesn't really know what courses I'm taking. I'll tell her the good news about saving a year before I get a Bachelor's degree. After that, I'll just have to tell her I'm not going to Seminary and I'm not going to be a minister." Evan grinned before he went on. "That's when she'll kick me out of the house."

"I hope she does. You can't live with Mamma after you grow up."

"You did."

"That's different. She was all alone in that big house. Anyway, I'm a cripple." Mel smiled to let Evan know it was a joke.

Evan changed the subject. "Will you get your lawyer's degree any sooner with the new semester arrangement?"

"The semester arrangement in graduate school programs hasn't changed. Law is in the graduate degree program. I still have two more years."

Evan sat silently thinking about the timing of his own graduation date: "It might work out we'll both graduate at the same time."

"Maybe, if you work your butt off. You in that big a hurry?"

"Yeah. If it means I can get out of my Momma's house a year early." Evan grinned and went on, "I'll be twenty-one, all grown up."

"In your case, it might take another year or so of weaning." Mel was partly serious with his reservations about Evan's escape to the uncharted waters of self-support. He changed the subject. "Since you've given up God, what will be your new major?"

"I don't know yet. I'll spend the month at home making up my mind."

"Good luck."

During the summer month he spent at home, Martha was always aware of where Evan was, and left him pretty much alone, until it was time for the evening devotional. His acceptance of this ritual made it easier to think about what he was going to do when he got back to Milcrest.

Molly never left some part of his mind, and the idea of Music kept coming up when he considered his new major.

When Evan's brother Henry was in eighth grade, Martha bought a second-hand upright piano and hired a teacher to give Henry once-a-week lessons. For almost a year, the piano-lesson agonies kept the untalented Henry on the piano stool until, much to Henry's welcome relief and Martha's dismay, the teacher pronounced Henry unteachable.

The strange piano melodies that Martha heard when she was in some other part of the house would send her hurrying back to the parlor to find no one seated on the piano stool. She would call Henry to come play something for her, until she realized the mysterious melodies didn't come from him. Henry didn't have an ounce of musical talent. It never occurred to her that the melodies had come from Evan.

Evan would listen to the tortured lessons given to Henry and, after the lesson was finished, go look at the keyboard chart on the piano music stand. He would finger the keyboard and silently practice the chords shown on the basic chord charts. When he thought everyone in the house was out of earshot, he would try some simple melody that was similar to something he had heard, correcting his mistakes as he went along. By the time Henry had taken his last lesson, Evan could play complete songs he had heard without the printed sheet music. He could not read the music he was playing, he was playing by ear. There came a time that, if he had heard it, he could play it.

Martha eventually learned about Evan's ability to play the piano, and when he balked at taking lessons, she didn't insist. Her experience with Henry had drained her musical enthusiasm.

When he was in ninth grade, Evan wanted an instrument he could play in the high school marching band. He wanted to play during the half of the football games and eventually in the dance orchestra that played for high school dances. He selected the clarinet because it was easy to carry and he liked the sound of it. He went through the motions of taking lessons from the band director, but he had learned the instrument so completely in three months, he didn't need the printed score, even when it called for harmony instead of the lead lyric.

The relatively simple marching band music and twice-a-year band concert program he played by ear. When the band director learned what Evan was doing, he lectured him on the necessity of reading music and challenged him to play more and more intricate scores he had heard only once on phonograph records. When Evan played them all note for note, he declared Evan to be a musical savant and began to feature him as a soloist in the band concerts.

He played in the dance band during his junior and senior years and had learned all of the big-band music that featured Artie Shaw's clarinet leads. When he stood up and played the infectious *Stardust* and *Begin the Beguine* and especially *Frenise,* the girls would take their partners as close to the band as they could and dance until the piece was over. With their impatient and jealous partners, they would stand in adoration until the next selection began.

Evan was adored but didn't seem to know it. He thought it was just about the music. While the hormones of every male and female at the dance were spilling all over the dance floor, Evan seemed to be unaware of how sexually attractive he had become to the girls who heard him play. Besides that, he was the best looking kid in high school. The girls began to think he was a little funny when it came to sex, even the few he had kissed. He was just painfully shy and didn't know of the social requirement that he be as horny as the girls who were his contemporaries.

While Evan was home during his June vacation, he played the piano enough to please Martha and the clarinet when he was alone in his room. When he went back to Milcrest, he took his clarinet with him.

Chapter Seven

The civilian undergraduates returned to the campus after a month of summer vacation to be astonished by the transformations that had taken place in so short a time. The Navy had commandeered the freshman dormitory as a barracks. The sailors were in full complement, almost four hundred, and drilled in squads wherever there was as patch of ground large enough to accommodate them. The cafeteria was partitioned and duplicate steam tables were installed. In the beginning, the sailors filed in, platoon at a time, until a third of the space was filled. The twelve hundred civilians used the remaining two thirds complaining sullenly of the crowded inconvenience. No sacrifice was a willing one.

The board of administrators leaned over backwards. It was their patriotic duty and their wrinkled old chests swelled with patriotism.

Classes began on July first and the male civilians settled down to silently cultivate their resentment of the intruders, and the sailors countered with their attitudes of superiority over those they considered unfit for duty. And there were many cries of anguish from the un-uniformed men who had been forsaken, and from the boys in blue, in their turn, as capricious females bestowed their favors briefly, only to tire and abandon one for another, younger or older, more hard whiskered or downy cheeked, darker or more blond, shy or impetuous.

In six months they all had begun to tolerate each other and a certain amount of intermingling promised a return of the days when hostility was a rare and frowned on emotion.

Evan was more concerned with the discomfort of the sullen, windless July heat that turned the classrooms into ovens full of baked students trying to concentrate on something other than the sweat that puddled in any belly crease or wrinkle. He had spent most of his nineteen Mississippi summers barefoot and in short pants, sitting in the shade of his front porch or under some oak tree in his neighborhood.

"You might just as well get used to it," Mel advised. "It will be almost October before it cools off."

Molly seemed relatively unaffected by the sweltering weather. She didn't seem to sweat like Evan did. As he thought about it, none of the girls seemed to be affected by the heat. Probably something in the female metabolism he concluded.

"Have you told your faculty advisor you're changing majors?" Molly asked.

"No, I haven't," he held up his hand to stop what she was going to say. "I just know I'm not going to continue with Theology. I haven't decided I want to major in Music."

"You're not considering Music because of me, are you?"

"Not really. I probably wouldn't have thought about it, except for you, but I do have a real interest in popular orchestra music, not classical. I just don't know whether I need to get a degree in it. I know I don't want to be a music teacher or band director." Evan paused and then said, "I play piano and clarinet, mostly clarinet. I brought my clarinet with me."

This was a revelation Molly didn't expect. "Can you go get your clarinet?"

"Sure. You want me to play it?"

"I want you to go to the music room I use and play for me."

The music room held two pianos, one upright for practice and a grand that could be rolled to the campus concert hall in the building. Molly took sheet music from a cupboard and spread the pages on the music stand on the upright piano.

"How about the grand?" Evan asked. "I've never played a grand."

"They don't really want..."Molly began to tell Evan about the restrictions on amateurs playing the grand piano. "Well, why not?" she said and moved the sheet music to the grand. "Have you ever played *Vilia*?" she asked.

Struggling to read the score, Evan began to finger the melody lines, but was so haltingly slow about it, Molly began to hum the melody. After six or eight bars, Evan began to play the complete keyboard. He had heard the song before. When he finished, Molly stood looking at him until he turned to her and waited for the question:

"You don't read music do you?"

"Not very well, but I can read it when I have to. I'm just slow until I know what it sounds like."

"Do you play mostly by ear?"

"Well, yeah, anything I have heard."

"Can you play *Vilia* on the clarinet?"

Evan took his clarinet out of the case and played the song with much more command of the instrument than when he played piano. His playing was so contagious that Molly began to sing.

What he heard was a voice so strikingly beautiful that he almost stopped playing just to listen.

"My God Molly, you sound like Jeanette McDonald!"

"I've always loved that song, since I heard her sing it on a record. Do you know *Kiss Me Again?*"

"Give me the first six or eight bars."

Molly sang until Evan held up his hand to stop her.

"That's a Kate Smith song." And he played it on his clarinet while he listened to her unbelievable voice.

When Molly stopped singing, Evan stood with his clarinet dangling from his right hand and looked with wonderment at the sublime expression on her flawless face. She sat down on the piano bench and waited for him to speak.

"I've never heard a voice like that, like yours, Molly."

"And I've never heard anyone play the way you do, Evan." She wasn't just returning the compliment; there was as much passion in the music he made as there was in her voice as she sang. "Has anyone ever told you that you have perfect pitch? That's the only way you can play by ear the way you do."

Evan had never been told that, and he didn't really know what it meant. He had never heard Molly even hum a popular ballad. As he thought about it, he realized that when she spoke in normal conversation, her voice was musical, perfectly matched with what she was saying.

"Do you have perfect pitch?"

"I've been told I do. I didn't know it until I got here and my voice instructor tested me in all octaves and said I did."

Molly had been, and still was, something of a sensation in the music school. When the voice instructor, assigned to her for preliminary testing, called the other voice instructors to come listen to her, they were amazed that her voice ranged from contralto, mezzo soprano, soprano, lyric soprano, to coloratura soprano.

"How many octaves do you have?"

"Five. But I have to work up to coloratura."

"I don't really know what that means."

"Think of the voices you may have heard. Contralto would be Gladys Swarthout singing *Carmen*. Coloratura would be Lilly Pons singing *The Bell Song*."

"You've lost me, Molly. That's opera, isn't it? I really don't know much about classical music. The songs you just sang were sort of semi classical. Do you sing any of the popular ballads?"

"Sure. Play *Blue Champaign,* I'll sing it contralto. Then play *I'll See You Again.* That's a Jeanette McDonald song, and I'll sing it soprano."

Molly could sing any of the popular songs Evan thought of to play for her.

"I think we better go, Evan," Molly said after a half dozen songs. The classes are changing and they'll be using this room."

"You've amazed me, Molly. You're no doubt majoring in Voice," Evan said as he put his clarinet back in the case.

"I believe we've amazed each other, Evan. I'm majoring in Vocal Performance and Operatic Studies. I'm here because this is one of the best Music Schools in the south. If you're really interested, I can introduce you to some of the faculty people. They could help you decide."

"I'm not ready for that, Molly. I need to think about it,"

When Melvin listened to Evan's excited and somewhat garbled account of the music-room session with Molly, he held up his hand to stop him in mid-sentence.

"Slow down, Evan; take a breath. You're leaving out stuff I want to know."

"Well, yeah. I'm just so amazed by the way Molly sings, it's hard to keep from jumping from one thing to another. I'll go back to when she sang *Vilia*."

When he finished, Melvin said, "I'm really not that much surprised about Molly. Aside from being the most beautiful female I've ever seen, she seems to be the most confident young woman I've ever been around. She seems to be more comfortable in her own skin than anyone I've ever known."

Evan wondered how many times Melvin had actually been around Molly. How could he seem to know that much about her with the few contacts he seemed to have had. But he thought of her comment when he had finally worked up the courage to talk with her. "I've been waiting for you," she had said, like it had been inevitable, just a matter time. He had told Melvin about the strange greeting, and he didn't seem surprised.

"How many times have you actually talked with Molly?" Evan

asked.

"Just a few times since you started seeing her a few months ago. I'd run into her on the campus and we'd talk about you. I think she knows more about you than you know yourself. If I said I thought she has some sort of unexplainable clairvoyance, would you know what I mean?"

"No, not really. Unless you mean some kind of insight people rarely have."

"That's about what it is. I think when she first met you in the woods; there was some sort of connection that made the relationship you have now, and will have in the future, inevitable. I don't think she has the slightest interest in any male alive but you." Melvin smiled before he added, "Not even me."

"Neither one of us knew about the music. I mean, I didn't have any idea that she even sang, much less that she has the most glorious voice I've ever heard."

"She didn't know that you have the talent you have either. I think that's part of the clairvoyance. There was much more to you than she actually knew. But she knew it was there. She just didn't know what it was, but she knew she would eventually discover it."

"I hope you're not making all this clairvoyance stuff up just to keep me from acting like a love sick sophomore, which I obviously am."

"You're lucky, Evan. Just let it happen, whatever it is. It may be the best part of your life from now on." Melvin had finished talking about it, playing the part of the wise older friend. "Now, play me something you like." They were sitting on a bench by the library that was out of sight of the rest of the campus quadrangle. Evan opened his instrument case and assembled his clarinet.

"What about *Begin the Beguine*?"

"Yeah, I like that one."

Melvin had a good musical ear and couldn't believe that someone who had practically no musical training could play like Evan

68

played. He thought of the big band instrumentalists he had heard. Evan sounded even better than he remembered them playing

"That's amazing," he said after Evan finished. "Play some other ones, whatever you like."

And Evan played. After fifteen minutes, he had begun to draw an audience. Students followed the haunting clarinet music and came, clutching their books, to stand just inside the hedges where they could see the player. A few of them sat on the grass, prepared to stay as long as Evan played.

Word got around about the guy who could play a clarinet like none of the students could remember hearing. He would play in his dormitory room when Melvin wasn't studying and would let him. When someone would ask for a song he couldn't remember, he would ask for someone to sing enough of it to remind him of the melody. If he had heard it, he would play it. There were a surprising number of students that had true enough voices to get him started. Sometimes there were so many rapt listeners that some would sit on the floor, if there wasn't room on the beds. Sometimes Melvin would come in and clear out the room and tell Evan to "Hit the books."

Evan's campus fame grew, and so did Molly's. Music students who had heard her sing would tell others, but she didn't sing in her dormitory room. Sometimes, when she was alone, she would spontaneously begin to sing a song she liked, but she didn't often sing without an accompanist. Her instructors discouraged it. They would tell her when she was ready for acappela vocals. If Evan was carrying his clarinet case across the campus, and Molly was with him, other students would follow at a respectful distance until they could hear the music. At first, they couldn't hear Molly's voice; she was singing softly, almost pianissimo, a strangely haunting blend of instrumental and vocal lyric.

One day in early October, they walked into the Seminary woods until they found an open spot in a stand of pine trees that was large enough for Evan to spread a blanket he had brought from the dorm. Evan wanted to talk with Molly about what he had decided about his major.

"Journalism," he said. "I've found out that all the classes I've taken will count as electives or part of a minor. I can take all the required courses I need to graduate in one more year after this one."

"Why are you in such a hurry, Evan?"

"I've told you how it is for me living at home. I want to get away from all that, go someplace where I can be what I want to be, maybe Memphis or New Orleans."

"Why journalism instead of music? You have an unusual talent that just needs the discipline you can get here."

"I like my music the way it is, Molly. I don't have any interest in being a concert performer. I know you do, you have the voice for it. I can play clarinet in dozens of places in a big city, but not make a living doing it. I just want to sit in at night or on weekends with some group that needs a clarinet lead. I never thought of music as a career."

"What is it about journalism that you like?"

"There are many different things you can do on a newspaper. You can be a reporter or an editor or a feature writer or an editorial writer. That's what the courses here get you prepared for. Not any of them right away; there's always an apprenticeship."

Molly leaned back on her arms stiff in back of her and looked at Evan so long he started to go on with what he had decided to say, but she leaned forward and said:

"I had thought we would graduate at the same time. I don't know that I can get my degree by the end of next year."

"Will you see if you can work it out? I don't want you to be here without me."

"It would be just another semester, if I can't."

"I don't want you to be anywhere without me." Evan leaned over, took both of Molly's hands in his, and pulled her toward him until their faces were close together. I'm in love with you, Molly."

"I know you are, Evan."

"Did you know I fell in love with you that first night in the woods?"

"Yes, I did, Evan. But I don't think you realized it at the time. That's why I said I had been waiting for you."

"Molly, do you—"

She put her fingers on Evan's lips to stop him, then she leaned forward and kissed him.

"Let's give this a little more time, Evan. We have a lot to do in the next year and a half."

Evan had not ever been in love before, had never even had a high school crush on a very available cheer leader or baton twirling drum majorette. His unwanted mental virginity was a silent embarrassment. He didn't have the faintest idea how to play the cavalier and wondered how Mel would handle the year and a half of waiting. It was probably something that he would not accept.

"You're just getting to the point where you should have been as a high school sophomore," he said, when Evan finally worked up the courage to tell him about his confession to Molly. "I don't think it would be a bad idea for you to let up for a while. You've got a lot of work to do, if you're going to graduate at the same time I do, which, by the way, may not be the best idea you ever had. I'm like Molly; what's your hurry? Why not wait until you're sure the two of you can graduate together?"

Evan thought about Mel's advice for a week and decided he was right. He could endure another semester, because there wasn't any vacation before the regularly scheduled last semester that would require him to go home for a torturous month of evening devotionals with Martha.

"You're right, Molly," he told her. "I'm not in that much of a hurry. Leave your schedule as it is. I'll slow down and not load up

71

with extra course work. It will be a relief, and I can be sure we'll graduate at the same time."

What he really meant was that he wouldn't be leaving her alone on campus without him. The prospect of a three-month separation was frightening. She might find someone else.

"I'm glad you decided that, Evan. That will give us both more time. I don't think I could have arranged to graduate early."

So they would go into the woods when they had the chance to play and sing for each other. Both Evan and Molly had a simple, almost childish, innocence about them. They really didn't know how to be anything else. They had not come to the point where they could, on hormonal impulse, change the way they approached each other. There was little physical contact, except for an occasional quick and spontaneous kiss when Molly was especially affected by their music together.

But regardless of their apparent innocence, there would come a time during their last year at Milcrest when they began to succumb to the smoldering urgency they felt whenever they were together, without the distraction of someone else.

Molly's voice became an ever-changing revelation to Evan. She seemed to put into the songs she sang when they were together everything that had been left out of her life. With her amazing range she would sing some songs in sultry contralto and others in soaring coloratura. In spite of her appearance of innocence, there was an intoxicating suggestion of sex in her voice she didn't know she had.

Evan seemed to unwittingly offer some sort of curative for whatever troubling insecurities that were in Molly's life. His playing became completely responsive to the moods of her voice. She loved the low register of the clarinet, and he would embroider what he played, never losing the melody line, until she would begin to sway and then dance as she sang. She knew the lyrics of the popular music and sang the ballads of the big-band female vocalist—

Helen O'Connell, Ginny Simms, Peggy Lee, Margaret Whiting—all of them. She had Evan listen to the religious music she liked and had him learn to play *Ave Marie, Sanctus,* and *Oh Holy Night.*

In the middle of May, Evan asked Molly if she were up to the two-mile walk all the way through the Seminary woods so they could have a picnic by the river neither one of them had even seen.

"I'll go to the deli and get the stuff to make sandwiches," she said immediately. "Can you get a little cooler for some pop?" As Evan was leaving, she added. "Bring that blanket and your bathing suit."

Middle-of-May afternoon temperature in Mississippi is often in the eighties. On this afternoon, it was more pleasant, never getting above the middle seventies. They didn't hurry and it took almost a half hour to get out of the woods. There was a good current in the clear, fifty-feet-wide river that was almost green in the deeper pools where the water moved more slowly. It appeared that where they stood, the riverbank had been sloped by erosion over time, and a small sand beach had been formed. In southern parlance, this was a perfect swimming hole.

"This is a gorgeous place, Evan. Do you know anyone who has been here? It seems a perfect place to swim and picnic."

"Mel told me about it. He said that the water can be treacherous, if you don't really know how to swim. Some students got into trouble down here when one of them, who didn't really know how to swim, almost drowned."

"Are you a good swimmer, Evan?" Molly asked.

"I swan across a mile-wide lake in Percy Quinn State Park."

"Good. I've been swimming since I was six years old."

They spread the blanket at the top of the sand beach. As Evan anchored it with the soda cooler, his clarinet case, and the picnic basket Molly had brought, she sat down and took off her shoes and socks. She pulled up her skirt and waded until she was about ten feet from the water's edge.

"The water's not as cold as I thought it would be. Let's go in."
She came back and stood on the blanket while she took off her
blouse and skirt. She had worn her bathing suit under her clothes.
Evan had started for the privacy of the woods, but turned to watch
her, anticipating her doing something so shameless that he couldn't
even imagine it. With her ebony hair hanging almost to her waist,
she was stunningly beautiful in a black one-piece bathing suit that
looked like it had been painted on her flawless body.

She smiled at him. "You didn't really think I was going to put
on a show, did you?"

Evan flushed. He hadn't been able to keep the image of Irma
Freeman out of his mind. Irma in the woods, with a body not nearly so perfect, even in complete nakedness. He admitted guiltily:

"Just hoped, Molly. The way you are, you're still the most
beautiful creature on this planet."

"Go put on your suit, Evan." She turned and walked back into
the shallows of the river.

They stayed in the water for a half hour, swimming with the
river's flow for thirty or forty yards until they turned and fought the
current back to the beach. They both swam strongly, but after several trips down river, they were tired enough to just dive and seek
the bottom of the closest deep pools. Then they would play and
splash around until Molly said:

"I'm hungry. Let's go have our picnic."

They both sat cross-legged on the blanket, facing each other,
while they ate their sandwiches and drank their pop.

"This is the first time I've been swimming in the river, Evan."
Molly said. "Is this something you do down where you live."

"When I was a kid, we'd go about once a week all summer. The
swimming hole, that's what we called it, was about six miles out of
town. One of the parents in the neighborhood would drive us there
and stay until we came home. When I was in high school, we did-
n't go nearly as much. There was so much other stuff to do."

"I learned to swim in a pool in Memphis. We lived in the city until we moved across the state line into Mississippi. I told you we lived in Southhaven. That's in a different state, but it's like a Memphis suburb."

Molly had stretched out and lay with her hands under her head while Evan sat cross-legged, looking down into her face. He would turn and slide his eyes down the length of her and marvel at her perfection.

"I love you, Molly," he said, as if he hadn't even heard her talk about how she learned to swim.

"I know, Evan."

Nothing else; not "I love you, too." Just like the last time. No commitment, just a one-sided love affair. Evan sighed his disappointment and stood up. "Maybe we should go back," he said. "Is your bathing suit dry enough?"

Evan's somber mood wasn't lost on Molly. She stood up and walked across the blanket to stand close to him, almost touching. She took his face between her hands, forcing him to look into her eyes.

"Don't be impatient with me, Evan," she said and kissed him more lingeringly than the short impulsive kisses when she was pleased with their music. "There's no one but you. We have a lot more time."

They didn't return to the river before they both left for their June summer vacation.

Chapter Eight

On June 6, 1944, Henry Sherman was killed on Omaha Beach in Normandy, France. He came in with the second wave of invasion forces. He fell out of the landing craft flat on his belly, got up and ran thirty yards up the bloody beach when a shell from a German 88 took his head off so cleanly that his dog tags weren't even pulled out of his skivvy shirt.

The medical corpsman, who examined his personal effects after he had been dragged from the beach, copied his name and dog tag number in a small notebook. He also read Henry's letter to a girl in England, and then tore it up.

When the telegram came that every parent dreaded twelve days later, Amos Sherman stood looking out the screened door as the delivery boy got on his bicycle and pedaled away. He couldn't open it. He went into the parlor and sat down on the sofa with the unopened telegram held tightly in his almost palsied hand. He did not have any idea how to tell Martha. It would be too cruel to just hand her the announcement of her son's death from the impersonal service that had unwittingly arranged to have him killed.

When he finally opened it, Evan was coming in from a bike ride into town to see a movie. The look on his father's face made him stop and then walk into the parlor. He looked at the opened telegram in his father's hand

"What's up, Pop?"

"Come over here and sit down, Evan." When Evan sat next to him, he said, "Try to be quiet. Your mother's resting for a while."

He spoke in a strained undertone.

"What is it, Dad?"

Sherman's face was gaunt and drawn. The meager light could not break the hold that shadow had on the irregularities of its surface, and what could be seen of his eyes in their suddenly deepened sockets showed hopelessness and retreat. He felt old and tired and defeated and he was struggling to say something and couldn't bring himself to it. He couldn't find the words.

Fear tightened Evan's throat.

"Is Mama sick? I mean real sick?"

"It's not your Mother, Evan. It's Henry." Sherman stopped for a moment, just long enough for Evan to realize what he had just said. "There's not any easy way to tell you, son. Henry's dead. He was killed twelve days ago in France."

When Evan finally believed that Henry was gone, that never again would he see his face, or lie in the dark and talk to him, or have the hard prod of his elbow disturb his sleep, or know the quick hatred of one brother for another or the quick love, or feel the kinship of that other blood, he despised God and he wept.

Evan and his father wept together, softly, because Martha was asleep.

They talked in solemn voices, halting to fight the emotion, choking it down, continuing as it strangled in their throats.

"When did you find out?" Evan asked.

"Twenty minutes ago." Sumrall showed him the telegram from the War Department.

"'—was killed in action on the 6th day of June,'" Evan read from the telegram.

"That's almost two weeks ago. Why did it take them so long? And Henry's been…it's been that long and we didn't know." Evan protested the terrible delay. Tears welled in his eyes and he almost cried again.

Twelve lonely days of death. A mound in a row of mounds in

a dreary French field where no one came to grieve. We have to wait twelve days to mourn him.

Amos Sherman got up and paced the room nervously. The strain had brought a sag to his shoulders.

"I regret the twelve days, Evan. I can't help but have a feeling of coldness and neglect and inadequacy for having him dead twelve days and not even being able to despair of it until now." Sherman's voice was soft and tired and thoughtful. "But there is a certain finality in having it this way that will make it easier, I believe, because he's too far away and it's been too long ago for us to disbelieve and try to resurrect him." Sherman was voicing his thoughts. He did not look at Evan and his voice was low, detached from this place. As he went on, still musing and contemplative, he continued to pace the room slowly in head-bent absorption.

"I don't think Martha will believe it. She won't let herself accept it."

Sherman stopped abruptly in front of Evan and looked down at him silently for a few moments.

"This was a blood bath in Normandy on the north coast of France. Thousands of casualties. They had to be sure, and they let us know as soon as they could, so let's leave that part alone. We'll wait until your mother wakes up and then tell her together. I think she'll accept it better if she realizes you know. But one thing you're not to do, and that's help her delude herself into thinking Henry will ever come back."

Sherman asked Martha to sit down with them when she came into the parlor. But she stood and looked from one of their faces to the other

"What is it?"

They both got up and stood close as Sherman showed her the telegram and told her about Henry. She would have crumpled to the floor if they hadn't both held her. They carried her back to her bedroom.

Amos Sherman sat by his wife's bed for an hour and then came back to where Evan was still sitting in the parlor.

"I don't want to leave her alone. Can you go in and just sit for a while? I think she'll wake up before too long."

"Yes, but I want you to come back in when she wakes up."

Evan got up and walked out into the hall. His shoulders sagged as if he were immensely tired. He resembled his father again.

Martha was still asleep when Evan went in, so he sat by the side of the bed where Sherman had been sitting. Occasionally a contortion of pain would cross her face and Evan would lean forward wondering what leering chimera she faced in her dreams. When relaxed in the reprieves that separated her nightmares, her face was slack and exhausted.

For a moment, Evan subdued his own sense of loss; he forgot to grieve and felt only strong compassion for his mother, for this woman he knew he could not comfort. As he sat waiting for her to waken he thought also of his father. They had spoken little, yet there was some strange understanding. There had been no greeting, but there seemed to be a stronger affection. To this man he had never really known, who came and went with the caprice of the railroad-call-boy, who entered and departed his life like a phantom, who looked at him strangely and made him uncomfortable, to this man he felt drawn and held by some new and astonishing bond.

He hated to admit any transience to this new found thing. He did not want to relinquish it. This was the first time they could stand together, pulled closer into each other to defend against some meanness of destiny.

Martha stirred. She turned to one side and moaned dismally. She lay facing Evan with her eyes still closed, and it seemed that she had lapsed back into complete sleep again when suddenly her eyes remembered something they had seen in the brief flickering when they had opened, and she sat bolt upright in the bed. Evan was startled. He leaned toward her gesturing with his helpless arms.

"Henry! Oh God! Henry!" she cried. She reached out her arms to him.

Evan felt himself buried in her as she pulled him to his knees beside the bed. She hugged his smothering and reluctant head to her breast and rocked to and fro.

"Mama. Please don't. It's Evan, Mama." He struggled to free himself as the panic mounted and blinded him. He took her arms and dragged them from his neck and held her so that she looked at him. When the recognition showed horribly in her face, he said:

"It's me, Mama. It's Evan."

Wary distrust pulled at her mouth. For five seconds longer she searched his pleading face. Then she rejected him. She lay down and covered her face with her hands.

Evan was still on his knees beside the bed. He sat back on his heels and stared forlornly at her until his legs cramped so painfully that he returned to the chair. There he sat poised on its edge, groping dumbly for the verbal anodyne that he knew did not exist. Desperately he wished that somewhere in his vast ignorance he could uncover just one comforting phrase.

For fifteen minutes he fidgeted nervously in the chair until he could stand it no longer; then he got up silently and left the room.

Evan stayed home four days. They were the most miserable four days of his life. At night he lay in the lonely bed and cried when he thought of Henry being dead. He whimpered like a small child, while he cast about in his mind for things to remember and torture himself with. If during the night he heard the familiar melancholy complaint of a train whistle, he sobbed unrestrainedly.

Evan didn't know what to do with the loneliness, the emptiness, he felt. His love for Henry had been so submerged that he had never realized how much of his life would be forever gone without him.

He left after four days because his father told him to.

"Go back to school, Evan," his father told him. "This house is not where you need to be. If you could hear him, Henry, wherever he is, is telling you the same thing."

Evan cried when he told Melvin. They stayed up most of the night and when they finally needed to sleep, Melvin got in Evan's bed and held him until he could hear the even breathing of unconscious relief.

Two weeks passed and Evan hadn't seen Molly, hadn't told her. Melvin stopped her as she came out of class and took her to sit on one of the benches by the library. He told her slowly, as kindly as he knew how, in a way that made Molly realize that Evan was very important to him.

"He can't tell you, Molly," he said when he had finished. "He adores you, loves you more than he loves his own life. He's so afraid you will pity him and tell him something you don't mean. Please don't do that. It seems that so many things have become one disappointment after another. He doesn't know what he believes about the religious things he has never understood. His home life is something he desperately wants to escape. He has a musical talent he doesn't know what to do with. He considers himself to be so flawed he will never deserve you. I know you will go to him. I have no idea how the two of you will get past this. I hope it's important enough for you to give him what relief you can."

Molly was standing in front of Evan's dorm when he came back from the cafeteria. It was after the evening meal and the long shadows of summer's twilight made Evan seem impossibly tall. He hesitated, almost stopped, when he recognized her. When he came to stand in front of her, she said:

"Go get your clarinet."

The moon had come up by the time they were deep in the woods, and Molly stopped in one of their favorite spots to play and sing.

81

"Play "*Kiss Me Again*," she said.

Evan stood looking at her as the gray of her eyes darkened to violet in the moonlight.

"Molly, I—"

"Let's not talk for a while, Evan. Just play for me."

There was so much more soaring emotion in her voice than there had ever been when she sang this song, that Evan stopped playing and just listened. She didn't seem to realize that he wasn't playing, and finished with tears running down her cheeks. She stood in front of Evan, put her arms around him, and looked into the eyes that were also bright with tears.

"Kiss me, Evan," she said.

There would never be another kiss like this for either of them. Their lips parted and they pressed together, exploring a passion neither of them had ever known, reluctant to let the moment end.

"I love you, Evan," Molly said and put her hand over Evan's lips as he started to respond. "I have loved you since we first met, the way you said you love me. I've never been in love before, and I was terrified, until I realized there never would be a life for me without you in it."

"Molly, do you know about—"

"Yes, Mel told me. But that doesn't have anything to do with how I feel about you. I just should have had the courage to tell you sooner."

"We're both twenty years old now, Molly. We're old enough to be in love forever. That may sound like a love-sick high school sophomore, but I don't think we need any more twenty-year-old love-sick agony. That's what it has been for me."

"Play *What Kind of Fool Am I*, Evan." And she smiled as she sang the lyrics, *What kind fool am I, who never fell in love.*

They kissed again, lingeringly, before they left the woods.

Evan told Molly about Henry the next time they played and sang together. He just told her the things Melvin had left out, how

Evan felt about his brother, because Melvin didn't know how to express them.

But Melvin detected a transformation in Evan that he couldn't quite define. So much of the pain had left Evan's face that Mel suspected Molly had given him whatever emotional therapy was necessary to account for it. And Evan couldn't define what had happened that day in the woods. He knew only that his overwhelming sense of loss was made bearable by his almost unbelievable discovery that Molly loved him and expected to always have him in her life.

Chapter Nine

Melvin's graduation had been delayed until the end of July to coincide with the regular undergraduate ceremony. Evan wanted to see him get his diploma and watched platoon after platoon of Navy V-12 sailors file into the auditorium—down both isles, two abreast, sliding in, row after row, part of the rhythm even after their feet had stopped moving, and they just stood waiting for the others. And then they all sat down in one vast movement and they were rows of orderly heads and blue shoulders. The Navy brass had made it mandatory that cadets attend.

Evan leaned forward and rested his arms on the balcony railing. He propped his chin on the back of his finger-laced hands and peered at the cadets distastefully.

The graduating class filed silently down both aisles, a mournful, rather straggling, single line on each side of the auditorium, a solemn unryhthmic procession in their depressing black gowns. The bobbing square hats looking ridiculous and the contrast between the gliding efficiency of the sailors and this unharmonious movement brought a smile to his lips.

The graduates formed two clusters on either side of the sailors, taking the front seats on both side aisles. Evan noticed with resentment that the Navy was on display for the public, the graduates flanking them like an honor guard.

Honorary pallbearers is more like it, Evan thought ruefully. *Damn Navy's taken this over, too.*

The deep rumbling of the organ filled his ears and he leaned back in his chair and closed his eyes. The balcony was hot, and he fought off the languid sleepiness until after the prayer then he sank down onto his spine and dozed through the president's droning introductions and commentaries. He awoke to hear a few phrases of General Henderson's graduation address, then succumbed again to be finally aroused by the booming chords of the processional. He watched until he saw Melvin get his degree and handshake and then noiselessly descended the balcony steps.

"You going to eat before you leave?" Evan asked. He had fallen in beside Melvin and they walked toward the dormitory. Melvin had stripped off his gown and held it bundled under his arm. He dangled the cap by the tassel, swinging it in playful little arcs as he walked.

"Don't have time, old buddy. Train leaves in an hour."

"You still want to catch the six-ten?"

"No reason to hang around." His amused eyes asked, "Is there?"

"No. I guess not." Evan reluctantly admitted.

Constant watering had kept the grass on the quadrangle a vibrant green during the drought of blistering summer heat. With a sudden fit of melancholy, Evan realized Melvin would probably never again walk across this symbol of university life. The feeling passed and he grimaced at the sentimentality of the thought. He glanced quickly over his shoulder to see the last handshaking phase of the mid-year graduation exercises. The sailors were milling about and began straggling off in aimless, slouching packs.

"Sailors must be on liberty tonight," Evan said dryly.

"They deserve it, poor bastards. They got it so tough. Anyhow, I couldn't have graduated without them. I'm grateful."

"A note of sarcasm has crept into your voice, Mr. Stuart."

"I love them like brothers." Melvin smiled broadly.

"You mean sons. They don't show a man your age the proper deference, especially since you were almost a full commander.

That fact alone should entitle you to a military escort to the depot, or at least one skinny sailor to carry your bag."

"At least," Melvin agreed and then promptly dropped the bantering tone. "You still don't like them any better than I do, huh, Mr. Sherman," he said, very serious now, turning to look at Evan.

Evan didn't answer, nor could he bring himself to look at Melvin. He never hid anything from Melvin it seemed.

"We're both fools, Evan, but I think I enjoy it where it torments you. If you can't beat them you can always join them." Melvin thought of his own case and amended what he had said. "Well, almost always."

"No, you can't. You can't and I can't. We're both fools, like you say, but one of us is no better or worse than the other. We just have different things wrong with us."

"Those guys don't have anything to do with what's eating you, Evan," Melvin said. It startled Evan. It was like Melvin had read his thoughts. "Or me either for that matter. They're probably good fellas, only most of them seem kind of stupid. Young and stupid. Well, that's better than being old and stupid." Melvin liked the remark. He turned to Evan and grinned.

"Anyway, my advice to you is to forget the sailors and, whenever you have a problem go over and talk with Mona after I leave. I believe it'd do you a lot of good. She'd straighten you out on what it's like to have a hero for a husband. You coming up?"

They had reached the dormitory steps. Melvin turned and waited for Evan to answer.

"No, I guess I won't. I better go over and eat something. I thought I'd go into town and see a show." Evan put his foot on the second step and leaned over to support his forearms on the bent leg. It was the casual and relaxed attitude of the upperclassman. He aped it now because he wanted his farewell to Melvin to be easy and painless. He wanted it to be unembarrassing and casual.

"Okay, Preach. Maybe you'll be so bored without me, you'll

come visit me at Stuart House; that's what my mother calls it. I'm not completely satisfied with the job I did on corrupting you. I don't believe you're through with the God thing." He started up the steps, but near the top he stopped suddenly, as if he had forgotten something, and lunged back down them until he stood before Evan's questioning face again. "You know, Evan, we're really the only true social parasites, along with the doctors, of course. Body misery for the doctors, soul misery for you, legal misery for me. We make our living out of human misery. Real professional men, answering the higher calling. Anyway, before long you can get out and, if you can't do anything with the journalism stuff, you can get in on some of the misery. Ain't that a hell of a way to put it, a real tender thought to leave you with." Melvin laughed and put out his hand. Evan shook it.

"So long, Mel," he said. "I don't agree with you about the God thing."

"So long, Preach."

Evan watched him bound up the stairs inside the building. The short leg made him pitch slightly from side to side. He realized he would miss Mel's cynical intelligence when he was gone.

Evan walked toward the cafeteria. He was suddenly very lonely.

Molly's senior recital was scheduled three weeks before her late October graduation date. It was more concert than recital, because word about her extraordinary voice had gone as far as Memphis and Jackson. Half of the tickets were available to Milcrest students on a first-come basis. The other half, available for sale to the general public, sold out the day after the recital was announced.

There was no other undergraduate voice student on the program and she would be accompanied by a faculty pianist—and Evan. Molly selected her own music and insisted on a segment where Evan would accompany her alone. The music faculty's reservations were overcome when they heard them sing and play together. It was such an unusual concert pairing, and Evan's playing was so infectious, they even agreed to a segment where he would play a medley of Artie Shaw music as Molly and the pianist rested backstage.

When Molly first told Evan of her involving him in her program, he resisted it. "Molly, this is your concert. I'm not a music student and I don't think the faculty will go along with it."

"Yes they will, when they hear us together. Evan, the time we have spent singing and playing together is the part of my music I have enjoyed most. I want this concert to show that a lyric soprano can sing popular music without trying to sound like a ballad singer from a dance band. I have the recital planned to separate more familiar music from the required arias most people don't realize they'll like until they hear them. All the arias I sing will be from the Italian operas that have the most lyrical music to match the voice of a lyric soprano."

"You'll sing them in Italian?"

"Of course. Italian opera doesn't sound the same when sung in English. Not one in ten people who love opera can understand the words. That's why you are given a libretto—the English translation of the Italian lyrics—when you go to a real opera house."

Evan was coming to the point where Molly was telling him more than he really wanted to know about the complexities of this particular part of classical music. He decided he should lighten the conversation. He smiled and said:

"I didn't know you could speak Italian. How are you going to manage keeping that touch of Irish brogue out of the lyrics?"

Molly was surprised. "You never told me you thought I had a brogue."

"I'm kidding, Molly. I just catch a touch of it when you get excited about something. I think it's wonderful. Don't ever lose it."

"I probably won't. I was brought up in the Little Dublin part of Memphis. I think every city of any size has a Little Dublin, where everyone has a brogue of some sort. I told you my parents came to this country so my father could eventually take over Sullivan's Irish Pub from his uncle, who had owned it for thirty years."

"Okay, Molly. Tell me the songs you want me to learn so we can practice. I want us to get them down cold, so I won't make a fool of myself when I'm up on the stage with you."

Molly's recital opened with an empty stage and the sound of clarinet music coming from somewhere the audience couldn't see. Evan, tall and handsome in a black tuxedo, walked from the stage wing playing *Villa.* The soprano voice came from backstage until Molly came from the other wing and stood by Evan. She wore a black, floor-length silk sheath and black heels that made her almost as tall as Evan. The only jewelry was a single string of pearls. The effect was electrifying, and set the stage for the evening's program. It wouldn't be an ordinary night.

Every undergraduate student in the audience had heard about Molly's glorious voice. Those who hadn't actually heard it were told of it by the music majors who had, and they knew about Evan and his clarinet. To them, it was a campus love affair long before Molly and Evan accepted it themselves. The people who came from off campus realized they were hearing something they would always remember. There was a rustling of anticipation in the audience.

When Molly finished singing *Only Make Believe* from the musical *Show Boat,* everyone in the audience stood during the ovation and stood again when *You are Love,* from the same musical, ended. Molly would take certain liberties during the program, as she did when she sang *Stranger in Paradise* from *Kismet.* The song was ordinarily a male lead, but she liked it.

In this part of her program, everything she sang was in the lower to middle range of her voice, from alto to contralto to mezzo-soprano. She wanted everyone to know she could sing popular ballads before the challenge of operatic music in the last part of the concert. To prepare them for what was to come, she sang *The Italian Street Song,* which ventured into the soprano range with such an infectious rhythm that there was another standing ovation as she left the stage.

When the applause subsided, Evan walked to the microphone and said, "When she returns, Miss Molly Sullivan will sing for you something you will tell your grandchildren about," and began to play *Deep Purple* and segued to *Stardust.* He started to play Summit Ridge Drive with such a driving beat that he suddenly stopped and, taking the microphone with him, went to the edge of the stage. He pointed to the several sections of under-graduate students and asked,

"Who'd like to dance?" He turned and pointed to the stairs on either side of the auditorium that led to the stage. "I need twenty couples." After twenty-two, he stopped the rush and said to the disappointed crowd who didn't make it the first time, "You'll have your turn."

And Evan played. He was back in high school, playing for the after-the-football-game dances. He let his clarinet wail and the dancers couldn't get enough of *Begin the Beguine* and *Frenesi.* They had to stop when Evan stopped playing. It had been twenty minutes.

"Molly Sullivan wants to sing for you," Evan told the audience. They all stood and applauded as she came on stage with her piano accompanist. Evan left the stage to sit in a place in the auditorium that had been saved for him.

Everyone in the audience thought Molly was singing for him, or for her. It didn't matter what gender. Those who had never heard opera in this form hated that it had taken this long to know what it could be. From the mezzo-soprano excitement of *Carmen's* most often sung aria, *Habanera,* she went to the lyric soprano of *Oh Mio Babbino Caro.*

For the moment, few in the audience knew, or cared, what operas contained these arias. There was almost disbelief that what they heard could come from the most stunningly beautiful young woman they had ever seen. Even the printed program that contained it all was ignored. It was just the voice. The lyric arias of *Cara Nome* and *Un Bel Di* led them to the final and almost unbelievable coloratura of *Mi Chiamano Mimi* from *La Boheme.*

When Molly finished, everyone seemed surprised, as if they expected her to sing on and on. The program had been over an hour and a half long. It seemed to them just minutes.

"Thank you." Molly said and bowed to the audience.

The spell was broken. The audience rose in a single sibilant movement. The wild applause was laced with cries of "Brava."

As Molly left the stage, the pianist stood and applauded her before following her into the stage's wing.

Evan left his seat in the audience and went back stage as the applause went on and on.

He started playing as he came back on stage for the encore. The melody, unfamiliar to the audience, had a lilting romance to it different from typical popular music. As before, Molly began to sing backstage, "*Speed bonnie boat, like a bird on the wing.*" She was singing *The Skye Boat Song,* an Irish favorite of hers since she was a little girl. The music wasn't a vocal challenge, but it was lovely, captivating, and so typically Irish that a touch of Molly's subdued brogue could be detected.

When she finished, and while the audience was again applauding so loudly it was evident they wouldn't leave before at least one more encore, she and Evan turned to smile at each other. The song was their secret. He was the only one who knew she would sing at least one Irish song. The applause didn't subside until Evan turned to the crowd and held up his hand.

"Miss Molly Sullivan will end this concert with a song I know you will love the way she does, and the way I do."

They stood facing each other and Evan began to play *Kiss Me Again.* This song was also a favorite of the romantics in the room and, after a brief involuntary spate of applause, the audience sat in almost reverent silence as Molly's voice soared.

At the song's end, Evan put his clarinet on the piano and turned to Molly. His arms enfolded her. They kissed the way young lovers kiss, unwilling for it to end. And the crowd went wild. Evan was right; they had heard and witnessed something they would tell their grandchildren about, something that would become known as "The Music Miracle at Milcrest."

The crowd, almost completely intact, waited for them to come to the front of the auditorium. They clustered in a moving group around Molly, eager to just touch her hand, to receive her smile, to tell how wonderful she was. A smaller group, mainly undergraduate girls, shuffled to get next to Evan, who, now that Melvin had left, was the most handsome male on campus. He also played the clarinet in a way that got their hormones dancing.

Many of the people in the crowd were from off campus, especially the music critics from newspapers as far away as the New Orleans *Times Picayune*, and they waited more patiently to talk to Molly. Their questions were brief and pointed. When they left, they knew of Molly's family background, her musical history, and her intention to follow a musical career. They would fill in the rest in their own particular style. They were obviously aware they had witnessed a very unusual evening in the genre of their newspaper specialty.

A half hour after the concert's end, Molly and Evan walked alone into the Seminary woods. It was refreshingly cool after the body heat generated in the concert hall. Molly stopped in a clearing with a pine straw floor they had used when they played and sang together. She lay full length and pulled Evan down with her. Both of them stretched their arms over their heads and lay supine, waiting for the release of the evening's tension of excitement. They could see each other clearly in the filtered light of a harvest moon. Evan didn't turn to look at her when he asked:

"Molly, do you realize what you have done?"

A full minute passed before her reply:

"I think I do, and it's a little frightening. I don't know whether I'm ready to commit to the career I told those newspaper people about."

"You can do anything you want to, Molly. We're both twenty-one now. According to Mel, we're grown up, or supposed to be. We can make our own decisions. Give this some time."

"Did I tell you my dad promised me a trip to Ireland for a graduation present?"

Evan was surprised. "No you didn't. When do you plan to go?"

"Probably in about three or four weeks. Not long after we graduate. Actually, I'm more eager to go now than I was. It will give me some time to think about the next thing I need to do."

"How long do you plan to stay?"

"I don't know. It's pretty much up to my mom. She's going with me. I think we'll stay quite a while. She hasn't been back but once since she left."

Evan turned on his side to look at the profile of Molly's face. "I won't know what to do while you're gone. I've been thinking about what we'll do after graduation, when we both go home."

Molly turned to him and smiled. "If you're thinking I might decide I don't love you anymore, there's not a chance that will happen, Evan. We both need some time to get on with what we're going to do. While I'm in Ireland, you can figure out how to escape your uncomfortable home life."

Before Evan could respond, she said, "Play *Clair de Lune* for me."

Evan retrieved his ubiquitous clarinet from the bed of pine straw where he had left it, and began to play the music with a title that couldn't have been more appropriate—*By the Light of the Moon.*

Molly sat up and leaned back on her straight arms as she hummed along with the music. When Evan finished, she said, "Play *Moonglow.*"

Halfway through the music, she stood up, walked several paces away from Evan, and, in one swift movement, stripped her sheath dress over her head. She hadn't worn anything at all under the dress. Standing in the moonlight, she appeared to be an ebony and alabaster apparition.

Evan stopped playing and just stared in disbelief.

"Come to me, Evan."

Thirty minutes later Molly and Evan walked out of the Seminary woods consummated and committed lovers, no longer strangers in paradise.

Chapter Ten

The newspaper accounts of Molly's concert were so rhapsodic, it appeared the music critics were in a competition to outdo each other. Although a little old to be considered one, Molly's amazing voice came from a vocal prodigy. The most knowledgeable and glowing account came from the New Orleans paper. The critic was not only knowledgeable about opera music—he reviewed the performances of the New Orleans Opera Company—he was a fan of the popular big-band clarinetists and compared Evan favorably with some of them and with the musicians who played in the Bourbon Street hotspots. He loved the alliteration when he coined the phrase, "Music Miracle at Milcrest," that would forever identify Molly's concert as the most well remembered musical event in the school's history.

Copies of all the reviews were given to Molly by the music faculty. They had begun to collect material for a "Molly Sullivan Archive." When Molly read them, she was with Evan.

"I hate for my parents to see this." She handed him the review from the Memphis newspaper. "I didn't think the concert would be such a big deal, so I didn't invite them. I didn't even tell them about it,"

"I sort of wondered why they weren't here."

"I know my mother will be livid. There's no way they won't read or hear about it."

When Evan began to speak, she stopped him.

"I wanted the night to be just for us, Evan. I don't regret not telling them."

"There's not one instant in that evening I would change, Molly. It was, and probably will forever be, the most important thing that has happened to me. If I were to become a complete family outcast, I wouldn't change a thing."

By the time the expected phone call came, Molly had braced herself for the lecture. The fire of her mother's voice seemed to leap out of the telephone into her recoiling ear. The blistering diatribe was liberally laced with choice Irish expressions Molly hadn't heard in all the years she lived in Memphis' Little Dublin. There was even a threat that Molly's parents wouldn't attend her graduation ceremony.

"She'll cool off in a few days. There's a lot of other stuff she promised we'd have a serious talk about when she and Dad get here. I know she wants to talk about graduate school. She's talked to the faculty here about it, and they told her, in spite of the success of the recital, I'm not nearly ready for public operatic performance. They don't have a graduate Music School at Milcrest, Evan. I'll have to go somewhere else."

"I've known since I first heard you sing you'd need more than you could get at Milcrest, but I've been afraid to ask you what you planned to do. I didn't think I'd like what you would tell me."

"Did you think it would make any difference in the way I feel about you, if we had to do separate things for a while?"

"I'm scared to death, Molly. I'll probably try to get some kind of newspaper job in Jackson or Memphis. I don't have any idea where you'll go to prepare for a performance career, probably New York for opera. That will mean at least two more years of training, just to learn a complete score in Italian, or whatever language the opera is in."

They were sitting on one of the benches by the library. Molly turned to Evan and took his face between her hands, forcing him to look directly into her eyes.

"Evan, if there was a choice that meant our separation would change forever the way we feel about each other, or me going directly with you wherever you are going, and it meant I'd never sing another note, I'd go with you. There will never be anyone but you."

Evan took her hands from his face and held them.

"Molly, we haven't talked about that last night in the Seminary woods, not really. I suspect you know I had never been with anyone like that. I know you hadn't either. We were a couple of twenty-one year old virgins hopelessly in love with each other. If it hadn't happened, I would still be hopelessly in love with you. I can wait forever for you to do what you have to do, as long as I know you will come back to me. You go to Ireland and come back with a brogue you'll have to get rid of. We'll talk about the rest of it later."

Molly smiled and pulled Evan close to her so she could kiss him. "Let's talk about what you're going to tell your mother when she comes to your graduation. Do you think she will ask you why your degree won't have anything about theology in it? Will she expect you to tell her you're going to start Seminary after you take a vacation?"

"I never have told her I planned to go to Seminary. She told me one time that I didn't have to go to Seminary to be ordained. Actually, I don't think you even have to have a degree to be ordained. I just never said anything about the degree. I'll just tell her the undergraduate degrees are all in Bachelor of Arts. I may have to dance around the subject of what I plan to do next."

"I can't make any decision about where I'm going either. I'll wait until I get back from Ireland. I just want us to spend as much time together as we can until I leave."

They didn't go back into the woods before graduation, even to just play and sing. There was too much to do. The graduation ceremony was at two o'clock in the afternoon on the last Saturday of October. Both of their parents drove to Milcrest in time to have lunch with their graduating children in the crowded cafeteria.

No effort was made to introduce the two sets of parents to each other. Evan and Molly decided things were complicated enough without having to go into the details of their relationship. They both had an almost adolescent feeling that there would be something about their behavior together that would alert their parents to their loss of virtue. They were unaware that the old folks might expect it was about time for that type of fall from grace. Of course an exception would be Martha. She would never admit accepting anything but complete celibacy before the marriage vows from Evan.

It was almost one o'clock when Evan and his parents got up to leave the cafeteria. On his way out, he was surprised to see Melvin and Mona sitting together at a table close to the door. His parents noticed his hesitation as he came up to them. He had to stop and at least acknowledge his old roommate before he passed them by. Melvin stood as they stopped.

"I have hoped I'd get a chance to meet Evan's parents on this special day." Melvin said before Evan could begin an introduction. "I'm Melvin Stuart, Evan's roommate until a few months ago, and this young lady is Miss Regan of the university staff. She has kept Evan and me on the straight and narrow about university rules and proper student behavior."

Mona accepted this inaccurate introduction with a twisted smile that Amos Sherman didn't miss. As far as he was concerned, Mona was the most interesting thing that had happened on the visit to Milcrest. He gave her a knowing smile and nodding of his head she didn't miss.

Martha was so impressed with Melvin's natural social grace, she pumped his hand with such enthusiasm he almost lost balance on his uneven legs.

"Evan told us how helpful you have been with his studies, Melvin," she said. "I understand you're a practicing attorney now."

"Well, not quite. I just passed the Mississippi bar."

"Evan tells us you live in the old Stuart Plantation house with your mother. Isn't your Plantation in the Delta up north of Greenwood?'

"Yes, Ma'm. There's not much left of the old property. It's not quite as fashionable as it used to be to live off the land."

Evan was becoming more and more embarrassed by his mother's fawning over Mel's perceived gentility. So he interrupted:

"Did you come down just to be sure I got my diploma, Mel?"

"Absolutely. And I thought it might be a good idea to have you come visit with me, before you got started on something that would keep you too busy to take a little vacation after all the hard work to get your sheepskin."

The idea of a visit to Mel's plantation house had enormous appeal to Evan, anything that would postpone his going home to the inquisition he expected from Martha.

"Will you be here tomorrow?"

"Do you still have an empty bed in your dorm room?"

"Yes, I do."

"Then I'll be here tomorrow."

It took a while for what had gone on between Evan and Melvin to register with Martha.

"I thought you were going home with us tonight," she said, after Evan had gone to his room to pick up his cap and gown. They were walking to the auditorium where Evan would take his assigned alphabetical place to go through the graduation line.

"Oh, I couldn't go home tonight. I thought you knew we have our big graduation dance. I'm playing part time in the dance band."

"Well, do you plan to go with Melvin for that visit he talked about?"

Bill Tucker

"I think he should go, Martha," Amos Sherman said. "He might not get another opportunity any time soon. Anyway, he can come home and tell us how the other half lives."

Evan appreciated his father's conspiratorial smile as he made this suggestion, and the cynicism of the last part of his comment wasn't lost on his grateful son. Neither was the look of betrayal Martha gave her husband.

"Well, yeah," Evan said quickly to keep a beat ahead in this opportunity to delay the inevitable reckoning he would have with Martha. "It'll give me a chance to wind down from three years of hard work. I suspect Mel has some good advice on how to work into a new life after you haven't done anything but go to school since you were six years old."

"I know Melvin is a nice young man, Evan, but I don't see why you can't do whatever this winding-down thing is at home. I know you need to relax for a while, but I was looking forward to having a good long talk about your plans for Seminary."

"We'll have a chance to talk, Ma. We'd better move along. I have just ten minutes to find my place in the graduation line. You and Dad go find your seats in the auditorium."

Evan saw Molly and her parents for the first time as he approached the graduation lineup. Molly was an amazing replica of her mother. Erin Sullivan was a little taller, by an inch or two. The few streaks of middle-age gray in the black hair she wore shoulder length, was the only indication that this slender, strikingly beautiful, woman was twenty-five years older than her daughter.

Barry Sullivan was a big and robust Irishman, taller than Erin by three or four inches and with the twenty pounds of midriff padding that went along with the owner of an establishment that served Guiness and Jameson to the enthusiastic patrons of a river-city Irish pub.

Evan's parents were not unattractive people, just ordinary in comparison. He suspected that this was the impression Molly had

100

when she saw them walk away as they went to look for auditorium seats. It didn't disturb him, but he was glad that whatever reaction the two sets of parents would have to each other was indefinitely postponed.

The V-12 sailors had been excused from this and future graduation ceremonies. The Navy had decided this was an unnecessary academic nicety, and the auditorium was almost full without them. The graduating seniors fidgeted in their seats, enduring the speeches that, to them, seemed endless. When their names were called, they hurried to the stage to shake hands with the university president and snatch their diplomas from his hand. They stood in an alphabetical queue in front of the stage and waited for the processional.

Because of their last names, Evan and Molly were close enough to have a few minutes together after they came out of the auditorium and waited for their parents.

"Are your folks going home tonight?" Evan asked.

"Yes, I told them I need a day or so to get packed up."

"Mine are leaving, too. Do you still plan to sing tonight at the dance?"

"Yes. The songs we talked about, unless you want something else."

"No, I like what we decided. Molly, I have some things we need to talk about before you go home."

"I know we do. If it's not too late we can talk after the dance. Maybe it will be better to wait until tomorrow."

Evan saw Martha hurrying toward him.

"Here come my folks. I'll pick you up outside your dorm at seven thirty."

Martha gave Evan a hug and a smacking kiss on the cheek as she reached for his diploma.

"Batchelor of Arts" she read and looked questioningly at Evan.

"I though it would say something like 'Bachelor of Divinity.'"

"All undergraduate degrees are Batchelor of Arts or Batchelor of Science, Martha." When Amos Sherman smoothly deflected his wife's probing into this troublesome territory, Evan realized his father was completely aware of his defection from the religious commitment he couldn't keep.

"Yeah, that's right. A chemistry major wouldn't get a Batchelor of Chemistry degree," Evan added, and while Martha was trying to figure out what the two of them had just said, went on, "I've decided to go stay with Mel for a while, Pop. Will you take the stuff I have packed up home with you?"

When Evan's parents left the campus at four-thirty in the afternoon for the two-hour drive home, Martha still had a puzzled look on her face.

Evan didn't sit with the band during the dance. He sat with Molly at one of the small tables next to the stage. When Molly went to stand in front of the band to sing, Evan went with her and played. He would stay when Molly went back to their table and play the infectious Artie Shaw rhythms that had the dancers crowding the floor, trying to dance as close to the band as they could. They loved to watch Evan as he made his clarinet wail to the boogie-woogie beat.

And Evan and Molly danced. They held each other as if they knew this would be the most time they would spend together for longer than either wanted to think about. The other dancers watched them, envying whatever it was Evan and Molly had that they didn't.

The dance was over at midnight and they went to sit on one of the benches by the library.

"What time are you leaving tomorrow?" Evan asked.

"Right after lunch, probably around two-o'clock."

"I told you I'm going to spend a week or so with Mel. When I leave depends on when he wants to go."

"We won't have any time together tomorrow, Evan. I want to tell you something that my parents just told me about. Apparently some northern newspapers picked up the story about my recital from the Associated Press Wire Service. My mother got a call from the Milcrest Music faculty that I would be invited to audition for two very prominent music schools.

"That's great, Molly. What schools are they?"

"Julliard in New York and Curtis in Philadelphia."

Evan was too surprised to react immediately. He was musically knowledgeable enough to recognize these two schools of music as possibly the most prestigious in the country. He wondered what her acceptance would mean for his place in Molly's life. He had no doubt that she would be accepted in either one, and it meant at least two years in an eastern city.

Molly knew what was running through Evan's mind.

"I haven't decided whether I'll go audition for them, Evan. I wanted to talk to you about it before I decide what to do. I know you're thinking about what we will do, if I go to an eastern school; it won't make any difference. It's just a question of whether I go to any graduate music school. No matter where I go, it won't make any difference between us."

"Of course you'll go. For God's sake, Molly! Julliard and Curtis. I know you'll be accepted in either one. I was just too amazed at what that means. When you go, I'll be right behind you. I can get a job in either of those big cities. When do you plan to go for the auditions?"

"If I go, it won't be until I get back from Ireland. I told that to my mother, and she's going to call the schools and tell them it will be a while before I can come to New York and Philadelphia."

"I'm glad you're not going to change your plans about Ireland. I know you've been looking forward to this trip for a long time. I'll probably spend at least two weeks with Mel, maybe more, depending on how we get along in that big house with his mother. I want to look for a job on a newspaper in Memphis or Jackson, probably Memphis. It's a lot closer to Mel's place."

"What will you do if you get a job, Evan? You'll have to get everything settled with your mother about not going into the ministry."

"I don't plan to go home again, Molly, not to stay. I'll just have to tell her and get it over with. I'm sure my dad knows already."

"Let's not talk about the future any more. I just want you to kiss me like we won't see each other for a long time."

They kissed and held each other for the thirty minutes they had left before going to their dorms for the last time.

Chapter Eleven

The day after graduation, Evan and Melvin drove to Stuart House in the 1941 Chrysler New Yorker that belonged to Melvin's mother. The black car was enormous and looked like the type Al Capone would have when his gang drove around Chicago assassinating his bootleg competitors.

When Evan made his admiring comments about the Chrysler, Melvin smiled and turned to look briefly at his passenger.

"I believe the reason my mother keeps this monster is that it represents just one more lingering reminder of the good old days. I'm going to buy a second-hand Ford about half its size."

"You plan to use it to drive to Hamilton?"

"I haven't definitely decided about Hamilton. We'll talk about that later. Tell me about how you and Molly plan to keep up with each other."

"I don't know now, Mel. She said we'd talk about it when she comes back from Ireland. She'll call me. I told her I didn't know where I'd be if I get a job in Memphis or maybe Jackson. She knows I don't plan to go back home."

"Did you tell her she can always find out where you are, if she calls me?"

"Well, yeah, I did. I didn't think you'd mind. Whatever we do depends on her decision on the auditions I told you about."

"I can't believe she'll turn down an opportunity to go to Julliard or Curtis. You could go to New York or Philadelphia and get some kind of job until she graduates, or whatever you do when you figure she's ready to go start a performance career."

"I've told her I would go anywhere she decides to study," Evan said.

"I guess you know, with a voice like hers and being as gorgeous as she is, she'll be a raving success." Mel turned and looked at Evan until he got nervous.

"What?" Evan asked

"How do you think you'll handle being known as *Mister Molly Sullivan?*"

"That'll be a hell of a lot better than being known as *Mister Nobody.*"

They left the main road and entered the long private approach to Stuart House. The property was wooded and, within a hundred yards of the columned antebellum house, the lawn was manicured. Evan had never seen anything that even approached the elegance of Stuart House.

Melvin's mother was sitting in a lawn chair, waiting.

Helen Stuart was an attractive fifty-year-old woman with auburn hair that undoubtedly had considerable beauty-parlor help. She was more fashionably dressed than would be expected of a widowed housewife who had relatively little social contact during the day. When she came across the lawn to meet her son and his friend, she walked with a well-practiced glide.

"I'm so glad you decided to come stay with us for a while, Evan," she said, and gave Evan's hand a welcoming squeeze. "Mel will welcome the company, and so will I. Country living does have its drawbacks now that just about all the social life is in the city."

"I'll welcome the change from the pressures of scheduled university life, Mrs. Stuart," Evan said. "I appreciate the chance to relax for a while in your beautiful home. It's very generous of you."

"I do wish you would call me Helen, Evan. We're all adults now."

When Evan hesitated, Melvin said, "You might as well, or

she'll poison your pancakes after the third time you call her Mrs. Stuart."

"Oh, Mel. You know that's not so. It was at least a half dozen times before that stiff-necked last fellow earned a little pancake lacing."

Evan looked from Melvin to his mother, and had to wait for their conspiratorial smiles to accept this type of leg-pulling humor. It was so different from the more somber, humorless atmosphere of his family's household that it required considerable courage for him to respond.

"I'm very fond of pancakes, Helen."

"I'll see that you have them tomorrow, Evan, *sans* arsenic."

Much to Evan's relief, the tone of his visit to Stuart House was set. He had never been a house guest in even a modest home. He would relax and enjoy the enormity of the place.

Melvin gave him a tour of the house pointing out the renovations that had taken place since the original construction in 1814. The kitchen hadn't been brought inside from a separate building until after the civil war. Bathrooms were added reducing the size of the eight bedrooms on the second floor and the four for house servants on the third floor. The center-hall first floor had an enormous ballroom, formal living room, a dining room that would seat thirty for dinner, a parlor, a study, a morning room, and the kitchen and pantry.

"We rattle round in the place, Evan, live in about twenty percent of it. But sweet Helen loves it. She knows we're the last of the family who will ever live here."

"Have you thought of any way you can keep it? It's such a wonderfully preserved old place."

"The Stuart fortune is about gone. The days of old money in the south are just about over now. The new guys with money want to live in the city. That's where the social action is."

"Do you plan to live in Hamilton, if you decide to practice

there? It's only twelve or thirteen miles from here."

"We'll talk about that later, Evan, maybe tonight after dinner. Let's go put your stuff in your bedroom upstairs."

Evan had brought two suitcases that held just about everything he owned in the way of clothes and the miscellany that would be needed if he never brought another thing from his home in Pineville.

The bedroom Melvin had selected for Evan was huge, the same size as his own, a suite with sitting area and a bath with an attached dressing room.

"I could get used to this, Mel," he said as he met Melvin in the hallway to go back downstairs.

"Better not. It'll be too difficult to go back and join the peasantry. I spent six years in a dormitory room to get used to the leavening effect that goes along with being relatively poor." Melvin's tone was humorous, without any upper-class bigotry in it. "We have stuff to talk about, but we'll do it after dinner. It's sherry time with Helen. I think I'll have a beer. What's your pleasure?"

"I've never tasted sherry. I'd like to try it."

Helen Stuart was a pleasant conversationalist. She didn't pry into either Melvin's or Evan's plans for getting on with their lives. She did suggest to Evan that perhaps her son could ease his passage into the world of journalism, without giving any unwanted advice.

After dinner, Melvin guided Evan into the mahogany paneled study where they sat in leather chairs facing each other.

"Can you tell me about this thing in Hamilton, Mel?" Evan asked.

"It's very tempting, Evan. I'll give you the bare bones of what I understand the proposition to be. There's a law firm with a senior partner who has been a family friend for a long time. He comes from old money, and he's managed to keep most of it. Actually, he's about ninety percent of the firm's practice. There are two junior partners that do all the scut work, but when it comes to anything that has to do with courtroom law, especially with a jury, the old guy takes over. He's getting to the point that he needs someone to give him a little relief in the courtroom. I guess it's because of his age. He's in his late sixties. He asked me to come in for a talk. I don't doubt it was because of the relationship our families have had for a few generations. I told him I didn't want to be a paperwork lawyer. I wanted to be litigator, to work in the courtroom whenever I could. Apparently that's what he wanted to hear. He said I had the voice for it." Melvin smiled and added, "The old guy has quite a sense of humor. He also told me the limp would work toward a sympathetic jury."

"Sounds like you could get what you want. Anything holding you back?"

"I'm not sure I want to spend the time building a practice in a small town, if I don't plan to stay. I was thinking more of Jackson or Memphis. Of course, if I go to Memphis, I'll have to pass the Tennessee bar."

"Will that be a problem?"

"Not really, just another delay. I'd probably be better off going to Hamilton. Mr. Bradford--that's a pretty big name in Hamilton-- told me there's a lot of money in this small town and a surprising number of cases that go to jury trial."

"When do you think you'll decide, Mel?"

"I thing I've decided. I do believe I just talked myself into it. Maybe I needed a sounding board. What do you think?"

"It sounds great to me, Mel. Just how big is Hamilton?"

"About twenty thousand."

"That's at least twice the size of Ridgefield." Evan chuckled and said, "That's a big town to me."

"You haven't given me any indication about what you're planning to do, Evan. It brings up another subject I want to talk with you about. What would you think about going to work for a daily newspaper in a town the size of Hamilton?"

"Well, like you, I've been thinking about Jackson or Memphis. I thought I might have a better chance of finding a job on a bigger paper."

"I mentioned to Mr. Bradford that a friend of mine would like to get started in journalism on a newspaper that would offer him a variety of learning experiences. I mentioned that this friend had graduated in journalism from Milcrest and had taken courses in creative writing, feature writing, newsroom management, reporting protocol, and everything else I could think of. The old guy picked up the phone and called Alex Garner, publisher of the Hamilton *Commonwealth*. Garner said send him over. If he liked what he saw, he had a job that would work the ass off of the journalism wonder."

Evan Sherman and Melvin Stuart both started their careers in the same week in Hamilton, Mississippi. They stayed at Stuart House for a month, until Evan got a paycheck that would allow him to share the rent on a two-bedroom furnished apartment in a comfortable old house on the outskirts of town.

The weekend before they moved to their new apartment, Evan took a Greyhound bus to Ridgefield. The confrontation with Martha was less explosively emotional than he expected. She sat grimly listening to his argument to justify the abandonment of ministerial studies.

"Your father told me you wouldn't go to Seminary. I don't know how he knew, if you didn't tell him."

"I didn't tell him, Ma. I think he knew all along that I wasn't really intended to be a minister."

"Did that Stuart boy influence you to change your studies?"

This was a difficult and unexpected question for him to answer honestly. Melvin had, in his own cynical way, condemned the religious hypocrites, like his own father. There was no doubt in Evan's mind that Melvin had made him look at his own real convictions— what he would have done without an emotional spasm on a summer night in an evangelist's tent. He couldn't tell her that her insistence that one of her sons become a preacher had brought him to the point of hypocrisy that Melvin hated.

"Mel didn't make me change my mind, Ma. He's probably the most intelligent person I have ever known. He helped me with all studies while he was with me at Milcrest. He showed me how to examine any philosophical question from a rational point of view. Maybe indirectly he made me realize that I was doing the wrong thing."

"Do you think your father knew you wouldn't go into the ministry?"

"I think he always believed I was doing the wrong thing."

"You don't plan to come home again after you leave, do you?"

"I have a job of Hamilton that is just what I want, Ma. You knew I wouldn't stay here for long after I graduated. There's nothing in Ridgefield for me, even if I had stayed and gone to Seminary. You knew I would eventually have to go somewhere else. I'll always come home when I can. I just can't stay."

"It seems I've lost both my sons." Martha said and left the parlor to go lie down in her bedroom to grieve.

Evan stayed in Ridgefield two days. Amos Sherman came home from the railroad late in the morning of the second day and Evan had a chance to talk with him alone.

"You knew all along, didn't you, Pop?" Evan asked after he told his father his plans.

"I knew you would eventually find out what an enormous mistake you were making. I hoped that when you figured it out, you'd have the courage to change what you were doing. You had to do it yourself, Evan. Now that you have, I want you to go back to Hamilton and get on with your life. I want to see you whenever you can come home for a while. Not soon. Your mother needs some time to accept what it's so hard for her to believe."

Evan wanted to tell his father how he loved and respected him,

but couldn't find the words he had never said before. He collected
a few things he had left at home and caught the bus back to
Hamilton the next afternoon.

As Alex Garner had promised, he worked Evan's ass off for two
months before he gave him a break and let him sit at a rewrite desk
and try his hand at breathing some life into some of the duller
reports about the daily social activities in Hamilton that the citizens,
especially those more socially deprived, waited eagerly to read.
Before that, he had Evan go with the newspaper's two reporters and
their lone cameraman to document anything that had the smack of
news about it. He ran errands for the old hands setting hot type in
the broiling hot typesetting room and handled the galley trays as
print proofs were pulled for the proofreaders. He performed every
menial task that kept the news coming and the press rolling.

He had time, sitting at the rewrite desk, to start wondering about
Molly, wondering when she was coming home. She had been
indefinite about how long she would stay in Ireland. It all depended on her mother. Molly seemed to suggest that it would be a matter of months before she came back. They had agreed not to write
each other while she was gone. It was more Molly's idea than
Evan's. She didn't have any idea where she would be or what she
would be doing. It depended on her mother. She didn't want to
promise Evan letters that might never come. He agreed reluctantly.
Now he regretted it.

"I know I've asked you before, but I just want to be sure," he
said to Melvin, when he couldn't stand not to. "You gave your
mother the phone number to our apartment, didn't you?"

"Evan, Helen has called here three or four times. If you think
maybe Molly called her and she forgot to tell us, give her a call and
ask her."

"I was just thinking, I've moved around a lot since I left
Milcrest, and—"

"Evan, you told Molly to call Stuart House when she got back from Ireland. That's what she'll do. She told you she didn't have any idea how long she and her mother would be gone. To me, that meant at least a couple of months. You said that yourself. She won't come back until her mother has soaked up enough of the old sod to last her until she can go back for another treatment."

"I know you're right about that. It's been over two months now. I'll wait another month and, if I don't hear from her, I'll call her father at that pub he owns in Memphis."

The chief editor of the *Commonwealth* took some of Evan's local news rewrites into Alex Garner's office and put them on his desk.

"I gave that kid you hired a shot at rewriting some of the local stuff everybody else hates to be saddled with. I'd like you to take a look at what he's done with it.

"Sit down, Burt. I'll look at it now," Garner said and motioned to the chair in front of his desk.

Garner read for ten minutes before he looked up at his editor.

"I hate to tell you this, Burt, but I haven't read copy this good from anybody else on this paper."

Burt Simmons smiled and said, "Including me."

Alex Garner laughed aloud and said, "You're an editor; you're not supposed to know how to write. You're just supposed to know how everybody else *should* write. That's why I pay you so much money."

"Yeah, it's nice being rich. Now that we're over the funny stuff, I have an idea I'd like to try on you. You have a few extra minutes?"

"Yeah. Let's hear it."

"We have three published novelists living in Hamilton. They're not native, but it's sort of the thing to do for novelists to live in small southern towns. Faulkner and Wilde and Welty and a half dozen others have set the pattern, and I think there's a great feature story series in interviews of the local writers by somebody who knows the language well enough to give the features some literary flavor. I'm thinking Evan Sherman. He showed me his college transcript and he's had courses in creative writing and feature writing."

Garner sat considering his editor's proposal. After a few minutes of weighing the idea, he looked up at his editor and said, "We haven't had a feature series in a long time that wouldn't put an insomniac to sleep. I like the novelist idea. Everybody in town would like everybody else to think they read something other than the funny papers. Try it out on Sherman and see what kind of reaction you get."

"I'd love to do a series like that," Evan told his editor. "As you know, I've never done any kind of feature story. I have all this other stuff I'm doing. How much time would I have to do the first story?" Evan asked.

"I like what you've done with the local news rewrites, Evan. I want you to keep on doing those and work the feature series in on as tight a schedule as you can. I'd say have something on the first series piece ready for me to see in about three weeks. I know it'll mean what amounts to overtime for a while but there's no such thing as overtime in the newspaper business." Burt Collins paused and waited for Evan to smile and nod his acceptance of this old newspaper cliché before he went on. "Choose one of these guys and go out and talk to him about doing an in-depth interview. I expect him to jump at the chance."

Evan had the feature's first draft on Burt Collins' desk the middle of the third week after his first author interview. It ran just over 1500 words after Collins made a few minor changes. He called Evan into his office and told him:

"Have it set in 10-point type and tell whoever does the makeup it will run under the fold of the front page." As Evan was leaving his office, Collins said, "Take Mack out with you and tell him to use that good portrait camera. I want some shots that flatter the hell out of this guy. He'll wet his pants if he sees his picture on the front page. It'll look like the New York Times to him."

Burt Collins took the feature copy in for Alex Garner to read.

"Where will you run it?" Garner asked.

"Under the front-page fold in Friday's paper. That will give the readers all weekend to talk about it." The *Commonwealth* didn't have Saturday and Sunday editions. "They'll figure out we've got something special for them to look forward to. It may even get some of them to read a book."

"Are you suggesting we have a basically illiterate readership, Mr. Collins?" This suggestion of mock criticism wasn't lost on the editor.

"Why certainly not, Mr. Garner. Every one of them has probably read the *Bible* beginning to end, even the *Begats*."

Alex Garner was through with the newspaper mechanics of getting the feature in print. He wanted to talk about Evan Sherman.

"Sherman wrapped his story around one of the best book reviews I've ever read. I believe he read all three of this guy's books, so he could give our readers a composite background on what literary value this author's books offer." Garner paused while he thought about how to phrase the suggestion he would make to his editor.

"I'd like you to think about what we're going to do with Sherman, if he keeps on giving us the quantity and quality work with the rest of this series and the other stuff he's been doing. He's been here just over three months now. After he finishes the series, give some thought to making him an offer with an editorial title and a salary that's almost double what he's getting now. That's your call, Burt, but I think we could lose him if we don't let him know he has a home here, if he wants it. Are you going to give him a byline on the series?"

"In 14-point boldface. If this series is as consistently good as this first part, word will get around we've got a writer that promises to become an honest-to-God journalist. I believe papers from Memphis to New Orleans will be on the prowl for his kind of talent. Let's see how quickly somebody comes knocking on his door. We may have to do something within the next six weeks, if the series stays on schedule."

The same week Evan's series ran in the paper, Melvin had his first courtroom case. It was a civil action in a contested estate settlement and tried without a jury. A panel of three judges listened to the arguments. Melvin sat second chair to John Bradford and was allowed to make the first part of the case's summation. The judges took less than thirty minutes to rule in favor of the Bradford client.

"Mel, you surprise me," John Bradford said as they walked out of the courtroom. "You sounded and acted like you've been in the courtroom for years. It's not just what you say, but the way you say it. And it's the way you stand and the way that you don't let your eyes waver when you address the judges. I do believe I've got me the makings of a trial lawyer."

Friday afternoon Evan worked until almost nine o'clock cleaning up the local events copy for Monday's paper. When he got to the apartment he and Mel shared, he noticed a 1947 Chevrolet sedan parked at the curb in front of the apartment house. Mel met him as he came in the door to their surprisingly large living room.

"We're celebrating, old buddy. I just had my first court case, and Mr. Bradford had me make the first part of the summation. We won, and Bradford laid some heavy compliments on me. Completely deserved, of course." Wearing a lunatic-type smile, Melvin pounded his expanded chest like Tarzan's celebration of victory.

"You seem to have gotten suddenly rich, if that is your Chevrolet out front." Evan attempted to match the lunatic smile.

Moonglow

"If you're suggesting I bought it with my Momma's money, which will be amply repaid, you are correct. It is necessary for you to understand, and fully appreciate, that you are cohabiting with this generation's Clarence Darrow."

Evan was about to ask if Darrow had won the "Monkey Trial" about evolution, but Melvin held up his hand holding a copy of the *Commonwealth* to stop him.

"You have outdone me, Evan. This whole town will read a brilliant examination of current American fiction in this feature bylined by none other than my roommate." Melvin became soberly serious as he said this. "I had no idea you could write like Thomas Wolfe. I have six extra copies of this landmark issue, and I plan to give one to Helen this weekend when we go to Stuart House and drink a lot of her sherry. I know you can get as many copies as you want, but I'm saving a copy for Molly, so, in case you don't tell her, she'll get to know someone she had no idea existed. And I have a copy for Mona, who, I think, sort of suspected it. She saw your grade transcript on the journalism courses you took. Have you sent a copy to your parents?"

"Well, no I haven't. If it's any good, like you say it is, my dad would enjoy it. But I don't want to do something my mother will consider trying to justify the decisions I've made that she hates." Evan was eager to change the subject, so he said," I'd love to spend the weekend at Stuart House. You can help me celebrate surviving my first four months out of the university's womb."

117

Chapter Twelve

Helen Stuart was well read, and she gave Evan a long, contemplative look after she finished reading his feature story.

"Evan, I know you've been told how good this is," she said as Evan was taking his first sip of her sherry.

"Mel said he thought it was good, and my editor seemed to like it. He asked me if I thought I could keep the same style and format for two more features. There are two more writers in Hamilton he wants me to do a story on."

"I've read the book, actually the books this man has written, and I'm amazed at how you have used the language to describe the work of someone I don't consider to have the same language skill you do. Do you think you can keep up the quality of what you've done in this piece?"

"I sure hope so. I'll be living with this generation's Clarence Darrow, who I'm sure will be my constant critic. He claims he has taught me everything I know."

"I haven't taught you nearly all *I* know," Melvin corrected. "For instance you don't have a clue about how to handle being in love with the most beautiful girl in the world with a mind of her own."

"Will you tell me about Molly, Evan?" Helen Stuart asked. "Mel says she's as talented as she is beautiful. He also tells me she's crazy about you."

"I don't know what Mel expects me to do that I haven't done," Evan said a little defensively. "Molly is an Irish girl born in this country to Irish natives. She has a glorious voice and has been invited to audition at Julliard and Curtis. She's gone to Ireland with her mother, a trip planned long before she graduated. She decided not to go to the auditions until she comes back. I just don't know when that will be. She said it was up to her mother. I knew it would be an indefinite time she would be gone. It has been over three months now. I guess I'm getting a little antsy."

"It seems there isn't anything you can do, Evan, except to tell Mel to mind his own business. I don't know of any wild success he's had with the ladies lately."

"I can't tell my love affair secrets to my Mamma," Mel said. "She's always been insanely jealous of my girl friends, Evan."

Helen Stuart was well aware of the magnetic attraction Melvin's good looks and social ease had for any woman past puberty and under fifty. There were only a rare few who hadn't at least heard the steamy exaggerations of the sexual pull of this storied heir to the Stuart fortune. It wasn't a complete lack of interest Melvin seemed to have for the sexual provender offered by the ladies of Hamilton that had led to his monkish life style the past three months. It was a determination to please the likes of John Bradford and his conservative friends, who wouldn't welcome into the legal brotherhood a town rake that threatened the chastity of their wealthy clients' daughters.

Although Evan Sherman didn't offer the charm of Melvin's claim to southern gentry, he had not gone unnoticed. He was four years younger than Melvin and immeasurably younger in sophistication. The yearning of the younger girls for Evan was just as intense as the universal yen all the women had for Melvin, and this sexual itch would amplify to include the older group when the effect of Evan's feature story became the talk of the town. It would be a rare occasion when the public appearance of either of them on the Hamilton streets didn't draw the attention of the available, and many of the legally unavailable, ladies in the downtown pedestrian traffic.

So Evan was unavailable because his unconditional love for Molly made him uninterested and unavailable, while Melvin was careful not to do anything with an over-zealous partner who might be enthusiastic enough to cause some sort of public embarrassment. He had another, safer proposal to offer Helen to satisfy her curiosity.

"Suppose, Sweet Mama, that I invite a special lady friend to come spend the weekend at Stuart House. Do you think you could be civil to a lovely sexpot you would no doubt think was just waiting for an opportunity to jump my bones?" he asked.

Helen didn't seem disturbed by this proposal that made Evan mentally gasp. She thought for a full minute before she responded.

"Only if Evan comes, too, and acts as chaperone. There should be at least one sane male in the house."

"I had that in mind all along. Evan knows this lady, who is on the Milcrest staff, and I believe they mutually admire each other. Isn't that so, Evan?"

Evan had no doubt Melvin's weekend guest would be Mona Regan and he doubted that she would decline the invitation. He knew the reservations he had about Mona were historical, based on one shocking night of discovery in his dormitory room, when he was still a virgin and thought he was entitled to religious indignation. Now, he didn't have the conviction or courage to express any serious reservations about Mel's proposal. As far as he knew, Mona was as constant a lover as Mel would ever have.

"I assume you are referring to Ms. Regan. And I do admire her. I will accept this invitation, as long as I'm not expected to take the part of protective father and bring along a shotgun. When do you have in mind for this interesting weekend?" Evan realized he was mimicking the Stuarts with his stilted response, showing off, trying to keep up. It seemed all their conversations when Helen Stuart was around sounded like dialogue from a bad play.

"The fourth weekend in March would be nice, the beginning of spring, my boy. That's when all the human juices begin to flow." "Your juices are always flowing," Helen Stuart said. "Don't push it, Mel. I might change my mind."

Later in the evening, when Melvin and Evan were upstairs sprawled in the leather chairs in the sitting area of Melvin's bedroom, Evan said:

"Admit it. You got me up here just to keep your mother from putting up a big stink about bringing Mona here for a weekend."

"Evan, I invited you so we could celebrate the first really good things that have happened to both of us since we moved to Hamilton. The idea of bringing Mona to Stuart House didn't occur to me until I realized how long it's been since I've had any female companionship. It's been over three months now. I know I have to be very careful in Hamilton, so bringing Mona up here is the best solution for a while. I don't want to mope around like you do, waiting for Molly to come home."

The moping comment stung Evan. He thought he had been stoically unobvious while enduring the pain of waiting.

"My moping hasn't been any more obvious than your goody-two-shoes being a nice guy who wouldn't dare take advantage of some juicy high-school senior."

"I do believe I struck a nerve, Evan, and I'm sorry I said that. I know you're so deeply in love with Molly that any separation has to be painful."

"Are you in love with Mona? I know she's in love with you. Don't ask me how I know, I just know. I've seen her face when you're around, and I've seen her face when you leave her. It's like she just died a little."

Melvin took his legs off the chair arm and sat straight, looking intently at Evan.

"Yes, I am in love with Mona, Evan, and I don't know what to do about it. I just can't promise her anything now. I want to say the right thing when she comes up with us, but I don't know what the right thing is. I haven't really decided I will stay indefinitely in Hamilton. I'm not ready to get married. Hell, I'm just twenty-six, just getting started. I'm not ready to play house."

"Why don't you tell her that? Tell her you love her, but she'll have to make the decision about whether she can wait, and you don't know how long. I think that's really what Molly and I told each other. We have to wait. I know I'd marry her tomorrow, but that's not going to happen. She needs a few years to get ready for the rest of her life, the part where I'll just be an observer."

"By God, Evan, I believe you're getting to be as smart as I am, smarter in some ways. I believe Mona will wait as long as it takes, and I think she will accept a long-distance love affair, if she is convinced I love her. You're right about what I should do when she comes up here. But you're wrong about being just an observer in the music part of Molly's life. You've got too much music in you not to be a very important part of what she does with the incredible talent she has."

"Let's go to bed, Mel. Molly's been gone over four months now, and I need some moping time before I cry myself to sleep."

Before Evan slept, he thought about the mother-son relationship Melvin had with Helen Stuart. The tolerance each had for the other's actions and opinions was so vastly different from the relationship Evan had with his mother, that they seemed to be contemporaries rather then a generation apart. Helen Stuart was a very attractive and desirable middle-aged woman, and Evan wondered how she tolerated the isolation of living at Stuart house with only the servants to keep her company. Everything about her argued for something other than playing the part of a spinsterish widow.

As he drifted into sleep, the thought came to him that his assumption of Helen's social isolation was probably far from anything this lady could accept. She didn't always spend her nights at Stuart House alone.

Moonglow

The second *Commonwealth* feature on novelists living in Hamilton was more widely read than the first one, and the flood of mail that came in to the paper's publisher and chief editor was so complimentary that Evan became more of a local celebrity than the writers themselves. As in his first feature, he had read all the books the writer had published, and the review of the quality of his work was so well done that Evan became something of a literary maven to the local book lovers.

The president of the local book club, a lady high in the social structure of the town, invited Evan to address the next meeting of the club on any subject he chose. His attempt to wiggle out of accepting the invitation was countered with a flexibility of schedule or whatever concession had to be made to accommodate such a busy newsman that he finally agreed to address the meeting in the third week of March.

Evan's principal reading of fiction had been of the writers of lyrical prose, so he made that the subject of his lecture. He concentrated on Thomas Wolfe and F. Scott Fitzgerald. He practiced before the mirror, reading aloud selected passages of each writer that most appealed to him. If Evan had been a singer, he would have been a baritone, so his voice became more sonorous with each practice reading.

The book club members were all female and almost every eye was bright with tears after the reading of a passage from F. Scott Fitzgerald's *This Side of Paradise:*

> *For a minute they stood there, hating each other with a bitter sadness. But as Amory had loved himself in Eleanor, so now what he hated was only a mirror. Their poses were strewn about the pale dawn like broken glass. The stars were long gone and there were left only the little sighing gusts of wind and the*

*silences between...but naked souls are poor things
ever, and soon he turned homeward and let new
lights come in with the sun.*

And as Evan continued with his Orson Welles voice, the weeping became audible with his reading of passages from Thomas Wolfe's *Look Homeward Angel:*

*They clung together in that bright moment of wonder,
there on the magic island, where the world was quiet,
believing all they said.   And who shall say—whatever
disenchantment follows—that we ever forget
magic, or that we can ever betray, on this leaden
earth, the apple-tree, the singing, and the gold. Far
out beyond that timeless valley, a train, on the rails
for the East, wailed back its ghostly cry: life like a
fume of painted smoke, a broken wrack of cloud,
drifted away.   Their world was a singing voice
again: they were young and they could never die.
This would endure...come up to the hills, O my
young love. Return! O lost, and by the wind grieved,
ghost, come back again.*

Evan owned the ladies of the book club. He would forever after be remembered as the golden voiced young man, who in memory would stand taller than his six feet. The handsome young man with maple colored hair, who could sing the songs of prose that made them tremble.

The last of Evan's three-part series was published the week before he and Mel returned to Stuart House. Some considered it the best of the series, because the novels of this last writer were the most popular among the Hamilton readers. Evan managed to make it out of town before the book-club ladies had a chance to make him

124

lie about why he couldn't give a repeat performance.

When Melvin drove the seventy miles south to pick up Mona at Milcrest, Evan went with him. On the trip back and into the Delta country, they all three sat crowded in the front seat because Melvin and Mona had insisted. They weren't ready for any kind of one-on-one conversation that could very quickly get into the dangerous waters of personal commitment. So Evan was an insulator sitting hip-to-hip with a woman who was almost as physically provocative as Molly. He inwardly groaned during the eighty miles to Stuart House.

Melvin had asked Evan to bring his clarinet with him for the weekend. He wanted to have as much diversion from the moment-of-truth talk he would eventually have with Mona. So Evan played all the popular music that Helen and Mona liked, and they even sang along, a little off key, when he played something they especially liked enough to learn the words. Mona knew how Evan could play any music he had heard, but he astounded Helen.

"Mel tells me you can even play classical music if you have heard it," she said in a tone that really made the statement a question.

"Well, not really. I think he means that I learned the melody line of some of the arias Molly loved from the lyric operas. I have a hard time without a strong melody line."

On the second day of the weekend, Melvin was ready to talk to Mona about their future, and he wanted to do it without Helen around. When the opportunity came, he asked Evan to play *Kiss Me Again* and then leave. He knew Mona had heard him play and Molly sing at her concert and the kiss at the end had an electric effect on everyone in the concert hall, including Mona. Before the last note had faded, Melvin took Mona's face softly between his hands and kissed her as Evan had kissed Molly. Mona began to cry. She was silent and helpless, with her arms at her sides.

When Melvin said, "I love you, Mona," Evan had already left

the room.

At the end of what Melvin told Mona about his inability to make any commitment other than at some time in the future he wanted her to marry him, if effect, to wait for him, she said, "I'm not going anywhere, Mel. I'll wait as long as it takes. I just want you to be honest enough to tell me if you change your mind."

As they were preparing to leave on Sunday afternoon, Helen embraced Mona and said, "Please come back again, Mona. I think you're the best thing that has ever happened to Mel. I hope he's smart enough to know it."

When Molly had not called to announce her homecoming after five months, Evan called the Sullivan Pub in Memphis and asked to talk to Barry Sullivan. After he had explained to Sullivan that he and Molly were close friends at Milcrest, Sullivan said:

"Oh yes, Evan. Molly told her mother and me about how fond she was of you. The ladies have decided to extend their stay in Ireland. I really don't know exactly when they'll be back. I'm sure Molly will let you know when she returns."

"I thought I might write Molly a note, but I don't have any kind of address. Could you tell me how I can address a letter?"

A detectable tinge of irritation seemed to amplify the already rolling brogue in Barry Sullivan's voice. "They aren't staying any particular place, Evan, keep moving around. You'll just have to wait until Molly gets back. I'm sure she'll call you." He hung up the phone while Evan was thinking about his next question.

Burt Simmons was sitting in Alex Garner's office ten minutes after he heard that one of the junior editors from a Memphis paper, the *Commercial Appeal*, had been systematically collecting information about Evan Sherman to show his publisher.

"How long has Sherman been here, Burt, six months?"

"In two weeks it'll be seven months. In that time, our circulation has increased over fifteen percent, a lot of it out of town."

"Our advertising income has increased more than that, about twenty percent. We can't afford to lose Sherman, Burt. What do you have in mind?"

"I want to double his salary, maybe more. He's being paid less than the guy who cleans up around here. I know the offer on a paper twenty times the size of ours will be a temptation hard to resist, but I think he enjoys being the hottest thing in Hamilton. I'd also like to give him a title. I believe Associate Editor on the masthead will mean more to him than the money."

"Put his title just under Managing Editor and pay him ten percent less than Emery's making. That will more than double his salary."

"I've got some other stuff in mind for Sherman, maybe a monthly column to go along with any feature series he would be working on."

"Go tell him what we're going to do, but don't say anything about the Memphis guy. I want him to think he earned everything he's getting."

Burt Collins gave Alex Garner a big smile, as if he had just said something funny, and said, "If he didn't put all that extra advertising money in your pocket, Alex, who did? I don't think you have any doubt that he earned what we're giving him, even if he doesn't do anything special ever again."

Evan waited until he had gotten his second check with the salary increase before he went to a used-car lot and made a down payment on a Ford sedan of the same vintage as Melvin's Chevrolet. He hadn't had much driving experience, so he spent the next several weeks taking excursions into the countryside around Hamilton.

"I'm going to drive to Memphis this weekend," he told Melvin. "I want to talk to Molly's father in person. Want to come with me?"

"You don't plan to beat him up, if he doesn't come up with the right answers, do you?"

Melvin's attempt to make light of something very important to Evan was completely ignored.

"I'll take my clarinet and see about some places where I might be able to play on weekends," Evan said. "I think we'll have to stay over Saturday night. Can you do that, if you go?"

"Well, yeah, I'd like to go. I didn't mean to kid about your talking with Molly's dad, Evan. I know it's been almost seven months now without a word of any kind. I think it's time for Sullivan to pony up some answers to a few questions. And I'd like to prowl around Beale Street with you and see what kind of action we've been missing. You know it's an hour and a half to two hours drive to Memphis, don't you?"

"I'll have all the stuff for the Monday paper done by Friday afternoon. I'm thinking about driving to Memphis after work Friday. Would that be okay with you? It might mean we have to stay two nights.

"I think my crushing social calendar can work it in. I know a nice little hotel in the Beale Street part of town where we can stay. It's not very expensive."

A little after seven-thirty on Friday night, Evan and Melvin walked into Sullivan's Pub. On the far side of the pub from the entrance, Barry Sullivan was sitting at a table with his wife, Erin. Evan recognized them both immediately, and he stopped and stared at Erin Sullivan. She and Molly were back from Ireland, and Molly hadn't called to let him know.

Evan and Melvin walked past the crowded U-shaped bar, that took up half the space in the pub, into the area that held six or eight tables for four. Besides the table where the Sullivans were sitting three others were occupied. As they approached their table, both Sullivans looked up curiously at the two men they had never seen before.

"Mr. Sullivan," Evan said and turned to say, "and Mrs. Sullivan. I am Evan Sherman and this is my friend, Melvin Stuart. I talked with you by phone some time ago about letting me know when Molly returned from Ireland. I guess she's home now, since you are." He turned to look at Erin Sullivan.

"Sit down with us, Evan and you, too, Melvin," Erin Sullivan said and nodded toward to two empty chairs at their table. "Molly is still in Ireland, Evan. I got back a few days ago and intended to call you. I just put it off, so I'm glad you're here. Molly's not through with Ireland yet, Evan. She doesn't know whether she will ever have a chance to go again, so she is determined to stay until she's visited with as many of her relatives as she can and she's seen everything about the island that she wants to see."

"Do you have any idea how much longer she plans to stay?" Evan asked.

"No, not really. It will be a while. We're not going to hurry her." Erin Sullivan paused while she was thinking of a way to end a conversation that would do very little to placate the young man who was hopelessly in love with her daughter. "Evan, I know how close the two of you are, and the time she spends getting saturated with the Ireland she didn't know anything about won't change that. I promise to call you when I know for sure when she is coming home."

"Is there anywhere I can write her?"

"No. I don't know where she will be. I left her pretty much on her own." When it was apparent that Evan would have to accept what she had said, and there really wasn't anything he could do but wait, Erin Sullivan asked, "Can I get you and Melvin a Guinness of maybe a gin?"

"No, thank you," Evan said as he stood up. "Mel and I have several places we need to go."

Barry Sullivan leaned over and shook hands with both Evan and Melvin. Neither he nor Melvin had said a word during this meeting that only succeeded in further frustrating Evan.

Chapter Thirteen

In the two more years Evan waited for Molly to call, he never contacted the Sullivans again. He had become a Hamilton journalist respected for his unusual analytical talent for interpreting the news that was considered important to the local citizenry, and was recognized throughout the state for his talents as a sometimes columnist and feature writer. On weekends, he played clarinet with a half dozen groups in Memphis and stayed over Saturday night, never returning home on Sundays in time for church service. Many of the local ladies who hankered for him almost to the point of despair formed a loosely knit group that assumed he was satisfying his carnal needs in some Memphis cathouse. They collectively forgave him his apparent ungodliness with the generous assumption that he attended services at some church in Memphis. Not for one instant did any of them really believe this.

Evan thought of Molly every day—and waited.

Melvin became more and more comfortable with his law practice and his life in Hamilton. He was also sought after by the marriage candidates who tended to be a little older than Evan's group that extended to high-school seniors on the brink of no longer being considered schoolgirls. Like Evan, he ignored them.

Melvin took Mona to Stuart House at least once a month. On a rare occasion, Evan would play only on a Friday night and drive down to join Melvin and Mona on Saturday. Nothing had really changed in their arrangement.

Mona was still waiting.

One evening in the early spring of 1949, Evan and Mel were sitting in the living room of their apartment when Evan asked, "Do you plan to stay in Hamilton, Mel? We've been here two and a half years, and I'm thinking it's time to decide one way or another if I'm going to stay here or go to a bigger place."

"I've thought about it, a lot. I'm a pretty big frog in this pond, and so are you. I admit I've thought about a big time law practice in a big city. I'm not so sure big is all that important to me anymore."

"Mel, you don't resemble the guy I met the first miserable day I spent trying to learn how to go to college. That was the guy who took me down into the woods for a cockfight that was apparently important to him for some weird reason I never understood. And I didn't have any idea what that was all about or what I was getting into when I went to the dormitory with him that night. That Mel would be in a big city in a heart beat. I can't believe the little-town kid you decided to raise in college had that kind of leavening effect on such a world-class cynic."

"I'm still a world-class cynic," Mel said with a big smile. "I'm just a lot more selective about who I let know it. You can't be too careful in a town the size of Hamilton. And you can give me some credit for taking a lot of that little-town kid out of you. You now have the social grace I've been trying to teach you for over five years."

"Does the relationship you have with Mona have anything to do with your decision about staying here or moving on to a bigger place?"

"No it doesn't. She told me the same thing Molly told you; she will go with me anywhere I want to go. Actually, I think she might be happier in some place other than Hamilton, some place bigger. I don't think she can picture herself sitting around gossiping with the town matrons." Mel sat thinking and realized he was preparing to say something else. "I've been taking Mona to Stuart House for almost two years now. Helen already treats her like one of the family. She wants me to set a date, get married and come live at Stuart House. I know Mona would love it."

"That doesn't seem all bad to me. It's only about a twenty-minute drive from your office. What do you think about it?"

"What do I think about me living with my new wife and my momma in the same house? Actually, that part doesn't bother me. I just don't want to divorce myself from the social life of Hamilton, if I plan to practice law the rest of my career here. I think the natives would come to resent it. I'll make the decision in the next month or so." Melvin hesitated a moment before he went on. "Have you given up on Molly? I haven't heard you even mention her name in months."

Evan waited so long to answer that Melvin regretted he had asked, that he had invaded some privacy too sensitive for Evan to discuss.

"Mel, I don't think I'll ever give up on Molly. I just don't know how long I can keep on living without someone close to me besides you. As it is now, I know it would be terribly unfair to some girl who would just be some sort of substitute for a Molly who might not even resemble the lover who left me almost three years ago. That's why I think I'll be moving on to somewhere else before too long."

Evan left Memphis on Sunday morning the following weekend to spend the rest of the day at Stuart House with Melvin and Mona, and Helen, of course. It was Helen who answered the mid-afternoon phone call. They all heard her gasp before she said "Yes, he's here. Just a moment." Wordlessly she handed the receiver to Evan. She then said to Mel and Mona, "Let's go out to the sunroom."

"I love you, Evan," Molly said as she hears Evan breathe into the phone, before he even said "Hello." Evan couldn't speak. He was stunned by a voice he had thought he might never hear again, the same voice he had heard say, "I love you, Evan" when they were in the woods so long ago.

"Evan, will you please talk to me."

"Molly, I thought I had completely lost you. I didn't think you would ever—"

"Evan, you will never lose me. Do you still love me?"

"I will always love you, Molly."

"Will you come to South Haven as soon as you can?"

"I'll come this afternoon. Tell me how to get to your house."

Molly met him at the front door of the Sullivan home on a street of houses that were the visual testimonial to the financial success of their owners. She was as beautiful as when Evan last saw her, but she seemed thinner, almost fragile, compared to the girl of three years before.

When Evan stepped into the foyer, Molly pulled him to her and took his face between her hands and kissed him until his mouth opened to match hers.

After the kiss, they still held each other, reluctant to retreat to the people they were a few moments before, afraid the future they both wanted would evaporate before they had a chance to secure it.

"Molly, will you—" Evan began, but Molly turned away and took his hand to pull him along as she went down the center hall of her parent's home.

"I have a wonderful surprise for you, Evan, a wonderful gift."

She opened the door to a bedroom and waited for Evan to come stand beside her.

"This beautiful little boy is your son, Evan, yours and mine."

A baby boy was standing, holding onto the side of a playpen on the bedroom floor. He had curly hair as black as Molly's and seemed tall for a baby that could hardly be two years old. Again Evan was unable to absorb what Molly had said. He couldn't speak.

He just looked wordlessly to Molly for something else.

"We made love once, Evan. I suppose I seduced you the night of my concert. Maybe we seduced each other. I know I don't regret it. When you get to know Daniel, you will be forever grateful we found each other and together produced something so perfect."

As Evan sank to his knees beside the playpen, the little boy held out his arms, wanting to be picked up. He was irresistible, and when Evan lifted him, Molly came down to kneel beside them. When little Daniel put his arms around Evan's neck, Molly said:

"You'll never be the same, Evan. This little boy will love you forever and he'll change your life. He has changed mine."

"My God, Molly, he is beautiful." Evan spoke for the first time since he entered the room. He pulled Molly into an embrace that included their son and kissed her with more love than passion. "And you named him Daniel."

"I wanted him to have your name, not Evan, but part of it. I named him Daniel Sullivan. I hate to say it now, but I didn't really know whether you would accept us after I had seemed to fail you by not coming back for so long. I gave him my family name because my mother said it could always be changed, if you wanted it that way."

"I think I understand why you stayed away so long, Molly. But did it take over two years to work up the courage to come back after Daniel was born. You knew you would eventually have to come home and live with what we had done?"

"My mother knew about what happened the first month we were in Ireland. She made the decision I would have the baby in Ireland, and we went to stay with her sister, Kate Flannery. She and her husband, Larry, live in Cork. Kate had been unable to have children, and she was delighted. I didn't come back because it was so easy to stay in Cork with my aunt. You can't imagine how much she and my mother supported me. There was never one word of disapproval. Neither of them ever criticized me about the decisions

I made. When my mother called home to tell my father he was going to be a grandpa, he was elated. His only concern was what I was going to do about my music, the same single thing that bothered my mother."

Evan stood up and lowered his son into the playpen. The little boy held out his arms for Molly to take him. But Evan pulled her up and guided her to sit beside him on the bed that she apparently used when she slept by Daniel at night.

"I talked to your mother after she came back. Mel and I went to your dad's pub and she just told me you weren't through with Ireland, that there were things you wanted to do. She didn't give me any indication it would be another two years before you came back." Evan tried to keep his voice from sounding like he was blaming someone for the agony of his long wait.

"It was easy to stay in Ireland, Evan. After mother came back home, she called me in Cork and told me she talked to you and Melvin at the pub. She actually didn't know when I would work up the courage to come home and face being an unmarried mother in a small southern town. She couldn't really tell you anything, just that it would be a while. And my Aunt Kate was so flexible with her time that she encouraged me to explore the Island while she played mother to Daniel." Molly smiled as she thought about her aunt telling her to go stay a week or so with relatives in Killarney. "I think my Aunt Kate wanted me to go home and leave Daniel with her. She loves this little boy."

"He's almost two now," Evan said, after he had done the mental arithmetic, beginning with the last time he and Molly had been in the woods.

"He'll be two on the sixth of June, Evan," Molly said and waited for the reaction she knew Evan would have, after the date penetrated the wall of other thoughts that crowded his mind. When it came to him, he seemed momentarily startled and then said:

"That's the day Henry was killed in France five years ago."

Molly took both of Evan's hands in hers and pulled him up to stand again by the playpen while they looked down at Daniel. "If you still believe in that God of yours, Evan, you can believe, as I do, that Daniel is his gift, his atonement, for allowing Henry to be taken away. Maybe you'll find some part of Henry in this little boy."

Evan couldn't speak. His eyes were bright with the tears he didn't even want to control. Molly had seen him cry before, when he told her about Henry five years ago.

"My parents left so we could be alone when you first came to see me, Evan. They'll be back in another hour or so, in time for dinner. Let's go sit in the living room and let Daniel take his nap. I've been keeping him awake until you came."

They sat together on the living-room sofa until Evan put his arm around Molly to pull her closer to him. He wanted to kiss her again, but Molly resisted and turned to him.

"Evan, I will do anything you want me to do. I will go to bed with you right now, if that's what you want. If you're anything like me, you can hardly wait. And I don't believe my parents would strongly object to our sleeping together while you're here, but I want that to be a decision you make after we've talked about what we're going to do that can't be postponed." As Molly spoke, the burr of dialectical speech that her exposure to the Irish brogue had brought to her voice became more and more evident, and Evan became more and more captivated by it.

"I love the part of Ireland you brought back with you that gives a lilt to your voice that will forever protect you from the southern-belle drawl. I can hardly wait to hear you sing *The Skye Boat Song.*"

For the first time since he has been with her, Molly smiled. "I try to catch it before it creeps into what I'm saying. It will take a while."

"Don't ever change it, Molly. I love it." Evan changed the tone of his voice to show that he was getting back to what Molly had just said. "I would like to postpone our sleeping together until you decide whether it will be forever. I want you to marry me, Molly, and I'd like for it to be tomorrow. I just realized I've never asked you. Will you marry me?"

"I told you before, Evan, married or not, I will go with you anywhere you want me to go. I will marry you anytime you want me to after we've done one thing I want you to do as a favor to me. I want you to take me home with you, I mean Ridgefield, so we can try to make whatever peace with your parents we can."

Evan sat and thought about what Molly had asked him to do. The prospect of bringing home with him the mother of his out-of-wedlock-born son was a chilling thing to consider, when it came to his mother. He had no doubt that his father would be as accepting as he needed to be. He then thought of Molly's parent's behavior when he and Mel went to talk to them at the pub.

"Did your mother know that I was Daniel's father when I went with Mel to talk to them two years ago?"

"Yes, I told her as soon as we both discovered I was pregnant."

"And your father knew, too?"

"Yes, I don't think my folks keep secrets from each other. If my mother said he should accept you for what I said you were, he would. Neither of them gave you any kind of hard time when you talked with them, did they?"

"No, they didn't. Now that I realize they knew all along who I was, I'm surprised by the way they acted. I know there's no way my mother will be anywhere near as civil to you. That's why I have to give some thought to your idea of coming home with me." Evan paused for a few seconds, then asked, "When your folks come home, do you think we will have any kind of question and answer session with them?"

"I know we won't. As far as they're concerned, you are part of the family, a sort of son-in-law in waiting." Molly pulled Evan around to face her more directly. "How much time do you need to answer me about going home with you before we do anything else?"

"I can answer you now, Molly. I'll arrange for you to come, but I need some time to work out the details. I live in Hamilton now, and I have a very good job that I probably will give up. So I'll have to work out what we're going to do after you leave your parent's house and I leave my job."

"Will you stay with me for a while? I want you to spend some time with Daniel before you go back to do whatever you have to do."

"I want to stay with you and Daniel for a while, Molly. I have a lot of catching up to do. I want Daniel to know who I am before I leave, so he can remember me."

That evening Evan called Melvin and asked him to call Burt Simmons at the paper and tell him he needed a few days to take care of some family matters. Melvin didn't ask any questions about the reunion with Molly. He would wait.

Evan stayed with the Sullivans until Wednesday morning. Barry and Erin Sullivan didn't ask a single question that would seem to be a request for Evan to justify himself for anything that had happened between him and Molly. Evan slept in the guest room, and every night Molly came into his bedroom to lie down with him. They didn't make love; they just held each other until the last lingering kiss and Molly went back to sleep beside Daniel.

Evan spent hours on end with his son. He couldn't get enough of him. He thought often of the time he had missed while Molly waited to come home. By the time he was ready to leave and start rearranging his life, he had discovered something about how a parent feels about a child---he could love someone else as much as he loved Molly. He wondered if it was because there was so much of Molly in him.

"Are you sure about this Evan?" Burt Simmons asked after Evan told him he would be leaving the *Commonwealth*. Evan was sitting in the editor's office on Wednesday morning. "You know you have become a very important part of this newspaper's family. That won't be easy to duplicate somewhere else."

"I do know that, Burt, but I don't have any choice; I have to leave Hamilton. The only thing I can tell you is that I haven't done anything illegal, and I don't have some outraged daddy after me with a shotgun."

"Alex Garner is going to be very disappointed if you leave."

"I hate it that I have to leave. Both of you have been very kind to me, something I will never forget."

"Alex told me that if you're determined to leave, to do whatever I could to help you, wherever you go. Do you have any other newspaper in mind?"

"I'm going to try the *Clarion-Ledger* in Jackson. Is that a problem?"

"Not really. They're far enough away that what they do does not really affect our circulation or our advertising. I know their managing editor; do you want me to give him a call?"

"I'd love to have something lined up as soon as possible, so I will really appreciate anything you can do."

"Go in and talk to Alex; he's expecting you."

After his talk with Evan, and Burt Simmons told him of Evan's interest in the *Clarion-Ledger,* Alex told Burt to get copies of every feature Evan had done and samples of his smoothing out the local news and send it to his friend on the Jackson paper.

"Send it overnight mail. I want to know that Evan is set as soon as possible."

When Simmons sent the package, he wrote a note saying that the *Commercial Appeal* in Memphis had made some inquiries about Evan. This was part fact and part fiction, but Simmons padded it by saying Evan had shown a strong preference for working on a

Mississippi paper.

While Evan waited for a response, one way or another, from the Jackson paper, he finished everything he had started for the next few issues of the *Commonwealth*. He called Molly to tell her about his application to a paper in Jackson and told her he really didn't expect an answer for at least a week.

"If that doesn't work out, I'll try the *Commercial Appeal* in Memphis," he told her, a confidence in his voice he didn't really have. They made telephone love and Evan always wanted a report on Daniel, detail by detail.

"Do you have any idea when we can go talk to your parents?" Molly asked.

"Molly, when I leave Hamilton, I won't be looking back. I'll be ready to go wherever I find work as soon as we walk out of my parents' house. Until I find out where the place is we start our lives over, I can't arrange for us to go to Ridgefield. You'll just have to be ready when I know."

Three days after Burt Simmons sent the package of Evan's work to his friend on the *Clarion-Ledger*, he got a call from him:

"Can you get Sherman down here by ten o'clock tomorrow morning?" he asked.

"He'll be there whenever you want him. Do I tell him to go directly to your office?"

"Yeah. The people downstairs will know he's coming and send him right up."

"You're going to like this guy, Walter. He's the best newspaper writer I've read in a long time. He may have a little too much class for that rag you work for."

"He'll be lucky if I don't send him back to the sticks where anybody who can spell is a good writer to you guys."

Evan was interviewed by the managing editor and the editor-in-chief and was offered a job as Features Editor before noon. He immediately accepted and went out to lunch with both editors to work out the details. He told them he needed a week to ten days to straighten out the details of leaving Hamilton and finding a place to live in Jackson. He didn't mention that he would have Molly and Daniel with him, and they didn't ask about his family.

The first night after he came back from his three days in the Sullivan house, Evan spent the hours between eight and midnight talking with Melvin.

"I've been about to wet my pants waiting for you to tell me what's going on," Melvin said. "When Helen told me it was Molly on the phone, I had a hard time believing it, after all this time. I hadn't really given up on her; I guess I just wasn't ready for the change it would mean when she came back."

It took almost three hours to tell Melvin all of it. It was so difficult for him to accept as fact the bizarre developments in Evan's life, Melvin would sit mute for minutes on end trying to put it all together in an acceptable composite of what Evan's life was now, compared with what it had been three days before. Most difficult to absorb was the shock of Evan's being the father of a two-year old child. As sophisticated as Melvin was, he couldn't get his mind around this thing between Molly and Evan. To him, Molly had been the most beautiful and virginal young woman on the planet, and Evan was the most unlikely threat to her virginity he could imagine. Not because she didn't love him enough, but because she evidently did. Melvin thought Evan was just too innocent to have sex complicate his relationship with someone he adored. He didn't know how spontaneous their lovemaking had been, what a surprise it was to both of them.

The last hour was spent dealing with the change that Evan's leaving would force into their lives.

"You know why I will be leaving Hamilton, don't you, Mel?" There was a note of apology in Evan's voice. "Even if we got married before I came back, I couldn't explain a two-year-old son to people in this town. That is not what I led them to believe about me for the almost three years I've been here. We'll be starting over in Jackson."

"I knew last Sunday, as soon as Helen told me it was Molly on the phone, you'd have to leave Hamilton. In fact, it made me think about what I would do when you left. I plan to give up this apartment at the end of the month and move to Stuart House. I decided that while you were gone." Melvin paused, composing what he would say next, something important enough to be said so that Evan would understand and accept it without question.

"Evan, I asked Mona to marry me last Sunday, after you got the phone call from Molly. I wanted to ask her when Helen wasn't around, so I asked her on the drive back to Milcrest."

"She no doubt accepted," Evan said. It was more of a question after Melvin didn't give Mona's response.

"Yes, she did. But there was a strange hesitation before she did. She asked me if I had waited to ask her until Molly came home to you. I think she had an idea that when you leave, she would just be taking your place in my life. I explained to her that you and I needed each other for entirely different reasons. You would wait the rest of your life for Molly, and you needed somebody to help make the waiting bearable. I was just waiting to find out whether I had grown up enough to love someone as completely as I love her, as completely as you love Molly. When she accepted and before she began to cry, she said 'Promise you will never leave me.' I can't imagine that I ever will."

"Have you told Helen?"

"She's already planning the wedding." Melvin's broad smile indicated the comfort he got from his mother's enthusiasm for his marriage to Mona. She thoroughly liked the girl her son has elected to marry. "She wants us to be married at Stuart House. She knows neither of us have a religious affiliation of any kind, so she wants a civil ceremony, have some important judge John Bradford might recommend. She plans to invite everybody of any social standing in Hamilton and have a garden party on the Stuart House grounds for a reception. Social event of year she calls it."

"Have you set a date?"

"Not exactly. Helen says we need a couple of months to do the wedding stuff, so I think it will be sometime around the first of September."

"I think we will be well settled in Jackson by then. We'll come up for it, if we're invited. We won't exactly be the cream of Hamilton society. Probably be an embarrassment when all the Hamilton socialites, who thought I was Mr. Wonderful when I was working on the paper, see me with a wife and hear the rumors of a two-year-old son."

"I not only want you here for my wedding, I want you, Molly and Daniel to come up and stay at Stuart House for a long weekend, or however long you care to stay. Mona and I don't plan to go away after we're married. She just wants to stay home."

"I think I'm having a little trouble accepting another major change in my life, Mel. We've been together, for the most part, for almost five years. I hope I've grown up enough to go from the comfort of the no-responsibility relationship we have to the responsibility of the husband-and-father position I will have in a few weeks."

"I think you'll revel in it. For God's sake, Evan, you'll have your Molly back and a son who's already out of diapers. I think your only problem will be how to get Molly back to the training she knows she needs to control a voice that is so rare it comes to very few in an entire generation."

"I've thought about that. I doubt there is a music school anywhere near Jackson with a voice department that even approaches Julliard and Curtis."

"Not every opera singer was trained at those two schools, Evan. Molly's voice will be the same no matter where she goes. I got interested in what she would do about her music and drove over to

Oxford and talked to the people in the voice department of Ole Miss. Every one of them said that there were many music schools with faculty who could train Molly, but some, like Julliard and Curtis, demanded more of the student. There is a great amount to performance technique that must be learned, especially in opera. The voice is the natural talent that has to be trained. Most teachers with a good ear can do that. It's a musical play with dialogue that must be learned."

Evan looked at Melvin in disbelief. He couldn't even imagine that Melvin had taken so much interest in the problem Molly would have developing her voice in the musical outlands of Middle Mississippi.

"I didn't know you had ever heard Molly sing, Mel," he said.

"I haven't really, just some of the spontaneous stuff she sang when she walked around the campus. But I read all the reviews she got after her concert. Remember, the Musical Miracle at Milcrest?"

"When did you get a chance to go to Oxford?"

"I went Monday afternoon after I called Burt Simmons for you. I just wanted to satisfy myself that you didn't have to take Molly so far away, like New York or Philadelphia, for her to keep on with what she has to do."

"She said that it would take at least two years at either of the eastern schools before she would be ready for a performance career. She thinks she's getting too old to postpone much longer getting back into her training program. I don't know what she means by too old. She's only twenty-five."

"I also made some inquiries about the music schools at Belhaven and Milsaps, both colleges are in, or near, Jackson. They got surprisingly good reviews from some of the faculty I talked to at Milcrest." Mel held up his hand to stop Evan from commenting on his music school research. "I know it seems like I'm meddling in something that's none of my business, Evan. I probably am, so that's the last I'll say about it."

"Don't worry about meddling, Mel. I think what you found out about Belhaven and Milsaps will be good news to Molly. I'll tell her about them when I call tonight.

Before they went to bed, Evan told Melvin he thought he should be able to leave Hamilton in about a week. He realized he had more to do at the paper, more than he first thought, before he finally walked out the front door for the last time.

When Amos Sherman answered the phone, Evan breathed a sigh of relief. "Your mother is at one of her circle meetings," Sherman said, even before Evan asked for her.

"I wanted to talk to both of you, Dad. I've taken a new job, and I'm moving from Hamilton to Jackson. I'd like to come home for a brief visit before I move, and I want to come when you're sure to be home. I'd like to come on Friday, if I can."

"I haven't looked at the board, Evan," Sherman said and after a pause, "I can arrange to be here."

"Will you tell Mom about it, or do I need to call back?"

"I'll tell her. What time Friday? There are two afternoon trains."

"Actually, I'll be driving down. I bought an old Ford sedan. I'll probably get there in late afternoon."

Amos Sherman would have been so much more receptive than Martha to the revelation of Molly that Evan hated the lack of courage that kept him from at least mentioning her. He almost called back to tell Amos Sherman he needed his support when he brought Molly into his house. Evan wanted his father to tell Martha about Molly, so the reality of her could marinate for a few days in Martha's always simmering disapproval of everything he did.

But he didn't call back. Instead he called Molly to tell her about the arrangements he had made for the both of them to go to Ridgefield. She would arrive on the coming Friday night on the 9:30 train.

"That will be awfully late, Evan," Molly said. "We probably wouldn't get to your house before ten o'clock. I'll be pretty tired by the time I get there."

"I don't intend to have you go directly to the house with me, Molly," Evan said. "Anyway my folks will be in bed before ten o'clock, and I want you rested and as relaxed as you can get before we face my mother's fire and brimstone predictions of our future together."

"Is that supposed to be funny?" Molly asked with a little petulance in her voice. "No, just a little dose of reality about the way things are at my house. Don't worry about it. My dad will be on our side."

"I think I like your dad already."

"Good. I know he likes you already. Molly, I'll meet your train and we'll go directly to the crummy hotel on Main Street where you will stay overnight."

"I don't care how crummy it is, as long as there is a bed without bed bugs."

"No more attempts at humor tonight," Evan said. "We're both too tired to be funny. Go to bed, Sweetheart. I'll see you tomorrow night."

Chapter Fourteen

Martha Sherman sat in her living room staring at her son. Her face was so expressionless it was apparent she hadn't absorbed what her son had just said.

"For God's sake, Martha, all Evan said was that he was bringing his girl friend home to meet his parents." Amos Sherman was impatient with his wife's obstinate refusal to accept the simple fact that their son had grown up.

"I told you about Molly when you came to commencement, Mom. The girl with the marvelous voice who gave the concert the newspapers called the Music Miracle at Milcrest."

"That was almost three years ago. I don't remember any girl you introduced me to when we came to Milcrest."

"You didn't meet her then. We just didn't have time in the rush to get ready for commencement. You remember we barely had time for lunch."

"What's your big hurry to get married now, after waiting around for three years?"

"We were only twenty-two then, Mom. I loved Molly then and I still love her. We plan to get married very soon, and I just wanted you and Dad to meet your future daughter-in-law." Exasperation was beginning to show in Evan's voice and Amos Sherman recognized it.

"She's getting in awfully late, Evan," he said. "It will be close to ten o'clock when you bring her here.

"I've reserved her a room at the Sanderson Hotel. She'll be too tired to come here tonight. Anyway, you'll both be in bed by ten. I'll get her here by midmorning tomorrow."

"You could have told us a little sooner, Evan." The underlying complaint was evident in Martha's voice. "We could have had her—"

"I think Evan has gone out of his way to please us, Martha," Amos Sherman interrupted. "It seems Evan's Molly is a brave girl coming to visit her prospective in-laws in their not too happy home. I can't believe that your son hasn't forewarned her about the lion's den in Ridgefield."

Evan recognized a streak of Melvin-like cynicism in his father, something that had been there as long as he could remember. He wondered how long it had been since his father was truly happy, or at least content, with his life. He thought about his own life as he walked to town as he had done hundreds of times before he ever left Ridgefield. He thought about his life in a small Mississippi town, a place he was determined to escape.

The dappled shadows slipped across Evan's white shirt. His own shadow leapt before him as he passed from under the trees that overhung the sidewalk to the unshaded moonlit patches and back under the trees again. He passed the anonymous front porches where summer voices speculated and passed judgement, not only on him but on everyone and everything, and promptly forgot the speculations and judgements when the pitcher of lemonade was brought, and his footsteps were mind-lost echoes in the oppressive night. Walking with head-bent urgency, as if fleeing some unpleasantness, walking away from something obscure and painful, Evan stepped on the foot of his shadow and on every crack in the sidewalk. He had counted the sidewalk cracks a hundred times, seven hundred and thirty-two between his house and the first block of Main Street. His gait was exactly measured to the five feet separating the cracks.

He passed the high school building, silent and cavernous, without even the rumors of a day of voices to give it memory. Squatting, old-bricked, three-storied, and lightless, grained and painted floors, the pungent smell of strong disinfectant mixed with sawdust burned in Evan's nostrils. Worn floors, foot-cupped wooden steps, hard, knife-ruined desks, obscenities on the lavatory walls; he conjured his own soundless rumors. He saw the study hall on the third floor as he had seen it for the first time almost eight years before. That first time, it was huge and threatening, filled with hostile and truculent faces. He saw himself thin and afraid, and this view of himself was so intolerable he erased it, mentally sliding forward four years to the time when he saw it for the last time, not so huge, with faces friendly and familiar. Now, outside in the darkness, he pictured it as smaller still, and the faces were gone, there were only rows of empty desks.

As Evan reached Main Street, he glanced up briefly, surveying the street before him. Nothing stirred, nobody in sight. The storefronts were dark, punctuated only by a sheet of light that fell through the doorway of the Sanderson Hotel. Hurrying past dirty, finger-marked display windows, he turned down Railroad Boulevard and diagonally crossed the brick-paved street to the station waiting room. As he approached, he could see that it was empty. He paused momentarily in front of a soot-grimed window and peered intently inside. Only the ticket agent was visible behind the iron bars of his window. One uncomfortable, back-to-back bench bisected the dimly lighted room, and it was empty. Evan glanced at the clock on the wall above the ticket window. Nine-twenty. The *Flyer* was due in ten minutes.

Everybody must be outside where it's cooler, he thought. He continued around the station house to the Beanery and stood facing the tracks with his arms folded across his chest. A small clot of prospective passengers waited, in too many clothes, perspiring and impatient, for the air-conditioned railroad coach.

A strange uneasiness stirred in Evan as he began to feel the pulsing approach of the train. He began to fidget nervously, shoving his hands into his trousers pockets only to remove them immediately and then shove them in again. He turned and walked to an iron bench that was pushed against the wall of the Beanery; he sat down. A cross bar in the back rest dug painfully into his shoulder and he squirmed down so that he could support his weight by leaning sideward, wedging himself between the back rest and a pile of mail sacks thrown against the Beanery wall. Crossing his legs, he bounced his right foot rapidly, like a nervous woman. Across the north and south-bound tracks on a service spur stood a diesel switch-engine. He stared into the open service door trying to identify the bulk of steel that formed the ponderous heart of the dormant brute. A little reflected light made bright spots on the oily surface, and with this deceptive lambency he tried to force his sight into the blackness, tried to identify something that to him would have no identity in broad daylight.

From four miles away, Evan heard the sound of the diesel horn. With the wind from the south, the horn could be heard as it blew for Stillman, and each succeeding crossing could be anticipated almost to the second. Evan mentally followed the train as it approached, and a tremor ran up his spine as he waited for the deep-throated bellow to announce the last crossing at South Yards. The bench was no longer bearable, and he got up and walked to within ten feet of the tracks. When the roving spear of light bounced between the round house and the car shed he stepped back from the tracks and turned so that the cinder dust wouldn't blow in his eyes. The engine sections, sleek and powerful, slid past him and the train braked smoothly to a stop.

Fifteen or twenty people got off the train, dribbling from the cars at sixty-foot intervals. Evan was standing midway along the train's length, and he turned one direction and then the other as they came toward him in single file, bent under the weight of suitcases and packages.

A group of passengers approaching from the rear of the train veered toward the parking lot and he saw her, carrying a small overnight bag the size of his mother's purse. Among the other passengers, she seemed taller than he remembered from just the days before, and thinner. When she saw him hurrying toward her, she put the bag down on the asphalt and waited.

Her face was pale in the frame of her dark hair, almost ghostly in the peculiar violet of the mercury arc lights. Evan looked into the blue eyes that the light had robbed of color. She's as beautiful as a cameo, he thought. Still as beautiful. A gray-eyed Athena.

She seemed to be standing in a state of arrested motion, waiting for him to speak. Thin lines of determined self-control about her mouth took some of the fullness from her hips. Her eyes explored his face for a few moments and she seemed ready to turn away from him when he spoke:

"I know this will be difficult for both of us, Molly. I thought maybe we could postpone it until after we were married."

"It's been over three years," she said as if she hadn't heard him. She had said what she was thinking. Because of her, they had waited too long. The thought made her face serious, but as she looked at him, her expression changed to mild surprise. "I remember everything about you. You're just the same."

Evan didn't know what she meant. They had rediscovered each other ten days ago. They spent their days falling in love again. It was as if she had forgotten.

They stood so close that Evan could not really see her. He stepped back slightly and looked at her completely and then came close to her again.

"No, I'm not," he said, "and neither are you."

He reached up with one hand to run the back of his fingers over her cheek. He held her face with both hands and kissed her until he could feel the strain leave her mouth. The train began to pull away from the station.

Four men were sitting together at the Beanery counter and their heads came up from between their sagging shoulders and turned in unison to watch Evan and Molly when they came in the door. Steam from their coffee cups added to the greasy, stratified air, wispy streamers that struggled to take their places in the haze at the ceiling. The stools at the L-shaped counter were unoccupied except for those curious trainmen. Along the front by the window were four booths and two more were around the corner on the short end of the L. All were empty. Through the short-order window could be seen the Negro cook. A huge shapeless woman sprawled in a chair that was tilted against the wall by the stove. The man who waited on the counter was sitting on a high stool behind the cash register.

The men at the counter were old, part of the streamliner crew that had been relieved by another crew of old men. They had to be old, with many years of seniority to have such a run. They looked at Molly with the boldness and insolence of old age. They looked at her unsmilingly and completely, and their eyes lingered near the floor because her legs were so beautiful.

"Two coffees," Evan said and slid the overnight case against the wall by the door. Molly went to one of the booths around the corner and sat down while Evan waited for the counterman to draw the coffee into the heavy cups.

"Are you sure you don't want something to eat?" Evan asked when he was seated opposite her in the booth.

"No. I had something on the train; I'm just not hungry," she said and then smiled. "Do you think I'm too thin?"

"I think you're perfect," Evan said and, amused at his ready gallantry, added, "I'm not trying to fatten you up. Anyway, the old goats at the counter didn't seem to think you were too skinny. Did you notice?"

"I noticed," she said and they both laughed quietly, so the old men couldn't hear them. They ducked toward their coffee cups and took little tentative sips of the scalding liquid. Molly added more cream to her coffee, let it cool a moment and then drank half of it.

"I told my folks about us this afternoon," Evan said. They know we plan to get married. My father understands it, and I'm sure he approves it. My mother doesn't understand why we want to get married now; she thinks it's a spur-of-the-moment thing. She can't believe I could have been in love for over six years with someone she didn't know existed."

"When did you say you'd take me to see them?"

"Mid-morning tomorrow. I just want to get it over with, Molly. We'll talk together, and no matter how it comes out, we'll leave. I hope you will be satisfied that we at least tried, no matter how tomorrow goes."

"I'm glad it won't be before tomorrow morning." Molly seemed relieved. "I know I look a little bedraggled tonight, Evan. I've been staying up with Daniel the last two nights. He's had a little fever and is so restless that it takes a long time for him to go to sleep."

Evan had wanted to ask about Daniel, and Molly's mention that he wasn't well was disturbing.

"You think he might have the flu?" he asked.

"I don't think so; maybe a cold. Babies get sick, Evan. Daniel's had colds and a little fever before. I just have to stay up with him until he can sleep."

Molly took another sip of her coffee and then asked, "Where am I going to stay tonight, Evan?"

"I got us a room at the hotel," he said, and, although he didn't look up from stirring his coffee, Molly could see that he was flushing lightly. She waited a few moments before she spoke again.

"You want to stay with me tonight?" She was surprised, and it showed in her voice.

"Yes." Evan looked up and held her eyes. There was a deeper

flush on his face.

"Everybody in town will know about it in the morning."

"We'll be gone by tomorrow afternoon," Evan said. There was a hint of triumph in his voice.

While Evan answered, Molly had become strangely agitated. She leaned across the table, straining up on her elbows to get close to him. Her voice was low and urgent when she asked: "Do they know about Daniel?"

"No. I haven't told them."

"Do you plan to tell them tomorrow?"

Evan hesitated, and when he answered his voice was defensive. "No, I don't, Molly. Why should we go through all that now? They never really knew anything about us. I was twenty-two years old and they thought I was just a kid with his first case of heartburn. They didn't know your name. They kept saying you were the girl I got upset about when I was in my senior year at Milcrest. That what they told everybody, they said a girl got me all upset. They laughed about it. They thought that's all it was."

Molly sighed, letting her breath out between pursed lips. She sagged a little between her table-supported elbows and then sat back in the booth. She seemed very tired.

"I thought they would blame me for keeping you out of the ministry. I don't know why, but I thought they knew." Molly paused and then said, "I thought everybody knew."

"Why, Molly? You said your parents never knew about me."

"Not your name. No, I never told them that. They just knew there was someone who was the only boyfriend I had the whole time I was at Milcrest."

"We don't have to talk about this now, Molly. Let me get you some hot coffee," Evan said; Molly held his arm as he began to slide out of the booth.

"Evan, was it the way you felt about Henry that kept you out of the ministry or was it me? Was it what we did?" She leaned forward and raised her arms while she spoke, as if she were going to take his face between her hands. But she didn't hold his eyes after she had forced him to look at her. She leaned back in the booth again and lowered her arms so they rested palm-up on the table. Evan looked at her slender fingers, which she seemed to be examining herself. "I always thought you were afraid of one of us," she said without looking up.

"Henry thought I was afraid of the war," he said after a long pause. "The last time we talked before he left, he called me a coward, Molly. I wanted to be able to explain to him that he was wrong; I just never got the chance. But I'm not agonizing because Henry got killed in a war I didn't think I should have anything to do with. Whether I was right or not is beside the point."

Evan stopped talking and waited so long to speak again that she thought he wouldn't finish it, but he went on, "Do you know what I heard an old woman who lives down the street say about me? She said, 'There goes that Sherman boy who's going to be a preacher to stay out of the army.' But the one she was talking to, this other old woman, said, 'No, that wasn't it. His momma wanted him to be a preacher; she decided before he was born. He didn't have anything to do with it.'" He paused and looked at her directly, looked to see if she understood what he had said. "The last one was right, Molly."

Railroad sounds drifted in through the screen door of the Beanery. Outside the front windows the sporadic blue of an arc welder flashed like summer lightning over the roof of the car shop. Molly seemed to be watching it.

"You don't want me to stay with you tonight do you, Molly?" Evan asked. His voice was gentle, but the question surprised her. She thought a moment before she answered him.

"I'd like to start off differently this time, Evan."

"You want to wait until we get married?"

"Yes. I just want you to take me home with you tomorrow morning. We can try to make them understand, and hopefully

Bill Tucker

accept, what we are to each other. If they can't accept that, I know they won't understand about their grandchild. You decide whether or not to tell them about Daniel. I want to just do what we can, and then leave."

Evan's eyes roved her face; they saw the mute pleading in the drawn lines of exhaustion around her mouth. No softening of expression changed the great question she was asking him with her flawless face. He waited for the constriction in his chest to ease before he said:

"All right, Molly. I'll come to town about eight-thirty and we'll have breakfast. I want you strong enough to do battle with Martha."

Amos Sherman stood at the screened front door and watched Evan and Molly as they turned from the sidewalk in front of his house to walk to the front porch steps. She was wearing shoes with enough heels to make her almost as tall as his son. He realized that he was looking at the most beautiful woman he had even seen. He marveled at her long black hair, her cameo skin, and the perfectly formed body. He made a silent resolution not to make a fool of himself in a situation that was critically important to Martha and these two young people.

"Evan tells us you have been sweethearts since you were both freshmen at Milcrest," Amos Sherman tried to get the history of the hard-to-understand relationship straight.

"Well, not really sweethearts, Dad," Evan dissembled. "We just knew there was something between us we didn't really recognize until we were juniors. I think I realized it when I first heard Molly sing. Because of my interest in music, I knew we had something in common besides just being physically attracted to each other." This was a stretch in Evan's effort to justify a relationship that had lasted, in one form or another, for over six years.

"You've both been out of college for over three years," Martha said. The unspoken accusation was 'Why haven't you done any-

156

thing in all that tine? Now you come and tell us you're planning to get married.'

"Mrs. Sherman, I've been in Ireland for almost all of those three years. I planned to go even before I started college. My parents promised the trip to me as a graduation gift. I'm Irish to the core, Mrs. Sherman. Both my parents were born and grew up in Ireland. They married before they came to this country. They love it here, but they wanted me to know where I came from. I am an American citizen because I was born here. Both my parents are American citizens now. They were naturalized over ten years ago. They both love this country, but they both still love the land they came from. My mother went with me on the trip and stayed for almost a year. She told me to take as much time as I needed, because I might never have the chance to come back. So I stayed until I knew that Evan and I could be together forever without me wondering about the land that would always be a part of me. Now I'm home, and Evan is my life. We both hope you can accept us as we are."

Evan was impressed with Molly's very believable justification of her three years in Ireland. But he knew that at some time in the future they would have to somehow explain how Daniel was involved in almost the total time of Molly's Ireland odyssey. The simple arithmetic of the three years would come back to be explained.

Martha Sherman was being elegantly lectured, and she knew it. This American girl who said she was Irish to the core was too much for her, too reasonable. The storm cloud that had gathered in Martha's face began to fade, and, before she could say anything, Amos Sherman said:

"If you didn't have any of it before, you certainly brought back a lot of Ireland with you. If your singing voice is as lovely as the lilt of Irish brogue in your speaking voice, there is no doubt you will thrill anyone who hears you sing."

The flattery made Martha wince and made Molly smile.

"I suppose I get a little carried away sometime." Molly was still smiling as she admitted she had been somewhat emotional in the comments she had made. "Ordinarily, I don't let that much of the Irish burr come into my voice. My parents still have Ireland in their voices, but I had hardly any at all before I left on my trip." Molly paused briefly and then went on. "I can see Evan smiling at me. He says I had a little bit when I got excited, even before I left."

Martha brushed aside the comments about Molly's Irish brogue Amos had made. To her it was a non sequitur. The simplicity of Molly's request--that she and Evan be accepted as they are--seemed to be an attempt to eliminate any further questioning or criticism about their plans. To her, it seemed she was being shut out of her son's life, even more than she had been when she thought that, in effect, she had been rejected when he told her he would not become a minister.

"Evan, your father and I would like to know something about this plan of marriage you and Molly have. Is it something you plan to do soon or will you have a church wedding. I assume you are Catholic, Molly. I understand everyone in Ireland is Catholic." The obvious distaste for the Catholics in Martha's voice wasn't lost by Molly.

"Not everyone, Mrs. Sherman. But well over ninety percent in the Republic of Ireland are Catholic. In another section of the island, Northern Ireland, there is a much larger percentage of Protestants. My parents are Catholic, but they are not devout. In my memory, they have always said that they don't let religion get in the way of their faith."

Martha struggled with the meaning of this very foreign-to-her idea—that there is a difference between faith and religion.

"I've not had the pleasure of meeting your parents, Molly, but I certainly want to. I've never heard my own sentiments described so succinctly," Amos Sherman said before Martha had come to grips with such an alien religious concept.

Before Martha could construct whatever argument she could, the telephone rang and Amos Sherman went into the hallway to answer it.

"It's for you Evan. Your friend Melvin Stuart is on the line."

"Evan," Melvin said, "Barry Sullivan just called me, because he didn't know how to get in touch with you and Molly. Little Daniel has been taken to John Gaston hospital in Memphis. He didn't give me any details; he just wants you and Molly to come now, as quickly as you can. He wants me to call him back as soon as you tell me. He won't be at that phone very long."

"Tell him we will be at the hospital in four hours. I'm driving; there isn't a train until three this afternoon."

Chapter Fifteen

Not-quite-two-year-old Daniel Sullivan died of bulbar polio before he could have his last name changed to Sherman, before his father and mother could see him again, before they could tell him goodbye.

Barry Sullivan's tear-streaked face told Molly and Evan they were too late. Before her father even had a chance to put his arms around her, Molly went down on her knees in the hospital hallway. Evan was too stunned to do anything but go down beside her and look into the face of this strong man who had endured the last hopeless hours of his grandson's short life—saw the pleading in the eyes of the little boy he thought was more his own than even his beloved Molly had been. Barry Sullivan sat down on the hallway floor in front of Evan and Molly. He seemed to not notice several small groups who walked around the three of them.

"God, we loved your little Danny Boy. Erin is still sitting by his bed. I can't get her to leave him. She's waiting for you."

Molly looked at her father as if she hadn't understood anything he had said. Her face was so expressionless that Evan, whose crumpled face expressed so much despair, knew she was in a state of shock so severe that she wouldn't accept Daniel's death. She stood up and walked down the hallway with her father. She didn't even look back at Evan, who was following them, dreading what he knew would be the most difficult act of acceptance in his life. He would have to see the still form of the son he had just barely gotten to know.

Barry Sullivan moved to the side as they entered the hospital room where Erin Sullivan sat beside the bed that held the baby boy she couldn't stand to leave alone. Molly stood at the foot of the bed and looked at her son and then at the grief savaged face of her mother. When Erin Sullivan moved from her chair to come and put her arms around Molly, there was no response from her daughter. She stood with her arms at her sides and waited for the physical act of comforting to end.

When Evan came to stand by Molly, she looked at him with so little recognition in her expressionless eyes, he knew he was a stranger to her in whatever place she had gone to avoid the pain. She came to the side of the bed and reached down to pick up her son, but Erin Sullivan quickly moved to hold her hands.

"He's cold now, Molly," she said as she looked into Molly's questioning eyes. "You don't want to remember him like that."

Evan had a strong impulse to hold his son in his arms just one more time. He had so little to remember. But he knew Daniel wouldn't put his fragile arms around his neck and lay his head on his father's shoulder ever again.

Molly sat down in the chair her mother had used for the lonely vigil, enduring the long wait for her daughter to come. After fifteen minutes of complete silence, Barry and Erin Sullivan both forced their way between Molly and the hospital bed and stood until she looked up at them.

"They will come soon, Molly," Barry said, "They'll take care of Daniel. We can't take him with us. There's nothing we can do now. I want to take you and Evan home to get some rest. You two need to be together for a while."

Molly looked up at her father and shook her head.

"Do you want to wait until they come for him?" Erin asked.

Molly didn't answer, not even a nod of her head. She just sat back in the chair and looked at her son. Evan pulled another chair from the other side of the bed and sat with her.

"We'll wait," he said.

They sat silently for over an hour before the people who take care of such things came to get Daniel.

Molly had not spoken a word for the two days before the very private memorial service for Daniel. Only the priest from a Memphis Catholic church and three couples of the Sullivan's very best friends spent the thirty minutes of traditional remembrance in the Sullivan living room.

Molly didn't speak to any of them. She didn't go with Evan and her parents to the cemetery to watch the tiny coffin lowered into the ground.

At night, Molly would lie in her bed beside the crib where Daniel had slept. After midnight, Evan would come and lie down beside her. She didn't reject him, she just didn't turn to him or respond to any attempt to hold her. And she didn't speak.

Barry Sullivan knew how Molly's silence was destroying Evan.

"I know how much you're hurting, Evan. You've lost the most precious thing you will ever have, other than Molly's love. I can't tell you where Molly has gone, but I know she's not hurting you on purpose. I think she blames herself for letting Daniel die. Neither of you, or Erin or I, could have done anything that would have saved him. If you don't know that, neither of you will ever get over blaming yourself for something you couldn't do anything about."

"I know that now," Evan said. "When I left yesterday, I went to John Gaston and talked to the doctor who treated Daniel. He explained how bulbar polio very quickly gets beyond anyone's control. Daniel's paralysis was quick and complete. The muscles in his chest were so quickly paralyzed that we couldn't have gotten him on an effective respirator if we had been clairvoyant enough to recognize the simple symptoms as polio. He said he probably would not have known it either." Evan stopped because Barry apparently wanted to say something.

Moonglow

"I had a similar talk with the doctor, and I'm glad you can now accept your own lack of responsibility for something that was, at some point, inevitable. I haven't tried to get Molly to understand what that means, but I don't think she will come back to us until she can begin to forgive herself."

Evan stayed with Molly until her silence was unbearable. On the sixth day, a Friday, after Daniel died, he took Molly into the privacy of her father's study. He sat in a chair facing her and, holding both her hands to keep her from turning away, said:

"I will be leaving you for a while, Molly. I know you hear what I am saying to you, and I don't expect you to say anything to me now. I know you're not ready yet. But when you can accept that neither of us had anything to do with the death of our son, you will remember that I love you now as much as I've ever loved you. I've never loved anyone else and I never will. I'll wait as long as it takes for you to come back to me. Maybe it will be easier when I'm not here." Evan leaned forward and kissed her unresponsive lips. He got up and called Melvin at his office to ask if he could spend the weekend at Stuart House. Molly heard what he said and had no reaction at all. Evan wondered if she would even know that he was gone.

The Sullivans understood Evan's need to get away from a house so full of despair that his own recovery from personal tragedy was jeopardized. They knew that Molly's retreat into some protective limbo would only add to Evan's need to be somewhere else.

"I think it's a good idea for you to go spend some time with your friend, Evan." Erin Sullivan agreed with him about giving Molly some space. "We can stay in touch by phone. I don't think Molly is ready to come back from wherever she is. If I see any sign of it, I'll let you know."

Evan saw Helen Stuart waiting for him as he drove up to the front of Stuart House. She came to the side of his car and said:

"Pull up to the end of the circle, Evan. Mel's not here yet. He's bringing Mona for the weekend, and I think they're bringing some of her stuff. They'll unload it and take it through the front door." Evan moved his car and came back to give Helen the expected hug and kiss on the cheek. He always looked forward to it. He wished he could greet his own mother like that. Before Evan could say anything, Helen held up her hand to stop him.

"They should be here in about a half hour, but before they come, I want to tell you how the loss of your little Daniel has hurt Mel. I hadn't seen tears in his eyes since he was a little boy."

"When I called to ask him about coming down this weekend, I didn't know whether he had heard that Daniel hadn't survived the polio. We didn't talk about it. He just said 'please come.' That made me think he probably knew."

"He called the hospital about every hour after he called to tell you and Molly to come to Memphis. I think he knew Daniel hadn't made it before you did. After the doctor told him that Daniel was gone, he had trouble telling me about it. I'm so glad Mona was here. I think she eased some of the shock he felt."

"I don't know whether you had known it or not, Helen, but Mel and I didn't start out like we would ever be close friends. We were different in so many ways that I thought after the first semester, when we were in the dorm together, I would move out and room with someone more my own age. You'll never know how grateful I am that I didn't. It took me a couple of years to realize how strong Mel is and to understand what he was talking about when we discussed what we expected out of our lives."

"I think Mel is right where he wants to be, Evan," Helen smiled to show how pleased she was with the thought of Mel staying in Hamilton and coming back to live for a while at Stuart House. "I'm not sure, but I don't think he has the big idea anymore about becoming a hot-shot big-city lawyer."

"I guess you know why I can't stay in Hamilton. We need a

new place to start over, and Jackson isn't very far from Stuart House. When the time comes I want to bring Molly here. I need you and Mel to help her get her life back.

Evan waited until Melvin came, and they finally could talk together, without the choking impulse to cry, to tell the three of them about Molly's retreat into some place he couldn't go.

"How long can you stay with us, Evan?" Helen asked

"I really don't know, maybe as long as you'll have me. Erin Sullivan agrees with me that I need to give Molly as much room as I can to help her get over the self-blame that has sent her to some place where no one else can come. She said we can talk every day by phone until she sees that Molly is coming back. It may take just a few days; we'll just have to wait and see."

"You know you can stay here as long as it takes, Evan," Melvin said. "I moved my stuff here last week, and I wouldn't want you going back to stay alone in that apartment in Hamilton. What do you plan to do about your job in Jackson?"

"I'll call the editor who hired me and tell him I have a family problem that will delay my coming there for at least a week, maybe more. I don't think timing is critical, because the job they gave me didn't really exist on the paper before. They know my strength is in feature writing."

The calls Evan made to Erin Sullivan on Saturday and Sunday weren't encouraging. Molly still hadn't spoken a word. But on Tuesday there was some excitement in Erin's voice.

"Molly looked around and, for the first time, seemed to know where she was. She looked straight at me and said one word. She said 'Evan?' and it was a question. She wanted to know where you were." Erin hesitated for a few moments and then said, "I asked her if she wanted you to come stay with her, but she shook her head. She's seemed to drift off again and she didn't say another word. I want you to be patient for a few more days, Evan. Molly's coming back to us, but I believe it would delay things if you were to come here now."

Evan detected an uneasy restraint in Erin's voice the next several days he talked with her. There seemed to be more that could be said, some reluctance that kept Erin from reporting fully on Molly's recovery.

On Monday, the tenth day Evan had been at Stuart House, when Evan called, Barry Sullivan answered the phone.

"I know you think we've been putting off giving you the full details of Molly's recovery, Evan, and you're right. We have. Molly is completely aware of her world now, but she can't accept her place in it. She wants to be somewhere else. Erin didn't have the courage to tell you, but Molly went back to Ireland yesterday. She made us promise not to tell you she was going until she could be someplace no one could find her."

Evan didn't say anything for so long that Barry Sullivan asked, "Do you understand what I just said, Evan? Molly has gone back to Ireland, and she won't tell us where she will be. I gave her enough money to go wherever she wants. She said she will eventually tell us where she is. She asked us not to try to find her and asked me to tell you she still loved you deeply but didn't want you to try to find her."

Evan hung up the phone without saying a word.

All Evan said before he left Stuart House was, "Molly's gone back to Ireland." He didn't elaborate. The only one who said anything was Melvin who just repeated the word as a question "Ireland?" and Evan said "Yes" and told the three of them goodbye.

On his way south in his old Ford, packed with everything he owned, Evan stopped at Milcrest after nine o'clock in the evening. He parked in the visitor's parking lot and took his clarinet with him when he walked into the Seminary woods. He didn't stop until he got to the river. The moon was full and the water glinted in the shallow spots where the current made the surface ripple.

He sat down on the small sandy beach and began to play. Not until he had played *Begin the Beguine, Claire de Lune,* and *Kiss Me Again,* and had begun to play *Moonglow* did he feel Molly's presence behind him. He glanced over his shoulder to see the glimmer of her in the fringe of trees at the beginning of the woods. He turned to see more clearly that she didn't have on any clothes, and he seemed to hear her say, "Come to me, Evan."

When he stood up and began to walk toward her, she retreated into the woods and the unbelievably beautiful nude form began to fade, to evanesce like smoke, the closer he got to where he thought she would be. When she was completely gone, Evan sat down again and played for another half hour before he put his clarinet back in the case and left the woods. He didn't know, but another couple had been deep in the woods and listened to the strange music that they had no idea was coming from a heart-broken lover who had no real place to go.

Evan got in his car and drove the two hundred and fifty miles to New Orleans. The apparition of Molly, naked in the woods, stayed with him as he drove in the moonlight of a southern night. He realized that he would see her this way for the rest of his life.

He explored the unfamiliar city streets until he came into the French Quarter, where he parked his car at the curb on St. Ann Street. It was six o'clock in the morning, so Evan slept for an hour in the back seat of his car. There was a for-rent sign on the front of the building where he was parked, but it was too early to go in and ask about it. So he walked the few blocks to Cafe du Monde to get coffee and donuts before he went in and rented the one bedroom furnished apartment

Later in the morning, Evan called the editor of the *Clarion Ledger* in Jackson and resigned the job he hadn't even started. He just apologized and told him family considerations made it too difficult to come to Jackson. The editor didn't inquire about his problems, but he did ask if he would be staying with the *Hamilton Commonwealth.*

"No, I won't, but I will be looking for newspaper work some place out of the state. Would it be too much to ask if you would send me the collection of my work Burt Simmons sent you?"

After the pause that Evan expected, the editor said, "Sherman, you've got balls, I have to give that to you. But sure, I'll send you the stuff Burt sent me. Maybe you'll get famous and come back and work at this little old country newspaper because it's in vogue for writers to live in Mississippi now."

A week later Evan took the samples of feature writing to the editor of *The Item,* one of New Orleans' afternoon newspapers. He didn't go to the much larger morning paper, *The Times Picayune,* because he thought it would be harder to get a job, and he would be required to work in the evenings to get out the morning edition. The feature writing samples got him the job at the *Item,* with the provision that he would start out at the lowest salary level until he could produce quality feature stories and give local news stories the same flavor they had at the *Commonwealth. The Item* had an undefinable flavor, something like a tabloid, in its approach to the way the news and feature stories were presented. It was more fun to read than the other two papers.

The first day Evan was in New Orleans was a Monday and, compared with the weekend, the evening traffic was comparatively slow in the jazz joints on Bourbon Street. There weren't enough people listening to get any enthusiasm out of the groups of fill-in musicians who took the places of the more experienced weekend bands. When Evan walked into the first nightclub, the players were just going through the motions of playing something that nobody was listening to.

Evan sat at the first table after the entrance and took his clarinet out of its case. When the players stopped, Evan stood up and, walking toward the tiny stage where the band sat, started to play *The Muscat Ramble.*

Every member of this group of professional musicians, who accepted their somewhat limited talents, recognized a very talented instrumentalist. Several started to play along, harmonizing as best they could, but there was no doubt where the talent was. As Evan was about to finish, a thin dark-skinned man in a tuxedo came out of a door by the stage and walked up to him.

"Play something else," he said.

"Does it have to be New Orleans Jazz?"

"Play anything you like."

Evan played a medley of Artie Shaw and New Orleans specialty songs that blended amazingly well together.

"Do you play everything by ear?" the thin man asked.

"Yes, well, almost."

"Does that mean you can read music?"

"Yes, if I have to, if it's something I haven't heard."

"What do you want to do, sit in with this group?"

"Do you have a different band on the weekends?"

"It'd be up to them. They would have to hear you play."

"What do you think the chances are they could use another clarinet?"

"I like your stuff. We need something other than straight jazz. We don't have room for a dance floor, but working in some dance music will get the kids coming in off the street. You come back Friday night and bring your stick. I'll get them to let you sit in and see what happens."

Over the next three days, Evan arranged to get tryouts with four other weekend groups. In three of the four nightclubs, he had arrangements to either be added to the group or replace a clarinetist with a mediocre talent.

It wasn't until the next weekend, after he had spent a week finding his way around his job at the Item and had played Friday and

Saturday nights on Bourbon Street, that he called and found out that neither Erin nor Barry Sullivan knew exactly where Molly was in Ireland.

"We truly don't know, Evan," Erin Sullivan said in a tone that made him believe her. "I know Molly will get in touch with us one way or another before too long. When she does we'll call you and tell you what we know. Now that you're working some nights in New Orleans, what will be the best time to call you?"

"In the afternoon either day on the weekend."

After three months neither of them had called.

Chapter Sixteen

Kate Flannery sat in her parlor with Molly's head in her lap when she cried for the first time after her son had died. Kate knew the baby she had come to love, as she would have loved the one she couldn't have, was gone. She couldn't say anything to help Molly, so she cried with her.

Larry Flannery wasn't impatient with Molly's lack of interest in the very ordinary life he and Kate lived in Cork. He could understand it. Even though Cork was the second largest city in Ireland, it was probably the most boring. Larry knew and accepted the lack of what people who weren't Irish called "Irish charm." This was the place he had found to make a very respectable and comfortable living. But he thought Molly had to get away from the confining and pedestrian life she would lead if she just stayed with them until whatever happened that would allow her to go home again.

"Molly," he said on the fourth day she was in Cork with him and Kate, "I know your mother told your Evan the reason you did not come back with her was because you were exploring Ireland while you had the chance. Now he knows you weren't doing that at all; you were staying here to bring up your and his son until you could work up the courage to go back home. I talked with Kate and she agrees with me that you should get out of this house and see the Ireland you didn't see before. Kate said she would go with you for a while."

"If you want to just stay here with us, that's fine," Kate said when Molly sat looking vacantly past her and didn't react one way or another to Larry's suggestion, "but I've been thinking of going over to Killarney and spending a day or so with Rose and Kevin Laurel. Rose is your father's niece, Molly. I know they would be delighted if you came with me. Kevin is a singer, a baritone with a lovely voice, and I'm sure you will like him, and Rose too. They're childless, like we are, and seem to be content doing whatever they do. Even we Irish agree with the tourists who say, 'If you want to know Ireland, go to Killarney.' I would add, 'especially to *Laurel's;*' that's the name of the pub and nightclub Kevin owns and performs in every night, except Sundays."

Kate had gotten Molly's attention.

"Mr. Laurel's a singer?" Molly responded for the first time she had shown any interest in anything either of the Flannerys had said.

"I'm sure he's not the same type singer you are, Molly. He doesn't sing classical music, but he sings all the popular Irish songs, especially the ones the tourists like, and popular music, the ballads, from the American bands."

"I think I'd like that." Molly was showing real interest in something for the first time she had been in the Flannery's house.

"Kevin's singing isn't the only entertainment," Larry said. He wanted to elaborate to pump up Molly's interest. "He always has a number of variety acts to go along with his vocals. He doesn't have a real restaurant, just a kind of light supper. His customers go there for the entertainment and the Guinness, not the food."

"You're sure they wouldn't mind me staying with them for a night or two?"

"They'll probably want us to stay longer," Kate said, "you just wait and see. We'll go tomorrow afternoon. It's just a two-hour bus ride. I'll call Rose tonight and tell her we're coming. You get your clothes ready to stay away for a week or so. We'll probably go somewhere else."

On the bus ride, Molly discovered why Ireland had been named

"The Emerald Isle." The woods along the way to Killarney had undergrowth that was so deeply green Molly kept wondering if this was just an enormous manicured park. Along the edge of the road flowering rhododendron bushes, so large and tall they filled the ground under the trees and rose to half their height. Molly was seeing a part of Ireland that matched the way her parents had described it when her mother's eyes would be bright with remembering. She was beginning to know more about who she really was. And the more she learned, the more her heart ached for Evan, for him to know more about who she was.

The Laurel's house was much bigger than the Flannery's. It was located in the heart of Killarney, which was not a very large city, compared to Cork. There was not much land surrounding the house, which was fine with the Laurels. They weren't city people like the ones who lived in downtown Cork or Dublin, but they liked being close to what action there was in a popular tourist town. And Kevin considered himself to be an entertainer, which, of course, he was, and the country life was inconsistent with what he did.

Both of the Laurels marveled at Molly's beauty. Kate Flannery had tried to tell them how stunningly beautiful she was, but, like everyone who had tried to adequately describe Molly in the past, failed. The Laurels knew of Molly's crushing loss of her two-year-old son, and wondered if the perfect, but unsmiling, face would be any more beautiful if it reflected anything other than the forlorn look of unbounded sadness. They knew they would have to wait for a while to know.

"Your father told me what a wonderful voice you have, Molly," Rose Laurel said. "With that raven hair you'll get everybody's attention before you sing a note."

Rose's comment hadn't been gratuitous; she just said what she was thinking, and it wasn't intended as uncalled-for flattery. But Molly had almost forgotten the adulation she had received after her concert. It had been too long ago, and too much had happened to dilute her memory.

"Are you my aunt, Miss Rose?" Molly asked as if she hadn't heard her.

"No, Molly, we're cousins. Your father is my uncle. I know I'm probably ten years older than you are, but we're equals in the relatives' pecking order. So don't call me Miss Rose, just Rose. Miss Rose makes me sound like an old lady."

Rose didn't look anything like an old lady. She was thirty-four and looked younger. Kevin was forty-two and looked it; most people would have guessed at least forty. Both were very attractive and had the kind of personalities that suited them perfectly for the business of entertaining people for a living. Rose didn't perform as a traditional entertainer, but she was the perfect Maitresse de. All those who came to Laurel's more than once were convinced that Rose remembered each of them when they showed up at the door. They could hardly wait to call her "Rose" loudly enough for everyone around them to hear.

The first night Molly and Kate were in Killarney was a Friday, a very busy night at *Laurel's*. Molly and Kate stayed at the Laurels' home, resisting their hosts' urging to join them at the nightclub. Kate told them she wanted to discuss with Molly a possible tour-bus trip around the Ring of Kerry. She had convinced herself that Molly must be kept busy to keep her from relapsing into the mute gloom she had just barely escaped. It was easy for Kate to show her enthusiasm because she had taken the Ring of Kerry tour over ten years before, had loved, it, and was eager to do it again.

The tour-bus route would be from the Ring's beginning at Killarney, at the center of the land-connected side of Iveragh Peninsula, and follow the peninsula's edge counterclockwise from Killorglin on the north to Kenmare on the south. The bus would stop for twenty to thirty minutes at both these towns on either end of the strip and at a half dozen other small towns in between. If the tourists, mostly not native to Ireland, found any of the towns of especial interest, a few extra minutes would be added to allow for more shopping at the specialty shops that featured novelties that could readily be identified as a piece of Irish memorabilia.

In Kate's telling of the trip, there was so much enthusiasm that Molly showed her aunt what modest interest her somber soul would allow.

"It's lovely, Molly," Kate said. "You probably never heard it, but Killarney has been called 'Heaven's Reflex' by somebody I don't remember. All of county Kerry is considered one of Ireland's loveliest districts. You just wait and see."

Kate hadn't oversold the glories of the tour around the timeless Ring. The mountain slopes, green to the water's edge, seem to slide into the sea to form a landscape so consistently beautiful that Kate could hardly wait to point it out to Molly.

Most of the time allowed at each small town where the bus stopped for shopping, Molly would walk the few streets of shops and into the surrounding areas where the villagers lived. She would occasionally see something in a shop window that seemed to interest her, and she would go in for a brief look at the shop's offerings. She never bought anything, and her lack of interest prompted her fellow travelers to wonder why she had come on the tour at all.

Kate didn't make any effort to interest Molly in the shops' Irish novelties, but she observed her closely to detect any return to despondence caused by boredom with the excursion. But Molly wasn't bored; she was soaking up this beginning experience in her search for the grail of Ireland her parents had described. She had seen the fields of heather flecked with wild flowers and the shepherdless, wandering sheep. She had almost waved to the countrymen who drove the carts along the banks of Killarney Lake. But the thing that impressed her most was Muckross House, a magnificent Victorian home comparable in size and splendor to the chateaux of the Loire Valley in France. This architectural anomaly was located on a land rise just a few miles from downtown Killarney and was surrounded by fields of heather. The field to the west of the house sloped down to the banks of Killarney Lake. Molly turned in her seat on the bus and watched Muckross until it disappeared around a bend in the road.

The hundred-mile bus-excursion had taken almost ten hours, and it was close to seven in the evening when Kate and Molly returned to the Laurel's home. Both Rose and Kevin had left for the nightclub, but a note on the kitchen table invited them to come to the club for a light supper and watch the entertainment. Like Friday, on a Saturday night the entertainers were more talented, and the crowds generally overflowed the available seating.

"Let's go Molly," Kate was eager to accept the invitation. "I'm too tired to find something in this unfamiliar kitchen to cook for supper." Molly didn't answer, but she put back on a light sweater she had worn on the bus trip and walked to stand by the front door.

Rose Laurel was standing at the club's entrance and took Molly's hand to guide her and Kate to a small table at the edge of the entertainment area. There were small tables on three sides of the performance floor, where there was enough room for the unending troupes of young girls who could hardly wait to show their mastery of the intricate movements of step-dancing. The supper they were served was delivered to them unordered, because there was just the one unchanging menu available for every Saturday night. The one variable was what customers had as a beverage. Most of them had Guinness or a lager; a few had American soft drinks.

The tables were full and latecomers sat on benches in back of the tables to watch the show and drink their Guinness.

Promptly at seven-thirty, a six-piece backup band began to play as Kevin Laurel came to center stage and announced that a dancing group from Tralee would open the evening's show and introduced the dancers by singing *The Rose of Tralee*. For the first time, Molly heard Kevin Laurel sing. He had a truly magnificent baritone voice, and, for the first time in her mind-lost months and years, she loved music again.

The company of ten step-dancers was very accomplished. If mistakes were made, they weren't detected by the inexpert watchers who were especially pleased that, among the pretty teen-age performers, there was the always hoped-for gorgeous redhead. Actually, there were two. Step dancers dance with their arms straight at their sides and with no expression on their faces other than complete concentration.

The challenge to get at least one of them to smile is always the part the audience plays in the dancing act. Most often the dancers who smile first are the redheads. There seems to be something in their often freckle-faced composure that can't stand the challenge. This night was no exception. When it seemed the dancers had won the temptation contest, the face of the tallest girl in the troupe, a redhead who had been faced with the most comedic showoffs in the audience, cracked. Her complete face was such a smile that her eyes half closed, and she giggled. The dancing was over and the rest of the girls, smiling because they couldn't help it, walked around the floor to shake their scolding fingers at everyone in the happy audience.

"We have a group with us tonight, ladies and gentlemen," said Kevin Laurel, again standing in the middle of the performance floor, "and I believe many of them are strangers, not only to Killarney, but to all of Ireland. We have had some requests for Irish songs that many of them are familiar with, and would like to hear an Irishman sing them. They may have expected an Irish tenor, but will have to settle for an Irish Baritone."

The first song Kevin sang was *When Irish Eyes Are Smiling* and at the beginning of the second verse asked the audience to sing along with him. Everyone in the audience knew the lyrics, and even the Irishmen sang with Kevin. It was the thing to do.

The audience voices began to fade when Kevin sang *Mother Machree* and stopped altogether when he sang *The Minstrel Boy.*

They also were silent when he sang *A Little Bit of Heaven*. They realized his voice was what they had come to hear, not their own.

Before he began to sing his last selection, he addressed his audience.

"I suspect many of you have heard the popular opinion that 'All Irish songs are sad.' That, of course, is not true, but some of them are heartbreaking." He began to sing:

> *Oh Danny Boy, the pipes the pipes are calling*
> *From glen to glen, and down the mountain side.*
> *The summer's gone, and all the flowers dying*
> *'Tis you, 'tis you must go and I must bide.*

> *But come ye back when summer's in the meadow*
> *Or when the valley's hushed and white with snow*
> *'Tis I'll be here in sunshine and in shadow*
> *Oh, Danny Boy oh Danny Boy, I love you so.*

> *And if you come, when all the flowers are dying*
> *And I am dead, as dead I well may be*
> *You'll come and find the place where I am lying*
> *And kneel and say an "Ave" there for me.*

> *And I shall hear, tho' soft you tread above me*
> *And all my dreams will warm and sweeter be*
> *If you'll not fail to tell me that you love me*
> *I shall sleep in peace until you come to me.*

There were very few eyes in the audience that didn't shine with tears when Kevin finished his sad song. But before the last note of his song had faded, a voice an octave higher than his began the song again. It was a soprano voice so lovely and clear that it filled the room even more than Kevin's commanding baritone. Every head turned to see Molly standing behind the table where she and Rose had spent the evening. This was not the girl who had so captivated her audience at Milcrest. This was a dazzlingly beautiful woman who began to walk toward the stage as she sang. Kevin stood with her and was the first to realize that, in the middle of the song. Molly had changed the lyrics to take the place of Danny Boy.

*And if **I** come, when all the flowers are dying*
*And **you** are dead, as dead **you** well may be*
***I'll** come and find the place where **you** are lying*
*And kneel and say an "Ave" for **thee**.*

*And you shall hear tho' soft **I** tread above **thee***
*And all **your** dreams will warm and sweeter be*
*And **I'll** not fail to tell **you** that I love **you***
*And **you** shall sleep in peace until I come to **thee**.*

As the last note faded and everyone in the audience, who had never heard anything to compare with Molly's voice, stood as they applauded. There was a surge in the crowd to come and surround her, just to be close and touch her so they could better remember her face and try to describe how beautiful she was.

Molly turned her tear-streaked face to Kevin as he moved to take her away from the crowd he knew she couldn't handle. When he got to the table where Kate was standing, Molly walked past it and, without looking back, went directly to the club entrance and walked out into Killarney's star-filled night. Kate trotted a half block to catch up with her. Because she didn't know what to say, Kate didn't speak a word on the way back to the Laurel's house. She was as stunned as anyone in the audience by Molly's voice. Her Aunt Erin had told her about Molly's remarkable talent, but she wasn't prepared for what she heard.

Molly went directly to bed, but Kate stayed up to wait for Kevin and Rose to come home.

"It's hard to believe what I heard tonight," Kevin said when the three of them sat in the parlor to marvel at the thing that had happened at Laurel's Nightclub on a summer night in Killarney, Ireland. "I can't imagine how far Molly can go with a voice she can turn into an experience that a complete audience will never forget after they've heard it. I fell in love with Molly tonight, and I know Rose will allow it." He looked directly at his wife, who smiled her agreement that he could love Molly in a way that had nothing to do with his love for her.

"I know that song was a spontaneous dedication to her son. I just hope that now she's found the way to apologize to the little boy she believes she left to die alone, the music that defined her will be back in her life again. Hopefully, it will be the way she can regain the rest of her voice, the part that will allow her to talk to you and me. Maybe most of all to talk to the boy she loved, the Evan you told me about, Kate, the one who is probably slowly dying because he doesn't know if he will ever even see her again."

Both Rose and Kate had listened in complete amazement as Kevin dissected the cause and proposed a cure for Molly's interrupted life. They had no idea he could be that perceptive and analytical about a problem of the heart and soul so complex that it had dumbfounded everyone else who had tried to cope with it.

"Do you think she may begin to talk with us, now that she has at last begun to sing?" Kate asked.

"I think she will probably respond more than a 'yes' or a 'no' or a shake of her head. I believe we're the first to hear her sing since little Daniel died. And she knows that some sort of release came with her confession to us and all the people who heard her. I don't want any of us to press her."

"I'd like to have Molly stay with us, on her own terms, Kevin, until we can see she's on her way back," Rose said.

"I don't know whether she's ready for that kind of commitment,

Rose," Kate said. "I think she's determined to continue her wandering around Ireland. Let's see what tomorrow brings."

The Laurels and Kate slept in on Sunday morning, and when they got up, Molly was gone.

"All her things are still here, so she can't have gone very far. I suspect she's just walking around town," Kate said. "That's the kind of thing she did when we went around the Ring."

After breakfast, the three of them walked into downtown Killarney in a strolling search for Molly. They didn't find her, but they talked to many people who knew who she was. "That's the girl who sang at your place last night wasn't she, Kevin?" was the common question. Everyone knew about Molly Sullivan and the voice so wonderful that no one could adequately describe it to those who grieved that they had missed it.

In mid-afternoon the three of them had become more and more concerned about Molly's whereabouts. They were preparing to get in Kevin's car and start a wider range search when the phone rang.

"Is this Mr. Kevin Laurel?" a woman's voice asked.

"Yes it is."

"I am Ella McCormick at Harrison House. I've had a young lady visiting with me for quite some time, and it seems she's ready to come back to your house. She wants to walk the several miles into town, but I think it's best that I drive her home. It seems that she failed to tell you about her excursion, and I just wanted to tell you she's had her lunch and is fine, just a little tired. I have just one question, Mr. Laurel. Is she the young lady that sang at your place last night?"

"Yes, she is. Since you obviously weren't at Laurel's last night, how did you hear about her?"

"Mr. Laurel, everyone knows about the most miraculous voice that's ever been heard in Killarney. But nobody knows her name. Now, I know she's Molly Sullivan. She says your wife is her cousin."

"Yes, she is. I don't know how much she has talked to you, but I suspect you know by now that she's American visiting relatives in Ireland."

"She really doesn't talk very much. Seems so sad about whatever is troubling her. I found her sitting on a bench in the heather field leading down to the lake. I sat with her for quite a long time and I'm not really sure she actually saw me with those gray eyes that seemed to show such sadness."

"Mrs. McCormick, we were about to get in my car and go look for Molly. I'll be glad to come pick her up."

"I think she's content to let me take her home, and I'd like to do it. Is there anything you can tell me that would allow me to help her. She seems so lost."

"Do you know where I live in town?"

"I think I know where almost everyone in Killarney lives." Ella McCormick chuckled as she realized that she really meant where almost *everyone of any importance* lives.

"Plan to stay awhile when you get here. We have Molly's aunt from Cork staying with us. We can tell you what we know about what's troubling Molly."

While Molly was in her room sleeping, they told Ella McCormick everything they knew, and speculated about things they suspected.

"Molly is welcome anytime she wants to come," the mistress of Harrison House said as she was leaving, "I don't intend to intrude, but maybe she can let some of the trouble drain out of her with someone outside the family."

Molly wouldn't go back to Laurel's Nightclub. The third day after she had sung her sad song, she told Kate Flannery, "I'd like to go to Tralee."

Kate was relieved that Molly had kept her interest in seeing more of Ireland. There was a certain discomfort that had settled in and seemed to deepen daily as they stayed with the Laurels.

"I'd like to go, too. It's only about thirty miles, an hour on the bus. It's so close, but I've never been to Tralee. I think there is a bus we can take about nine in the morning and we can return in late afternoon. We would have most of the day to look around. That should be enough time. Tralee isn't very big."

"I don't mean to come back here, Aunt Kate. I'd like to go to Dublin after Tralee."

"Oh, Molly, Dublin's all the way across the island. It would take all day on the train. I don't even know whether there is a train from Tralee. Maybe there's one from Limerick. I'll have to ask Kevin when he comes home tonight."

"You wouldn't have to go to Dublin with me, Aunt Kate. I want to stay there for a while. I have enough money to rent a flat for a while."

"I won't let you go to Dublin alone, Molly. I'll go with you, but I can't stay more than a week. I told Larry I would be gone for no more than two weeks. I've never left him for this long before. He'll be about ready to jump out of his skin, if I stay much longer."

As she promised, Kate left Molly a week after they got to Dublin. The day they got there Molly rented a flat in Temple Bar, which isn't a bar at all, but a district near the river filled with very active pubs that all have music of some kind in the evening. During the week that Kate stayed in Dublin, they went to different pubs at night for a light meal and to listen to the music. Their favorite was O'Donahue's, a pub more than a century and a half old, which featured authentic Irish music.

The night before Kate left to go back to Cork, Molly stood at her table and sang for the first time since she became unforgettable when she stole the hearts of so many people in Killarney. And she sang alone because everyone else stopped to listen to her internal crying when she sang *The Soft Goodbye.*

Molly Sullivan, the strange American girl with the voice no one could even describe, had arrived in Dublin. She would stay until

Bill Tucker

the following midsummer and wander the streets of Dublin. She spent most evenings on Grafton Street where even the other street performers would stop to listen when she sang. She became known as Molly Malone because she would go stand by the bronze figure of the original Molly Malone and sing the song that defined her:

In Dublin's fair city, where girls are so pretty,
I first set my eyes on sweet Molly Malone
As she wheeled her barrow
Through streets broad and narrow,
Crying "Cockles and Mussel, Alive, Alive, O"

The streets and pubs of Dublin continued the cure of Molly Sullivan that began the night she told everyone in Killarney about her little Danny Boy.

Chapter Seventeen

Mel and Mona were married at Stuart House in late afternoon on the first Saturday in October. Evan rented a tuxedo and stood by Melvin as Best Man, and the peculiar arrangement for Mona's part of the wedding's formalities was to have Helen Stuart not only give her away but also serve as Matron of Honor. The early fall weather was perfect, and the reception for three hundred guests was held under a giant tent on the Stuart House lawn. In all of northern Mississippi, this was not only the social event of the year; it was the social event of the decade. Everyone in Hamilton, and the more elegant people living in the country with any claim to the nonexistent blue-blooded southern aristocracy, was invited.

Helen Stuart was accepted as the matriarch of the almost defunct clan of Scots who had owned this land for a century and a half, even though she and her son, the lone survivors, didn't have a drop of Stuart blood between them.

Evan, who had become more verbally clever because of his studied approach to the techniques he had learned in his college course on creative writing and his flair for newspaper feature writing, served very well as the toaster at the reception and as commentator on the virtues of the bride and groom. He was remembered fondly by the ladies of the Hamilton Book Club, who took what opportunities they could to rub against him during the extended cocktail hour, where they especially seemed to have a limitless capacity for the continually flowing French champagne.

A wooden floor was laid in the middle of the tent and a dance band from Memphis kept the party alive until the guests with the most stamina left just before midnight.

"I think I'll write a feature story about this bacchanalian blast for the Item." Evan said the next morning when the four of them were sitting in the sunroom for a late breakfast. I think my super-sophisticated Louisiana readers will especially appreciate your having the twelve-piece band sleep over at Stuart House."

"Good," Helen Stuart said with a broad smile. "Mel has subscribed to your paper and I've enjoyed some of the local news I know you wrote, even though it doesn't carry a byline. When it comes out, send two hundred copies to the Madison Pharmacy. I'll pay for them, but I'll get Alma Madison to hand them out free. She'll love it. I thought she and Adam were going to stay all night with us, sleep with the band, so to speak."

"Do you want me to see if I can include a complete guest list?"

"That would be wonderful, if you could. There'll be dozens of framed copies of your feature in Hamilton houses within a week."

Before Evan left Stuart House, he and Mel spent a half hour alone talking about Mona and Molly.

"Mona doesn't want to go on any kind of wedding trip, Evan. She says she has been on a three-month honeymoon just living here with me and Helen. She has never said anything about it, but I know she wants us to keep living at Stuart House, never sell it. For a long time now, we've had only two people living here to help Helen take care of this twelve-bedroom monster. I can afford to hire some more help now, and Mona loves just keeping things straight the other two girls don't have time for."

"You don't need to sell this place, Mel. I'd love to see you keep it forever. Then I'll have a place to go to grieve."

"Don't you think Molly is coming back to you, Evan? I absolutely believe she will; it's just a matter of time. I suppose it's also a matter of how long you can wait."

"I've told myself I can wait forever. If I have a soul, she is part of it, and always will be. I know I will never love anyone else the way I love Molly. But I am beginning to think I may have to learn to live without her. I hate to think that, because it means that in some way, I will be lonely forever."

"You wait a while longer, Evan. If she doesn't come back within a year, go to Ireland and find her."

"I don't have any idea where to look, Mel. Her aunt lives in Cork, the second largest city in Ireland; that's where she stayed until she worked up the courage to come back with Daniel. But I don't think she's there now. I don't believe her parents know for sure where she is either. They told me that as soon as they knew for sure, they'd tell me."

"Do you really believe they will?"

"Absolutely. I think they want me to go to Ireland and find her. They want Molly to come home, and they think the only way she will is for me to go find her and bring her back. They know she won't come back to them until she comes back to me from wherever she's gone to escape the demons she believes the both of us somehow invented."

"That's pretty heavy stuff, Evan."

"I've given it some pretty heavy thought, Mel. Every day I think about the Molly I knew three years ago. I've never known anyone with as much of the social grace you seem to have. I've never seen her uncomfortable with even the most offensive people a girl as beautiful as she is would have to endure during her life on a college campus. When she said she loved me, I believed her completely. I still do."

"When Molly comes back, and I know she will come back to you, Evan, I want you to marry her here at Stuart House, and I want to be your Best Man," Melvin said as he walked with Evan to his car when he was leaving.

"I think her parents would go along with that, Mel. So it's a promise. I might even bring my own band, and Molly can sing at her own wedding. I bet it will even make a feature in the *Item.*"

The comfort Evan always felt when he spent time at Stuart House began to drain away to be replaced by a numbing apprehension as he drove south to Ridgefield. It had been almost three months since he and Molly had left his parents parlor for the tragic drive to Memphis. They had left with no goodbyes, no explanation of why they were leaving or where they were going. Guilt was driving him back to Ridgefield to try to explain something he knew his Mother would never understand, a sin she would never forgive. When he drove up and parked in front of his old home, it took him five minutes to work up the courage to get out of the car.

Evan's parents didn't know he had a son who was dying while he was sitting in their parlor with Molly, trying to convince them that he was grown up enough to get married. They didn't know it until Evan's sense of guilt drove him to their parlor in Ridgefield over two months after he had come to New Orleans.

"It was polio, Mom. Little Daniel didn't have a chance," he told them as tears welled in his eyes.

Martha's face looked like it was carved out of stone. Amos cried with his son.

"Is Molly with you in New Orleans?" he asked when he knew he could control his voice.

"No she's not, Dad," Evan said, after considering what to say about Molly. "In more than one way, I don't know where Molly is. I believe she has gone someplace in her mind and spirit where no one else can go to find her. And she has gone back to Ireland to find a place where she can start over, the place where she can relive the almost two years she spent with our son."

"Do you think she will come back to you, Evan?"

"I have to believe she will, Dad. When she said she loved me and no one else, I absolutely believed her. I know there will never be anyone I love the way I love her."

Martha got up from her seat on the sofa and looked at Evan and Amos as if she couldn't believe the talk of undying love she was hearing.

"I hope she never comes back," she said and walked out of the room.

As Evan was walking to his car to go back to New Orleans, his father walked with him.

"It seems that the two women in your life have gone someplace you can't go, Evan," he said. "Your mother left us long before Henry died. I think it's something more than the religious fundamentalism that seems to be choking the life out of her. But don't ever doubt that she loves you. She's just forgotten how to show it. Give yourself some time and then come back to see us. Be patient with your Molly, son. I believe she's worth waiting for."

It took almost two weeks of solid argument to get editorial approval for Evan's feature on Melvin Stuart and Mona Regan's marriage at Stuart House to run in the Item.

Evan put so much rhapsody into the telling of it, that it was a mild sensation in New Orleans, but a blowout success in Hamilton, Mississippi. Besides the two-hundred more copies Alma Madison ordered for the pharmacy, over eight hundred more copies were scrounged from New Orleans news-stand leftovers to fill all the orders that came in the day after the flowery feature, with a complete guest list, was published. Helen Stuart had been right. Copies of the feature would be preserved in many households to be passed down from generation to generation.

The next feature Evan had run in the *Item* was a not-too-exciting description of the short-excursion riverboats at the foot of Canal Street as an attraction for first-time New Orleans visitors. It was well written, but there was limited interest to local readers in the entertainment value of something that had been a fixture of New

Orleans's nightlife for decades.

The subject was of special interest to Evan, because the most popular and largest of the boats was *The President,* which had a very large dance floor on the first deck and a band with some of the best musicians in the city. When they played big-band dance music, two hundred couples would be on the dance floor.

Although there were few places on Bourbon Street with any place to dance, Evan began to draw the younger people, the ones who liked to dance the boogie, in off the street. This was the same group that was attracted to the dance floor on *The President.* It would take another six months for Evan to feel comfortable enough with his time commitment to the paper for him to go audition for a chair in the boat's orchestra. He was added to the band because the clarinetist they had decided he'd like to take his riffs with a tenor sax. Evan didn't abandon Bourbon Street entirely. There were after-hours sessions where musicians would go to embroider on the melody lines of some of the most popular music of the times.

Evan wrote his feature articles for the Item and played his clarinet until he was known to every music buff in New Orleans. And he waited for the phone call from Barry or Erin Sullivan. It rang in the afternoon of the last Sunday in July, a year after he had last spoken with one of Molly's parents.

On the twentieth of July, more than a year after Molly left Killarney to go to Dublin; Ella McCormick looked out a window at Harrrison House and saw Molly sitting on the bench in the heather field. She came to sit beside her and waited for Molly to speak.

"I've come back here because I don't know where else to go."

After giving thought to Molly's confession of heart-breaking loneliness, of having no place she could find any kind of sanctuary, she said:

"Of course you do, Molly. You will stay here with me. I'm all alone, except for the servants. I know Kevin and Rose Laurel would welcome you back in their house, but I need you more than they do. I lost my husband, my lover, over three years ago, and I believe we need each other to begin living again in a way that is more bearable than what we have now."

"It might be better if I stay here, Miss Ella. I've brought my clothes with me," Molly said and indicated the suitcase by the side of the bench. "I guess I have to tell the Laurels I'm back in Killarney. They have been very kind to me, but I really don't want anyone trying to help me solve my problems, whatever they are. I'll have to do it myself, no matter how long it takes."

"I'll call the Laurels and tell them you're here and will stay with me a while." Ella McCormick paused and then said, "Molly, I won't pester you with amateur solutions to your troubles. I think just staying at Harrison House will offer you a great deal of comfort. This cavernous old house has been my haven, my escape from the almost unbearable loneliness of the last three years."

Ella McCormick waited for a week before she drove into Killarney and talked to Rose Laurel.

"She's been with me for a few days, Rose," she said. "I've waited until I felt confident she wouldn't run away while I was gone. She's still a very troubled young woman. I know you will have to let her parents know that she is in a very safe place, but she's not ready to come home. I want you and Kevin to come to Harrison House in a few days to tell her that what she's doing is just fine with the two of you. Will you do that?"

"Of course we will, Ella. I don't believe there's any place I'd rather her be than with you. I'll call my uncle Barry and tell him his daughter is in good hands. Of course, it's up to him what he does about it, but I'll tell him what you said about Molly not being ready to come home."

Every afternoon Molly would sit on the bench in the heather field and look at the lake the locals called Lough Leanne. There were a few rowboats with fishermen on the lake, and along a lakeside path an occasional donkey-powered cart the local farmers used to bring vegetables to the outskirts of the city.

Every afternoon Ella McCormick would come sit with her and they would talk about their lives, being careful to avoid any part that was in any way painful. Ella would tell Molly about the glory days of her life at Harrison House. Her husband, Sean McCormick, was one of the richest men in Ireland, and she would describe the dancing in the great ballroom, with a full orchestra. Those guests who were too far from home to return after the dance, sometimes as many as fifty, would stay overnight in the enormous house and leave the next morning after a full breakfast.

Molly was interested in the clothes the ladies wore and the music the orchestra played. She learned that Ella MCormick was an accomplished pianist, but Ella didn't tell Mona she had shown promise as a voice student. She did tell her she liked to sing when she was young. Ella remembered what she had heard about Molly's heartbreaking performance at Laurel's Nightclub, and this was the opening she needed to ask her to come sing something for her while she played the grand piano in the ballroom.

Reluctant at first, Molly finally agreed to sing a few Irish songs she liked.

"Do you know *The Skye Boat Song*?" she asked.

"They wouldn't let me live in Ireland if I didn't know that song, Molly," Ella smiled as she answered and then began to play.

When the song was finished, Ella put her hands in her lap and turned to look at Molly as if there was something she wanted to say. She seemed to change her mind and asked, "Do you know *May It Be*?"

"Oh, that's a beautiful song. I just learned the lyrics a few months ago."

Ella McCormick had the accompanist's skill that was necessary to feature the singer's voice, and Molly's soprano filled the huge room as if she were on stage at the Dublin Opera House.

Over the next several weeks, Ella had her sing more challenging songs to determine the range of her voice without any apparent strain or slipping into a quivering falsetto that no real professional would accept. "Have you ever heard a record of Lily Pons singing *The Bell Song?*" Ella asked after she had given Molly every other challenge to test the range of her voice.

"No, I haven't. I haven't heard *anyone* sing that aria. I assume it's an aria. But I don't even know which opera."

"That's not really important, but it's from a rarely performed opera, *Lakme,* by a fairly obscure composer, Delibes. I don't remember his first name. Come with me, Molly. I want you to hear this."

On the other side of the ballroom, there was an up-to-date phonograph that played the new 33 rpm records. Ella selected a record of opera music and found the place to lower the needle to the Lily Pons aria.

To most listeners, *The Bell Song* was more of a vocal exercise than a song with any melody line whatever. Much of it is sung with no instrumental accompaniment, so that the quality of the voice can be judged as a single musical instrument itself. Lily Pons' voice was perfection. The range of her voice was beyond anything Molly had ever heard. She didn't listen in the same way to her own voice, because the recorded voice that vocalists hear is different from the voice they hear as they sing. "I want to play certain parts of this over several times, Molly," Ella said. "When you think you've heard any part enough to sing along with the record, I'd like you to try it."

Most of the afternoon Molly listened to the recording, with certain passages repeated until she thought she could sing along with the recorded voice of Lily Pons. She didn't understand the language of the opera's lyrics, but she thought it probably was Italian.

When Ella realized that Molly was tiring from her effort to overlay her own voice to match such a perfect voice, she turned off the phonograph and led Molly to a sitting room that overlooked the heather field and lake. She decided she had to invade a part of Molly's life she had declined to talk about.

"Molly, I know you went to University in the United States, and I know you studied voice as your music major. Rose Laurel told me you had a wonderful voice and I want to tell you what I think about it. *The Bell Song* wasn't a fair test, but I am amazed by what you did with the exercise to duplicate certain passages." Ella stopped and turned in her chair to take both of Molly's hands in hers.

"You have a five octave voice without strain in the top octave. I've heard your contralto in some of the Irish songs. From bottom to top, you have a rare quality of tone. I feel certain some of your music school faculty have told you most of this, but you've just begun the training of what may be one of the greatest soprano voices of your generation. I think you're two years away from an operatic debut, which I predict will be *La Boheme*. You've got a Puccini voice and you'll sing lyric opera." Ella sat back in her chair and smiled at Molly. "Have I overwhelmed you? I didn't intend to, but you are an exciting find for an old-lady Irish piano player."

"You're not an old lady, Miss Ella. Fifty-three isn't that old. My Dad's almost fifty, and he certainly isn't old."

"You don't want to talk about more vocal training, do you, Molly?"

Molly put her hands in her lap and tightened them into fists. She seemed to be ready to shut down the openness she had while she was singing. Her eyes began to tear, and she looked away from Ella McCormick.

"I don't know whether I will ever sing more than I just did with you. I'm not ready now for that kind of training, and I don't know that I ever will be. I have to find the strength to find my way back to a place I can't even define now."

"Maybe we'll be able to find it together, Molly. And maybe I'll find my place along the way. Living alone, even if it's just in our minds, can't be the solution for either of us."

One afternoon in early September, Molly was sitting on the heather field bench when Evan Sherman came to sit beside her. At first, she thought it was Ella McCormick, her usual afternoon bench partner, and didn't turn to look.

"Hello, Molly," Evan said and leaned forward so she could see his face.

For the first dozen seconds, Molly just stared in disbelief. She then put her hand on Evan's cheek, as if to check the reality of what she was seeing.

"I love you, Molly," Evan said, and taking both her hands, pulled her forward. He kissed her until she yielded to her own instinctive passion and her lips opened.

Without a word, Molly stood and pulled Evan up from the bench. She took his hand and they walked into the heather field down the slope toward the lake. A quarter mile from the lake, Molly pulled Evan down to lie by her. They were almost completely obscured by the heather around them.

"I'm safe here, Evan," Molly said, not turning to look at him.

"Safe from what, Molly? What's threatening you?"

Molly didn't answer the questions. She just rolled onto her side and pulled Evan close to her.

"Hold me, Evan, just for a while."

For three days Evan and Molly would walk the halls of the Harrison House and marvel at the size of it. There were forty-two rooms, including a half dozen for servants. And every afternoon they would wander the fields around the grand house, sometimes lying in the heather and sometimes sitting on the bank of the lake, watching the few boats with languid and unenthusiastic fishermen.

At night, they slept together, an arrangement silently accepted by Ella McCormick. She would have been surprised if they hadn't. She was the one who had brought Evan to sit with Molly in the heather field. But as closely as they held each other the whole night through, there was no consummated sex. There seemed to be a mutual agreement that they were not ready for it, not yet.

When Ella McCormick had a chance to talk with Evan alone, she told him she knew of the tragedy of his and Molly's losing a child. She told him all she knew of what Molly had been doing for the past year, admitting that neither she nor the Laurels really knew what Molly had done in Dublin.

Evan was impressed with Ella's knowledge of music when she told him about the evaluations she had made of Molly's voice.

"Evan, I know enough about the human voice to tell you Molly has an extremely rare gift. A five-octave range, with no drifting into falsetto in any octave, will qualify her for training in any music school on the planet. I learned from her aunt Kate in Cork that she had been invited to audition for Julliard."

"Was it her Aunt Kate who called Barry Sullivan to tell him Molly was staying with you?"

"The Laurels called him first, later Kate and I talked to him when she came to Killarney to stay a day of so with the Laurels. I just told him Molly was safe and content staying with me."

"When did you find out I was coming to Killarney, rather than one of them?"

"Barry called to tell us to expect you. He thought Molly would be more receptive to the idea of coming home with you."

"What do you think, Ella? Is Molly ready to go back home?"

They were sitting in the morning room that faced the lake and Ella McCormick sat back in her chair and looked out the window, mentally composing what she would say to Evan.

"I don't believe Molly will be ready to go back home until she has exorcised the demon of guilt she has inside her. You can't do it, and her parents can't do it, and surely I can't either. After all the time I've spent with her, I have become absolutely convinced that the cure for her melancholy will be the music that's in her. And she can't just sing; she has to be successful; she has to perform. She has to know it's more than just the wishful dream of a talented but limited young woman. I don't think that Julliard would accept her as she is, and the rejection would be devastating."

"It's apparent you have given this a lot of thought, but you don't seem to offer any solution, any hope that I can expect Molly to come back to me."

"Evan, I don't have the gift of prophesy, but I sincerely believe that Molly will come back to whatever will be the rest of her life without the terrible pain she has had for so long. She hasn't said it in just those words, but I know she is deeply in love with you."

"Do you think it would be harmful for me to ask her to come back with me, if I stay a while longer?"

"No, because she won't go with you. It will probably pain her to tell you that. I don't want her to get the impressions that you have become so impatient with her that she has to make a decision she isn't ready to make."

"Where do we go from here, Ella? Is Molly going to stay here until something inside her just changes, and she's ready to come home?"

"I want to take Molly to Trinity College in Dublin, Evan. The College has an excellent Music School. There are still faculty people there who were there when I was taking piano. I know them, and I know there won't be any problem getting Molly into their voice program. And there are counselors there who can help her more than amateurs like her parents and you and I. She can live very close to the college in an area called the Temple Bar where she stayed before. It's safe and inexpensive. I will pay for her living expenses."

"I don't think—" Evan began, but Ella held up her hand to stop him.

"I'm a rich old Irish lady, Evan. I plan to go to Dublin from time to time, and I'll stay with Molly. So the flat she rents will be big enough for the two of us. It will also serve as a place I can go to get away from this big house that will be empty without her."

"Do you want me to leave?" Evan asked, a tone of defeat in his voice.

"No, Evan. I want you to stay until you know it's time to leave. If Molly says she will go back with you, and you believe she's ready to go back, I'll accept that. The decision will have to be yours and hers, not mine."

A week later, Evan left without Molly. The following week Ella McCormick took Molly to Dublin and enrolled her in the voice program of the Trinity College Music School.

Chapter Eighteen

The first phone call Evan made when he got back from Ireland was to Barry Sullivan. He explained, as best he could, why Molly didn't come back with him and why he thought it would be quite a while before she did come back.

"What do you think about this Ella McCormick, Evan? It seems to me she has a great deal of influence in Molly's life now. She's not some kind of crank is she?"

"Mr. Sullivan, I stayed for almost two weeks in Harrison House, a forty-two-room mansion that Ella McCormick owns. She is an enormously wealthy woman in her fifties. She is an accomplished pianist, and I believe she knows more about Molly's talent than anyone, even her teachers at Milcrest. I also believe she knows more than any of us about the mental and emotional demons that are haunting Molly. She is an intelligent and elegant woman and I can't think of a safer place for Molly to be."

"I know Molly told you she wasn't ready to come home, but do you have any idea what she will do, other than just stay where she is?"

"I believe Ella McCormick will take her to Dublin and enroll her in the Trinity College Music School. That goes along with her belief that Molly's music may be the road to her return to her normal life. She told me she would write both of us about Molly's progress. I can't think of anything more to tell you."

What Evan told Barry Sullivan was essentially the same thing he told Melvin Stuart. Mel's comments boiled down to "She'll come back" and "No shit! Forty-two rooms."

The *Item* editor, Hollis Edmonds, was a sentimental man and forgave Evan for overstaying the vacation he had earned by over a week when he learned the trip had to do with an affair of the heart.

The *Item*, like many other newspapers that leaned toward more entertainment to go along with the straight news, published serialized short fiction in much the same way as consumer magazines like *Colliers* and *Saturday Evening Post*.

Six months after Evan came back from Ireland, he proposed a story about a man tormented by a lost love.

"Show me the first thousand words," Hollis Edmonds said.

What Evan showed him was a thousand words of misery, the heartbreak felt by a twenty-eight year-old assistant professor at a southern college located in a large city. When his ladylove, who had sworn eternal devotion, drifted away from him—in less than a month of peculiar behavior--until she disappeared altogether, he began his search for her.

While Evan was in college, he bought a copy of "A Little Treasury of Modern Poetry" and he began to find short poems to give more flavor to the prose he was writing for his short story. When he wrote about the parting of the two lovers, he used a Lord Byron poem to start the reader toward having bright eyes:

> *When we two parted*
> *In silence and tears,*
> *Half broken-hearted*
> *To sever the years,*
> *Pale grew thy cheek and cold,*
> *Colder thy kiss.*
> *Truly that hour foretold*
> *Sorrow to this.*

Later in the story, when the young man's search had not

been successful, he continued Byron's lament:

...If I chance to meet thee
After long years.
I shall greet thee
In silence and tears.

Hollis Edmonds loved the story's beginning. He knew the New Orleans readers would speculate that there was some broken-hearted young college professor at Tulane or Loyola, maybe Sophie Newcomb, who was searching vainly for the woman who abandoned him. The editor almost choked with emotion when he read the two lines of Emily Dickinson:

Parting is all we know of heaven,
And all we need of hell.

Evan's story ran weekly in the Friday edition, because the editor wanted his readers to have extra time on Saturday to read each section of the story. Some sections would run as long as twelve-hundred words and he knew that when some of his subscribers read, their lips moved.

Evan's searcher would think he saw his fugitive lady riding on a city bus and would run along side of it until it stopped. He was always bitterly disappointed when his search proved to be futile. He would be convinced he saw her in a crowd of pedestrians on a busy shopping street in the city, but she was never in the crowd when he got there. Nor was she the owner of the voice he thought was hers in some smaller social group, where others would look at him strangely when he intruded. He used a poem by an unknown poet to illustrate this section of his story:

*If you but knew
How all my days seemed filled with dreams of you.
How sometimes in the silent night
Your eyes thrill through me with their tender light,
How oft I hear your voice when others speak,
How you 'mid other forms I seek—
Oh, love more real than though such dreams were true
If you but knew*

The beginning of the story's last section reflected a sense of total loss with an introducing poem by Francis Bourdillon:

*The night has a thousand eyes,
The day but one;*

*Yet the light of the bright world dies
With the dying sun.*

*The mind has a thousand eyes,
And the heart but one;
Yet the light of a whole life dies
When its love is done.*

The story ended with a ray of hope that the itinerant lady would somehow reappear in the life of her grieving lover. The reader reaction to the story's end was a mass appeal for a sequel in a barrage of phone calls and letters to the editor. Because of the story's popularity, circulation had a marked increase, principally from newsstand sales. The newspaper executives—who read the story segments with as much anticipation as their customers—were so pleased with the sales increase that they made Evan responsible for regularly scheduled stories, published in five or six segments. They also gave Evan a small private office, a substantial raise, and included his name on the newspaper's masthead.

"The lost ladylove was yours, wasn't she, Evan?" Hollis Edmonds asked after the series ended.

Evan didn't respond immediately. He looked at his boss to determine whether his interest was more than just curiosity about the unnamed and lost lady. The editor sensed Evan's reluctance to get involved with a subject that was as painful to him as it was for the searcher in his story, so he said:

"I loved your story, Evan, and I don't think you could have written it that way without being personally involved in a similar affair of the heart. I have sensed some sort of melancholy that has affected you for the year I've known you. You probably don't know it, but I've come a number of times to hear you play. I sense a sort of lost-love wail in your playing."

"Jesus! I didn't know it was obvious."

"I believe that is part of what makes your playing so beguiling. People like to be part of the tragic suffering the music reflects."

"You amaze me, Hollis. I didn't expect this from a hard-boiled newspaper man."

"Is your lady coming back, Evan?"

The question was so blunt, Evan didn't know whether he wanted to answer it. After an uncomfortable wait, Edmonds said:

"It's probably not fair for me to ask you that. I only want to know if I'm going to lose you completely the next time you go on a search for someone who is never coming back."

"Hollis, I admit the story was my own lament. I've seen Molly—that's her name—on the St. Charles streetcar when she wasn't there, and I've seen her standing under the clock at Holmes where people meet when they're downtown. And I've seen her in the crowd in front of Maison Blanch on a day when there was a big sale. It's always been some sort of unreasonable hope that deludes me. I don't do that any more. Do I think Molly will come back? I'm certain she will eventually come back. I just don't know whether she will ever come back to me."

"Evan, old friend, get yourself some female companionship. You don't have to marry anybody, but you need someone to hold you while you cry. She doesn't have to know exactly why you're crying."

When Evan talked to Melvin, he got some surprisingly similar advice.

"I've saved all the parts of your newspaper story," Mel said, "and I know it's a statement of your agony that's three or four years old by now. I'm not sure there seems to be a promise of relief in the future. I'm tempted to send the package to Molly to see if she can be jolted into realizing what she's done to you."

Evan began to say something, but Mel stopped him.

"I'm not going to send it to her, Evan. If anyone sends her that particular package, it should be you."

Evan waited on the phone, because he knew Mel wasn't finished with what he had to say.

"As far as I know, with the exception of one encounter with unforgettable results, you have remained a physical virgin. I say physical because I don't have any idea what runs through the virginal mind. But I don't believe man was intended to remain celibate the way you have. Get yourself somebody, Evan. It's been over three years, closer to four, that you have waited. Molly has made you wait for her too long."

Through no effort on his part, Evan did get someone to hold him when he cried. Over the months since his return from Ireland, he had noticed a group of younger people who seemed to frequently hang around the band while he was playing. They were dancers and were more dependable when he played on the boat. One girl in particular, a year or so older than the rest and the best dancer in the group, would dance as close to the bandstand as she could. When Evan would stand to take an especially long riff, she would stop dancing completely and hold her partner's hand while she stood and listened.

One night, when the band took a fifteen minute break after the first set, she came to talk to Evan before he left to go outside and stand on the deck where it was cooler.

"Are you the Evan Sherman who writes for the *Item*?" she asked.

For a moment Evan hesitated. The girl was very pretty, almost beautiful, and her honey blond hair fell a little past her shoulders. She had wonderful legs and wore three-inch-heel springalator pumps that made her almost as tall as Molly.

"Yes, I'm *that* Evan Sherman," he said and smiled. "Are you mad at me because you don't think I finished the story?"

"Oh, no," the girl protested. "I loved your story. It seemed that whoever was writing it was actually the miserable protagonist. I'm amazed at the way you, the writer, seemed to reflect the sense of loss that haunted this fictional character," she hesitated before she added, "if it was a fictional character."

Before she could ask the question Evan knew was on the tip of her mind, he said in his best conspiratorial voice:

"Don't tell anybody, but there will be a sequel. You'll have to wait to see how it all comes out."

That was the beginning of it. The next time he played on the boat, he learned that her name was Emily Harris and she was a twenty-seven-year-old doctoral student in Tulane's English graduate school.

A month later, she asked if he would come and talk to her graduate class about derivative fiction that comes from an actual event. That's when Evan became convinced that she had known all along that he was the tortured searcher in his story, although she never asked the question.

Without a graduate degree and only an accidental degree in journalism, Evan was reluctant to face a class of doctoral students.

"Some of the great writers had no degree at all," Emily argued.

"I don't know whether William Faulkner ever got a degree at Ole Miss. That doesn't seem to reflect in his acceptance as one of the great writers of his generation, maybe of this century."

Evan talked to the class of fourteen, and every one of them clung to every word he said. They were listening to a pro who, at twenty-six, had become a more-than-local success in the newspaper business. And that was important; he had become successful because he could write narrative prose that showed the music in the English language.

A week after Evan's talk to the graduate class, Emily Harris knocked on the door of Evan's apartment on St. Ann Street. It was six o'clock on a Wednesday evening, and Evan was boiling a pot of spaghetti to go with some canned Italian sauce.

"Did you come for dinner?" he asked before she said anything.

"Sure, what do you have?"

"Spaghetti?"

"Any red wine?"

"Yeah, dago."

"Perfect."

For several months, Emily Harris would come to St. Ann Street twice a week. She and Evan would cook dinner in the apartment or go to an inexpensive restaurant in the French Quarter. They never talked about the lost love in Evan's story.

The reports Ella McCormick had promised to send to Evan and the Sullivans came regularly at intervals of a month to six weeks. The reports were brief and contained only very dry, factual information. She would report on Molly's acceptance and registration in the Trinity School of Music and the beginning of a counseling program. As the reports continued, there was little to indicate any progress in understanding whatever repression still kept Molly in an emotional and mental limbo.

Six weeks after Evan's fiction series ended, the sequel began.

This time Evan decided not to use poetry again to add lyric to his prose, but selected a single line from Thomas Wolfe's novel *Look Homeward Angel*. This line—*O lost, and by the wind grieved, ghost, come back again*—repeated again and again throughout the novel, had puzzled Evan ever since he first read it. He didn't know who or what was lost. He didn't know whether the ghost was a young boy's youth, which was forever gone, or the elusive love of one of the young women that tormented him. Or it could be the vision lost by the boy's father, who made stone angel monuments, whose blind eyes looked on as the family disintegrated.

In Evan's sequel, it was the ghost of the love that had been lost and the ghost of the girl who had vanished and left only a tormented searcher. The readers stopped holding their breath when she was found in the last segment of the sequel. This last segment ran the week before Christmas, and was almost considered a Christmas gift to the readers. The *Item* management felt much the same way, because of the additional surge in circulation the story caused.

Three days before Christmas, Emily Harris moved to St. Ann Street. She brought only a suitcase and a box full of miscellaneous stuff she needed to keep up with her class work at Tulane. Evan and Emily slept in the same bed for three months, with no more than naked body fondling, until Emily finally said:

"Evan, I know the solution you had in your story isn't the one you need for your lost ghost. Will you search on forever, or will you ever think you can love me enough to make love to me?"

"I love you enough now, Emily. I know you think I've played the lovesick fool ever since you've known me. That's over now. You're the best thing that has happened to me in years. I want to make love to you, and now I think I know how."

But he was wrong. That night, after the first rush of passion had Evan inside Emily and she began her pumping response, he became impotent. As she turned on her side to look questioningly at her failed lover, he said:

"Why doesn't your hair smell like heather?"

Emily moved out of the St. Ann apartment the last Friday in February.

As she was leaving she asked:

"Do you think you will ever find her, Evan?"

"No, not really," he said. He didn't tell her he knew where his lost love was. He just meant he didn't believe she would ever come back to him.

Evan kept on playing his clarinet in the French Quarter and on the boat, and Emily kept coming to hear him and to dance, but there wouldn't be any more Emily Harris' sharing his bed in the apartment of St. Ann Street.

Chapter Nineteen

Ella McCormick stayed in Dublin with Molly for three weeks before she went back to Harrison House. She refurnished the flat they rented in Temple Bar to suit a taste much more extravagant than Molly's and to ensure a comfort level that would make her long visits to Dublin more pleasurable.

The Monday after they arrived, she took Molly to Trinity College for an interview with the people she knew at the School of Music and an afternoon audition with the faculty who specialized in Voice. When Molly had been through a rigorous hour and a half of testing, the head of the Voice group called in the department chairman and other faculty members for them to hear Molly sing as much of *Mi Chiamano Mimi* from *La Boheme* as she remembered. She remembered all the music, but she couldn't remember all the Italian lyrics. She also sang some of the more demanding passages of *The Bell Song.*

When she finished what the voice instructor asked her to sing, the department chairman, an internationally known violinist, sat a full minute without any comment. Then he asked:

"Have you tested Miss Sullivan in the contralto range?"

"Yes, we have. We've tested her by comparison with Gladys Swarthout's performance of *Carmen.* Miss Swarthout is a mezzo-soprano, but parts of some of her arias in the opera are in the contralto range. It may be presumptuous to say, but I believe Miss Sullivan's lower range is actually fuller and more controlled than the voice of opera's current reigning Carmen."

"Have you discussed with Miss Sullivan the full range of her voice?"

"Yes. She knows she has full control all the way through coloratura."

"Where do you plan to start her?"

"She had three years of training in a college voice department in the United States. We believe she's advanced enough to start training in concert and operatic performance, including language for opera."

"Miss Sullivan, we're delighted to accept you as a voice student at Trinity," the department head said. "We'll expect you here daily for the first several weeks. Then your voice faculty will schedule you on a permanent basis less frequently. Are you prepared to accept the constraints required of you to become a professional performer?"

Molly looked at Ella McCormick to indicate how she should respond. Ella nodded her head and Molly said, "Yes, Sir."

The next day Ella took Molly to the psychology group of the Arts and Science College to arrange a counseling schedule. Her objective was to find faculty with enough musical background to consider the effect the progress in Molly's voice training would have on their methods of mental and emotional therapy.

When they left Trinity College, Molly had a schedule that would keep her on the campus parts of every day in the Monday-Friday week. Her weekends would be free for whatever she could find to occupy her time. She waited until Ella McCormick went back to Killarney to venture out on Grafton Street and rejoin the street entertainers. They were happy their Molly Malone had come back. She drew crowds of local people and tourists who had heard her before or who had been told about the beautiful girl with the glorious voice. They would stay and be entertained by the jugglers, musicians of all sorts, mimes, and step-dancers. For some reason, their tips, dropped into the open violin cases or hats on the sidewalk, were more generous after they heard Molly sing. Maybe it was because Molly didn't accept tips.

And Molly sang in the pubs. She became such a draw that the pubs began to compete to try to get her to come more often. The question was asked all over Temple Bar: "Will Molly Malone be singing here tonight?"

Grafton Street ended very close to the main entrance of Trinity College. Many students and a number of faculty members would venture onto the street to see and listen to the entertainers after school hours. Several faculty members of the Music School stood unobtrusively in the back of a crowd listening to Molly sing *The Rose of Tralee.* She was accompanied by a violinist, who was a third year student of the Music School.

The faculty people, who were not part of the voice staff, had heard of the girl with ebony black hair and gray eyes who had an almost incomparable soprano voice. They had also heard that she had some sort of emotional problem that was serious enough for her to be in a very rigid counseling program.

"We are well aware of Miss Sullivan's activity on Grafton Street," the chairman said when the faculty members reported what they had seen and heard. "We know she also sings in Temple-Bar pubs in the evenings. Our friends who are counseling Miss Sullivan asked us to encourage it. They are convinced that what she is doing is helping her return to a reality she has denied for a very long time. This young woman will ultimately become a classical-music per-former. What she's doing now doesn't hurt her voice and it gives her the confidence she will eventually need to stand on a concert stage all alone except for a piano accompanist."

By the time Evan had said his sad goodbye to Emily Harris, Molly was only two months away from her first concert in the Trinity auditorium.

Of course, Evan did see Emily Harris many times again as she danced her way to the bandstand. She still would stand and just listen to Evan play when it was his turn to show off. Many times he would look at her and wonder what he had meant when he said he loved her and was unable to prove it. He knew he had come as close to loving someone other than Molly as he would ever come.

The reports from Ella McCormick became more interesting as Molly progressed through her voice training and her counseling sessions. The reports were still dry and factual, but they indicated that Molly seemed to be responding, slowly but surely, to the musical and psychological therapy. However, there was always the admonition that expectation of a quick cure of Molly's maladies would lead only to disappointment. It would take more time, and the time was unpredictable.

Evan was enjoying the success of the short fiction he had written for the newspaper. The carryover effect was an invitation to address a book club in the classy *uptown* area of New Orleans that includes the mansions along St. Charles Avenue and Tulane and Loyola Universities. Evan didn't pretend to be a gifted writer, but described himself as a journalist with a critical eye for well-written longer fiction.

The members of this and other book clubs in the fancier districts of uptown New Orleans were also well aware of Evan's musical popularity. Most of them had walked Bourbon Street to hear him play and danced on the boat along with Emily Harris. He was asked by one club to bring his clarinet with him to illustrate the marriage he had made of Jazz and big-band music.

Evan had subdued his Molly misery to the extent that he rarely called Barry and Erin Sullivan to speculate about any predictable time Molly might come home. He found several local writers who had had short fiction published in respectable magazines and contracted with them to write the fiction features in the *Item*.

Evan was not becoming a social butterfly, but he did accept a number of dinner invitations from the uptown younger set of married socialites. There was always an unattached female about his age who was acceptably, if marginally, attractive. On several occasions, he invited his dinner companion to dinner at a French Quarter restaurant. As a conversational gambit he told them he had bought an old upright piano for his apartment. Each of his ladies was unaware that he played piano and could hardly wait to be taken to St. Ann Street to hear him play and start unbuttoning her blouse. This resulted in some prolonged clinches--and almost passionate kisses on Evan's part--but the end result was always the same. Almost.

The voice faculty was very sensitive to the type music Molly would like to sing in her first concert at the Trinity auditorium. They knew she would resist anything that smacked of the religious oratorios that had practically no melody line. She did want to include some of the religious standards, such as *Ave Maria* and *Oh Holy Night,* and the faculty was pleased. They also approved Molly's selection of the lyrical arias of Puccini's and Verdi's operas. Molly insisted on *Vilia* and *Kiss Me Again.* The program was longer than the faculty had planned, but Molly wouldn't cut any of the songs she had worked so long to master. She was especially adamant about the arias where she had worked so hard to learn the Italian language lyrics.

When the concert was announced, it was made clear that there were a limited number of seats available to the general public. And when the general public local to Trinity, Temple Bar, and Grafton Street learned that their own Molly Malone was the Molly Sullivan who would sing, the available tickets were claimed on the first day they were available.

When Molly came on stage in a black evening dress to stand by her accompanist, the auditorium was jammed to the doors with Trinity students and faculty, Dublin's musical community of prominent performers and critics, dignitaries of some sort or another, and the Molly Malone people.

If it were possible for an audience to be more enthusiastically responsive than the audience at Molly's Miracle at Milcrest, this audience was. Next to the last of the songs in her repertoire was the aria *Caro Nome*, from Verdi's opera, "Rigoletto." The aria's name translates to "Dearest Name" from the Italian, and as she sang, her eyes became bright with unshed tears. Everyone in the auditorium stood and, with the shouts of *brava* on almost every tongue, applauded so long Molly's accompanist stood and left the stage. As Molly turned to follow him, the applause abruptly stopped and the pianist returned.

The last song on the program was *Kiss Me Again* and now the tears wet her cheeks. When Molly sang the incredibly tender *Caro Nome*, she was singing for Daniel. As she sang this last song, she was singing for Evan and a night in the Seminary Woods. She cried for what she had lost.

Molly Sullivan was again a phenomenon on a college campus. And on this one night, she was introduced to the musical influences in Dublin. The chairman of the Trinity Music School told Molly she had taken a very important step in the development of a classi-cal-music performer, but under no circumstances was she to accept any overtures to perform professionally until she had completed the Trinity musical program that had been designed for her. The street and pub performance was acceptable as long as it was basically recreational, a release from the more rigorous requirements of her voice development program.

For Molly's concert, Ella McCormick sat with some of the fac-ulty people she knew and learned for the first time about Molly's almost unlimited vocal talent.

"The most perfect musical instrument is the human voice," Molly's principal voice instructor opined as they were leaving the concert hall. "I'm certain others disagree with me, but I think the popularity of someone with an enormous vocal talent lends credi-

bility to my opinion. And I've never heard anyone with the talent Molly Sullivan has. She was born to sing opera."

Ella didn't know how to report Molly's concert to her parents and Evan. She believed that there was some sort of recovery milestone Molly had passed with this concert. Besides the tearful evidence, she instinctively felt that, when she sang her last two songs, Molly was singing to somehow salvage a life that had become lost in some way she didn't understand. If Ella had known Evan better, she would understand his puzzlement with:

O lost, and by the wind grieved, ghost, come back again.

So she really didn't know what to say about her opinion, and the somewhat supporting opinion of Molly's councilors, that an unexpected barrier to her recovery had been breached. She didn't want to suggest an accelerated return to any kind of normalcy that could not even be defined. So her report acknowledged that Molly's concert was a success, but it didn't come close to describing the euphoria that gripped the music lovers and the Temple Bar people who came close to worshiping their Molly Malone.

Ella McCormick wouldn't admit, even to herself, that she didn't want Molly to ever leave Dublin and Harrison House. She began to think of her as the daughter she didn't have. The thought of inevitably losing this young woman she had come to love encouraged Ella to extend her stays in Dublin. She spent more time there than at home in Killarney.

And she would spend more and more time with Molly on Grafton Street and in the pubs where she sang. She became more and more aware that, though none was anywhere near comparable to Molly, there were very talented entertainers capable of forming the cast of a musical review that would entertain even a musically fastidious audience. As an accomplished pianist, familiar with the music community in Dublin, she was also accepted as a sponsor by the small theater groups who presented musical reviews in small theaters throughout the city.

Two months after Molly's concert, Ella presented, under the name of *The McCormick Players,* a review of music and dancing that was so well received that most of the Grafton Street entertainers lined up for auditions, hopeful of joining the company.

Ella had found the answer to the loneliness of a middle-aged widow. She would become known as *The Angel of Grafton Street.* She had found her calling, producing musicals, and she always included herself in the show so that she could play the piano again.

Eighteen months after she had begun, Molly completed her course at Trinity College. She had learned the complete Italian librettos and musical scores of two Puccini operas—*La Boheme* and *Tosca*—and her graduation recital, which would include excerpts from both operas, was scheduled a week after her voice instruction ended. She would have her recital at the National Concert Hall three blocks south of the Trinity College campus.

The concert made the newspapers in every city in Ireland— papers that had at least enough circulation to have a daily issue— and in several London papers. Without exception, the reviews concentrated on the phenomenal voice of this unknown American. And it would be a rare review that didn't mention the departure from accepted classical music to the sentimental closing of the recital with *Kiss Me Again*, and the tears streaming down the vocal artist's face.

Unknown to Molly, Ella McCormick had invited Kate and Larry Flannery and Rose and Kevin Laurel to the recital. She paid their transportation costs and arranged for them to stay in the same building where she and Molly shared the flat in Temple Bar. After the concert, Molly was delayed for almost an hour by the seemingly unending applause, her reluctant and brief interviews by the critics and the newspaper people, and by the fans who waited to at least touch the hand of the beautiful lady with whom they all—men and women alike—had fallen in love.

For celebration, Ella took them all back to the Temple Bar flat

with a surprisingly large living room that she had beautifully redec-
orated. Everyone but Molly raised a flute of Mumms champagne in
tribute to the new musical icon—Molly Sullivan.

Molly was uncomfortable. These people who were related to
her in different ways—the Flannery's and Laurel's by family ties
and Ella McCormick by measureless kindness—seemed to be
demanding her to accept and behave like the iconic figure they had
created in their minds.

After a half hour of drinking champagne, eating the finger-food
Ella had prepared, and repetitive comments about the concert,
Molly made a suggestion:

"I think all of you should see the part of Dublin where I live."

She took them to Grafton Street where the late-night people
were still coming to see the street entertainers. Ella had become
almost as well recognized as Molly because of *The McCormick
Players,* and she mixed well with the late-night crowd. The
Flannery's were more surprised than the Laurels with the idea that
there was a Dublin street with only pedestrian traffic and given over
to street entertainers and the very successful shops that lined either
side of the street. The Laurels were in the entertainment business
and had been there before.

Molly wasn't mobbed, as she would have been after the first
concert at Trinity. Very few of the street entertainers had seen the
just completed concert—the tickets were too expensive—but they
had heard about it. They were all very proud of their Molly Malone.

"Molly and I have a favorite pub I'd like to take you to," Ella
said as they drifted away from Grafton Street and were walking the
streets of Temple Bar.

Many of the regulars at O'Donahue's Pub could afford the tickets to Molly's concert and were sitting in the pub to finish a wonderful evening. When she walked in, the band started to play and
the customers started to sing Molly Malone's song. Molly Sullivan
sang along with them. When the last line of the song was sung:

...cockles and mussels, alive, alive oh

the crowd rose and applauded Molly. Some of the concert-goers also distinctly, but not loudly, said *brava*.

Molly sang Irish songs for almost an hour, while the people in the pub fell in love with her all over again.

For the first time since Ella McCormick, or the Flannerys and Laurels, had known Molly, she seemed untroubled. It wasn't exactly a look of happiness or elation; they saw a beautiful cameo face that didn't register some indefinable fear, some guilt that seemed to cloud her eyes.

The report Ella sent to Evan and the Sullivans didn't suggest that Molly was fully recovered from her three-year emotional and mental malaise, but there was such a contrast with the former more, somber accounts, that it had a more positive and encouraging tone. Ella didn't know whether she would have the courage to send Molly home. She didn't want her to ever leave.

On the fifteenth of January, Molly was called by the chairman of the Music School at Trinity to come for an audition for Opera Ireland, the national opera company that performed principally in Dublin.

"Miss Sullivan," the Opera Director said, "we are to perform *La Boheme* in Dublin on the thirteenth of February. Our *Mimi*, Licia Albanese, will be unable to perform and her understudy and the soprano who plays *Musetta* aren't strong enough for the lyrics of the *Mimi* arias. I understand that you know this opera in its entirety. Are you willing to sing selections at random for me to get some idea how prepared you are to perform the Italian libretto and the score of the complete opera?"

The Opera Director had never seen anyone play Mimi's death scene at the end of the opera the way Molly played it. Neither had anyone else in the audience when the opera was performed at the Dublin Opera House. The opera was performed four times, on Friday and Saturday evenings the thirteenth and fourteenth of February and on the next weekend.

Descriptions of the magic of the Molly Sullivan voice and her dramatic performance amounted to something of a competition in Dublin music circles. The result was that, when the opera was performed the second weekend, there were no tickets available to the hundreds who went to the ticket office on the night of the Friday performance.

Molly had sung *La Boheme*. She had become more than she had ever thought possible. She had been lionized by everyone who had heard her sing. She had become the pride of Dublin and was dearly loved by the street people who called her Molly Malone.

But there seemed to be something she wouldn't let herself define that was lacking in her life. She wouldn't let herself believe Evan would ever forgive her or that she would ever bring herself to face a new life at the old place she had deserted. So she told Ella McCormick she wanted to go back to Killarney and Harrison House. She wanted to go back and sit on the bench in the heather field.

Chapter Twenty

Evan and Molly's parents knew nothing about her performance in the opera until they got Ella McCormick's report at the end of February. The three of them really knew very little about Molly's progress in the Trinity Music School and were amazed that she had mastered the complete opera. There was an unconfessed resentment by the three of them that they had not been witnesses to the most remarkable success in Molly's life.

Evan and the Sullivans talked on the phone for almost a half hour when they received Ella McCormick's report.

"I think the whole thing sounds pretty positive," Erin Sullivan said. "The way she acted after her concert, taking Rose and Kate and their two guys down to the pub where she feels comfortable and then singing the Irish songs, sounds like she's not avoiding everybody while she tries to work out her problems."

"I don't really know what Molly did before, Erin," Evan said. "Did she really avoid people, or maybe just go into some protective place where no one could reach her. She seemed to be fairly open when I was with her at Harrison House, but there were times when I knew she wasn't really with me. She would sit on the bench with me and pull me around to face her. She would hold both my hands when she said 'I love you, Evan.' But I've wondered if that was just a memory of how we were together before her heart was broken."

"I don't doubt that Molly still loves you, and she still loves Erin and me," Barry Sullivan said. "What I believe Ella McCormick is trying to tell us is the same thing she said before. Her music will be her salvation. The successes of her two concerts and her sensational performance with the opera were the things Ella believes have brought Molly into an absolutely new life where there isn't room for whatever guilt she can't even define that has been an emotional shroud for so long."

They all agreed that the report was positive enough to encourage them to think in terms of Molly's not-too-distant-future return home. But none of them could even speculate on what effect her musical success would have on what she would do in the near future. Would she go to France to sing in the Paris Opera House? Or would she go to Milan and sing in La Scala? Or best of all, would she come back across the ocean to New York and sing at Carnegie Hall?

According to Ella McCormick, she didn't want to go anywhere and sing; she just wanted to go back to Killarney and Harrison House. She wanted to sit on the bench in the heather field. This troubled Evan. She wanted to go back to where she had been, to retrogress into the never-never land where he had sat with her a year and a half before. Evan just wanted her to come back and sing in the moonlit woods while he played *Kiss Me Again.*

No one in the band that played on the excursion boat had any idea that Evan knew how to play the piano, until he volunteered when the keyboard guy got sick. Just before they were set to go on, he left the bandstand and didn't return. The band leader went to look for him and, after ten minutes, came back.

"We'll have to get along without Adrian. He's throwing up everything but his liver."

"If Quincy wants to come back to clarinet, I'll sit in for Adrian." Evan offered.

The band leader hesitated, then said somewhat doubtfully, "I didn't know you could play keyboard, Evan. Quincy will stay with the sax, but you take your stick to the piano so you can change over when it gets to something you can't handle."

Evan played piano all during the evening, and many of the dancers, including Emily Harris, danced up close enough to be sure that their clarinet guy hadn't left the band.

This became an attractive novelty and Evan became more visible and popular as an entertainer. He would play the piano once or twice during the evening while Adrian sat out. Because Evan played almost exclusively by ear, he was better at improvisation than Adrian, and he could combine the keyboard with his clarinet when the music had a strong clarinet lead.

March 17, St. Patrick's Day, was on a Saturday and the boat was jammed with temporary Irishmen from every ethnic group on the planet. The first Irish song every band in the land plays is *When Irish Eyes Are Smiling,* because everyone in the audience believes he, or she, sings it better than anyone else. After that, most often comes *My Wild Irish Rose* or *Sweet Rosie O'Grady* or maybe *Little Bit of Heaven.* The singing goes on until the more difficult songs, like *Minstrel Boy,* result in red faces, strangling sounds, and an almost epidemic threat of larynx hernia.

But the most challenging and best loved is *Danny Boy.* In any large crowd, there is always an acceptable voice or so that can meet the several octave challenge of the song. On this night in New Orleans, there were two who considered themselves to be honest-to-God Irish tenors and challenged each other in separate renditions so that the crowd could choose between them.

But before the last applause started, there was another voice—unaccompanied by the band that had stopped to allow the contest—that came from the back of the enormous room.

Oh, Danny Boy, the pipes the pipes are calling...

It was the voice, not the collective gasp of the crowd, that made Evan turn away from the deck rail where he was talking to the fully recovered piano player. He held up his hand to silence Adrian as he listened. When he walked onto the dance floor, the beautiful young woman in the black dress, the tall girl with the cameo face and the gray eyes that had become blue in the darkness of the dance hall and the raven hair that reached her waist—the young woman with the unbelievable voice, stopped singing.

"Play for me, Evan," she said as he came to stand in front of her to look into her eyes with all the unspoken questions gathered in his.

Evan turned and picked up his clarinet from the top of the piano. He began to play as she started to sing again. They walked toward each other until they were standing together, singing and playing the song for their lost son.

The hush that had come over the room was like a vacuum, a drawn breath that was only exhaled when she stopped singing and before the wild applause started. Everyone in this audience, privileged by circumstance, realized that this was an event that probably would never be duplicated. Something that would be described over and over again to people who didn't have any way of knowing what the experience had really meant.

Both of their faces were wet with the tears of remembrance when Evan began to play:

Kiss Me Again

No one coughed or whispered or raised a disinterested glass or looked away from the young man and woman who were making love to each other with their music.

When the song ended, Evan put his clarinet on the floor and took Molly's face in his hands. The kiss would never be adequately described either. It had to be felt as well as seen. It required a lump in the throat and eyes bright with unshed tears.

Evan picked up his clarinet and, taking her hand, led Molly onto the open deck at the bow of the boat. They were away from the lights of the city on the return from their trip up the river. As they stood in the light of a gibbous moon, Evan held Molly with his face in the hair that still smelled like heather.

"I've come back to you, Evan, if you'll have me."

"Will you ever leave me again?"

"Not if you'll marry me."

"You will have things to do with your life that won't include me, Molly."

"Everything in my life will always include you. Since I fell in love with you, every song I've sung has had you in it, even when I got lost and didn't know why. I believe that is the most important part of how I found my way back home again. Next to you, music is the most important part of my life. No matter where or when I sing, you will always be part of my voice, even if you won't come back to me forever."

Evan looked into Molly's violet eyes for so long that an expression of rejection clouded her face. Just as she was turning away from him, he asked:

"How did you know where I would be tonight?"

"Mel told me. I called Stuart House the night I got back from Ireland. He said you were still waiting for me. Were you, Evan, still waiting?"

Again Evan stood looking into Molly's moonlit face. After a long minute of silence, he said:

"You *are* my life, Molly. Mel knew I would wait for you because he knows there could never be anyone else. He knows that for all the years you have been away, there has been something broken in me only you could mend."

"Evan, I will never leave you again, even if you won't marry me. There is no way either of us can change what we are."

"Mel wants us to be married at Stuart House. Are you ready for it now?"

"Can we leave tomorrow?"

"Tomorrow afternoon. In the morning I have some arranging to do about my job."

"Do you want to stay with me tonight, Evan?"

"Are you checked into a hotel?"

"Yes, the Roosevelt."

"Take a taxi and go get some sleep. I have to finish this set before I leave. Be ready by noon tomorrow."

An hour and half after sunset, Evan drove into the parking lot in back of the Seminary building. Molly looked at him questioningly in the moonlight that filtered through the car windows.

"Are we going into the woods, Evan?"

"Back where it all started, Molly. I believe there's something we left in those woods; I want to find it again."

Evan reached into the back seat and picked up his clarinet before he got out of the car. As they entered the woods, Evan took Molly's hand, and he didn't stop until they got to the little beach by the river. In the cool Mississippi night, they sat side-by-side looking at the moon's reflection that sparkled in the ripples of the downstream rapids.

Evan took both of Molly's hands and turned her until they were looking into each other's eyes.

"Molly, do you love me the same way you did when we were here seven years ago?"

Molly pulled her hands free and stood up. As she began unbuttoning her blouse, she said, "Play *Moonglow* for me, Evan."

About the Author

Bill Tucker wrote his first novel when he was eighteen, sailing the Pacific on a merchant ship. He realized the book was so bad, he fed the pages into the wind over the South China Sea.. He returned home, became an engineer and scientist, a university professor, an industrial researcher, a professional editor, a publisher, a memoirist, and—finally—a published novelist. His first book, *Widow's Walk,* was a romance/suspense thriller. Then came a memoir, *Sing for Me, Betty Lee,* about his boyhood and the events of his adult life his son asked him to "put in hard copy."

His next novel, *Running Through the Sprinklers*, was profane humor described as a hilarious read.

This new book, *Moonglow,* is a tragic love story about two wonderfully talented young lovers who are separated by a common tragedy. It has been described as "a broken-hearted melody."

Bill lives and writes in Aurora, a small Midwestern town in the Western Reserve area just south of Cleveland, Ohio.